MARIA MERCURIO

EVERNIGHT PUBLISHING ®

www.evernightpublishing.com

Copyright© 2025

Maria Mercurio

Editor: Stephanie Marrie

Cover Artist: Jay Aheer

ISBN: 978-0-3695-1121-8

MARIA MERCURIO

DEDICATION

To the ones who live thousands of lives adventuring through spilled words on pages, dream while standing, and experience intense emotions birthed from worlds in your mind.

I see you.

MARIA MERCURIO

Books in the Survival Series:

Survival

In a much-regretted fit of rage, Chloe lost her dream job. Still needing to pay the bills, she resorts to tending bar. Embarrassment about the mishap forces her to take a job twenty-four miles from her home in a dive bar located in small town nowhere. Into this disreputable bar walks Raff and his intimidating crew.

Chloe's role in relationships has been the queen. She's worshipped and adored while maintaining tight control over what happens. Eventually, she loses interest and moves on to the next conquest. Raff is everything she stays away from. He's cocky about the effects he has on her, arrogant about his own importance, and calls her out on any of her bull. Despite all the warning bells, Chloe cannot help the unexplainable lust she feels around him.

After being drugged, abducted from her home, and dragged to the middle of nowhere, she realizes Raff and his crew are living two stops past crazy town. They are convinced she isn't human and have a plan to prove it.

Pack for a Lifetime

Chloe struggles to rationalize why she strolled past two friendly police officers and calmly walked away with her kidnapper. The intense attraction she feels for Raff is confusing enough, but the sense of belonging she feels around all the guys has her second-guessing reality. Can getting abducted, being injected with experimental drugs, and told you are no longer human be the best thing to ever happen to a girl?

Miles Away from Home

Miles is the villain in everyone's story. Raised by the most hated pack in the States and accused of abandoning his baby brother and leaving him to die, his reputation as a man to avoid has been firmly cemented. Miles could care less about his crafted bad-boy persona. Social niceties aren't his thing. His mate constantly rejecting him? Now, that's not just a sore spot—it's a festering wound. He could try the good guy routine to win Akela over, but the clock ran out on that option. Since nice guys finish last, he fully expects to win.

CONCEAL AND REVEAL

Survival, 4

Maria Mercurio

Copyright © 2025

Chapter One
Kate

"Please, Aaron," I pleaded, hating the desperation in my voice. "Don't go on this trip."

My husband glared at me, clearly exasperated. "It's my job. This isn't up for discussion."

I wasn't one of those women who nagged my husband when work obligations came up and cut into family time. The truth was trickier. He wasn't leaving for work. He was leaving to spend time with his latest side piece. I just lacked the courage to call him out on it. "They didn't give you any notice though. Can't you move it to next week? It's our son's first birthday party. We have around thirty people coming tomorrow."

He released a long-suffering sigh before glaring at me again. "You invited them all. You deal with it. Or better yet, cancel it. Tommy isn't going to know it's his birthday. He's one."

I wrung my hands. "I can't. What would people think?" My eyes welled with tears. I was only minutes away from truly begging. "I only need a little help. I can't watch the boys and pick up the food. The place doesn't deliver."

"Call up your sister or your mother then. I won't be here," he replied firmly with no apology.

I gulped. My mother wasn't the best person to count on to even show up on time, let alone help. Meanwhile, my sister had been pretty M.I.A. of late.

"I just don't understand why you have to leave right now? It's Saturday," I whispered brokenly. "The party's tomorrow."

Aaron patted me absentmindedly on the shoulder. "I'm sure you'll figure it all out. You always do. No one will be the wiser."

It was hard not to flinch at the remark. I was constantly juggling to little applause. If one more person smiled at me fondly and gushed, "I just don't know how you do it all!" I might break down and cry. Reality? I was living in a house of mirrors and the cracks were visible if one cared to look.

Aaron continued to pack his duffel bag, not sparing me a single glance. It was pointless to press him. He was leaving me more and more. Physically. Emotionally. The harder I tried to keep us together, the more he pulled away. I wasn't sure he ever truly loved me. Sometimes, I wondered if he even liked me. He must have liked the idea of me as his wife. I loved to cook and keep the house tidy. I ran my business from home, was always there to take care of our two boys, and never yelled. I always accepted whatever he spun. In short, I was a welcome mat.

It was hard to blame him entirely. After growing up with a mother who changed husbands as often as rolls of toilet paper, I wanted the white picket fence lifestyle badly. I accepted the first offer to come my way. I was nineteen, and Aaron was thirty when he proposed. My mother warned that I was too young and told me to wait and hold out for "the one." I sniggered. Hypocritical was what she was. People should work with what they have. Mom never tried to make any of her marriages work. There was no such thing as the perfect match. No fairy godmother was going to make my life better.

When Aaron and I couldn't have children of our own, I pushed for adoption. Aaron was perfectly fine with getting a dog. Being a mother was all I ever wanted. My own mother wasn't terrible. She was simply absent. I had a cavernous desire to nurture others. I dreamed of providing an ideal environment for a child. Aaron didn't mind my need for a family. He just wasn't as invested. I was expected to sacrifice any personal time and my career for the boys, sparing him any aggravations. I didn't mind doing it. Those boys were my world. I'd just hoped that he wouldn't act like spending time with us was unsavory. I wanted my husband to want to be with us. Aaron always made me feel I was asking too much. I should have known better than to expect more from him. He'd been clear from the start. He would put himself first, and I would need to accommodate. Nineteen-year-old me hadn't foreseen the difficulties this would cause.

Today felt like a deeper betrayal, though. Leaving me to do all the work was nothing new, but having others perceive our lives as less than picture-perfect was humiliating. I'd managed to cultivate this image that we were the ideal family. It would be awkward explaining to everyone why he wasn't here. I was a terrible liar. I wished it truly was because of his job. He used to cover up his indiscretions better, but lately, he barely even tried. His cell phone sat out on our nightstand while he used his watch to reply to texts. The messages flashing on his screen today were NOT from work. Unless sexting was a new form of communication his sixty-five-year-old, former marine boss was trying out.

I should object. Stop being a doormat.

"Alright, Aaron." My shoulders slumped, defeated. "I'll handle it."

He smiled, but no warmth reached his eyes. "That's my girl."

I left him to pack and checked on our little ones. Tommy was still on a two-nap-a-day schedule and should be out for at least another thirty minutes. Will had just turned three and stopped napping altogether. It freaked me out a little. I wasn't sure how I would get all my calls done for work with him awake all day. Will was my wild child. He already had a parkour challenge mapped out in our living room. I had to constantly stop him from jumping from the couch to the coffee table to the TV nook. Luckily, my little speed demon was still slumbering. I pulled out my phone and called my neighbor Mary. Her kids were teens and didn't require the same level of supervision.

"Hey, Kate," she answered on the first ring. "What's up?"

"I hate to ask, but can you watch the boys for about a half hour tomorrow right before the party? I need to pick up the cake and the pulled pork from that smoked meat place you recommended."

"Of course! It's no problem."

I sighed with relief.

"Where will Aaron be?" Her tone noticeably changed from sweet and caring to a tad suspicious. Mary had been my instant friend when we moved in five years ago. We didn't have kids then, and I'd been happy to help her whenever she needed a hand. She, in return, was everything a new mom could hope for in a friend. She organized a new mommy meal train with our neighbors when we brought our boys home, she offered advice when I freaked out about any colds they had, and she was never a gossip. She was my confidant. The only one I allowed to see the cracks in my marriage.

"He has to work," I replied, unable to say more without breaking down completely.

"Right." Her tone was terse. "You just tell me when. I'll be there."

"Thanks, Mary. You're the best. I do have a bouncy house getting set up on the lawn. I'll leave you some money to tip the guy. Other than that, I should have everything else ready."

"Do you need Lindsay to come over and help? She's grounded right now for taking out the car without permission," she huffed. "She's stuck home this weekend, and I've run out of chores to unload on her."

We both giggled. Her daughter was a great girl. Far better behaved then my sister and I were at sixteen, but she had a tendency to ask for forgiveness rather than permission. "Actually, I wanted to head to my sister's place and see what's going on with her. She hasn't answered any of my texts. I'm not sure if she's even coming to the party."

"That's strange. No problem. I can send her over now?"

The front door opened and closed. Aaron left without even a goodbye. My heart dropped to the floor. "Now works," I quavered.

Chapter Two
Kate

I texted my sister Chloe before heading to her place. It'd been nearly two weeks since I'd heard from her. It wasn't unusual for her to ghost me. Unlike me, Chloe was incredibly independent. She was never scared of being alone. She wasn't a typical big sister. I was the responsible one, the homebody. When our mother would go on her various dates, she usually left me in charge of the house and food, even though I was almost three years younger. My sister took care of me in her own way. She was often overly protective with friends or, when we were younger, boys. She never liked any boyfriend I had, including my husband. Chloe took after my mother in some ways. No one man was ever the right fit. She was also the opposite of my mother and myself in that she never tried to make something work when it didn't. Never in her adult life had she called any man her boyfriend. No guy could take up a permanent residence in her heart. However, Chloe was usually there for the big things, and that's why I was driving over to her place. She might not be my best friend, we certainly didn't tell each other everything, but she wouldn't miss my son's first birthday. Something was off.

I parked in her spot at the apartment. Her car wasn't there. My spare key got me in, and I made my way up the stairs and planned to leave a note. She'd feel guilty if she missed Tommy's party. Perhaps she hadn't seen the invite? As soon as I opened the door, though, I knew something was terribly wrong. There were flies everywhere. My heart thumped forcefully enough to leap from my chest. I pulled out my cell phone to dial 911, hoping my sister's dead body wasn't inside. With adrenaline pumping through me, I shoved the front door open with a crash and flinched. I needed a steady breath before I could force my shaking body inside.

Her apartment appeared bare. It was as if she'd been robbed. "Chloe!" I shouted as I stepped into the living room. It was an open floor plan. The kitchen, dining area, and living room were all in one space. The source of the flies was the kitchen. A half-eaten chicken rested on the countertop. I gagged at the smell and the wiggling maggots. It had to have been over a week to get this disgusting. Chloe didn't have a love for cleaning like I did, but she wasn't a slob. I couldn't help the compulsion that made me find some gloves and discard the mess, opening a window to let in some fresh air while I scrubbed at the counters to disinfect them. Once the task was done, I went to the back to search her room. The closets were empty as well as her dresser. Hangers and cosmetics littered the floor. I fell nauseous at the sight.

Backtracking to the living room, I scanned the place more carefully. Startled by a note on the dining table with my name on it, I lunged for it. The writing was messy as if written in haste.

Kate,

This is going to sound crazy, but I met someone. I know what you're thinking! But it was time for a change. Things haven't been great in my life. I believe I have a real future with him. I can see it clearly. The apartment is paid up for two more months, but I'm not planning to come back. Please tell my landlord for me. He can keep the furniture. Don't worry about me! I know how much you worry about others. I'm making the right choice. Once I decided, I couldn't wait a minute more to start my new life.

Love ya!

Chloe

I numbly pressed a number on my phone. It rang until I was sure it was going to voicemail. "Hey, baby," someone soothed.

"Mom." I tried hard not to hyperventilate. "Something terrible has happened to Chloe."

Chapter Three
Kate

My mom convinced me not to go to the police. She agreed the note didn't sound like Chloe, but it wasn't impossible to imagine my sister falling for a guy. Mom was adamant it could happen. Despite my misgivings, I went ahead with my son's first birthday. Everyone asked about Aaron, of course. I smiled through my lies till my cheeks ached. Mom didn't show up until it was time to cut the cake. Mary was a godsend, though. She helped me with keeping the trash cans from overflowing, making sure the coolers had ice, and encouraging the older kids to stay outside and play. The only big snag of the day came in a most terrifying form.

The bouncy house rental had booked me for the deluxe package. That apparently came with a of all things ... a clown. Everyone knew clowns should only exist in the seventh circle of hell. I couldn't find the courage to ask him to leave, even though I was sure it would have been preferred by everyone. I mean, what sane person hired a clown to come to your home? I took the coward's approach, though. I avoided all eye contact and walked in the opposite direction if I heard honking or saw overly large shoes in my peripheral.

Thankfully, my boys were all smiles. They appeared to have a blast. I welled up watching Will help Tommy open his presents. I took a million pictures. At first, I texted Aaron a few, not wanting him to miss out on all the cuteness. When he didn't reply after an hour, I stopped bothering. I'd wait to see if he would ask. I hoped he would.

Once everyone left, the kids became cranky.

They'd both missed naps due to all the activity. I happily put them to bed, even though it meant they would wake earlier than I liked. Finishing cleaning the house was next on the agenda. I braced myself to tackle the mess, but my endurance faltered. Instead, I grabbed a bottle of pinot, a massive slice of red velvet cake, and binge-watched a few reality TV shows. Sadly, the programs weren't entertaining enough to distract me. My mind was racing, filled with all the things that could go wrong with my marriage, with the kids, and with my little start-up.

I fretted about the future of my candle and soap company. Everything had been promising in the beginning, but cash flow issues kept me from doing the expansions needed to accept larger orders. There was nothing but roadblocks and no idea how to get around them. Often, I had to turn down big orders, unable to afford the ingredients large batches required. Even today, a few friends approached me at the party, wanting to buy for upcoming events. These were time-sensitive issues I could not avoid by pushing delivery. I needed to come up with a strategy.

From financial worries, my brain jumped to my marriage. I was plagued with images of what my husband might be doing. Picking up my phone for the twentieth time to call him, I sat it down, imagining him answering and gruffly telling me now wasn't a good time. He didn't call. He didn't text. The message was clear that he wasn't interested in talking. I drank more wine. I'd regret it in the morning when my youngest woke at an ungodly early hour looking for a bottle. For now, I wanted to numb myself. I wanted to sleep and not toss and turn all night, focusing on the empty spot in the bed beside me.

Stumbling into my room, I changed into an oversized T-shirt, washed my face, covered my body in lotion, put in my retainer, and blankly stared at my reflection in the mirror over the bathroom sink.

Did my sister truly drop everything and leave her old life behind to start something new? An ugly bolt of jealousy sprang up at the idea. I was disgusted with myself for it. I would never walk away from my boys, but I wasn't happy. It was a jarring realization. My entire life, I'd focused on putting everyone else's happiness before my own. If they were happy, I was content. Always a good girl for my mom. An excellent student at school. Attentive to my husband and a doting mother to our kids. I should be happy.

Shouldn't I?

Chapter Four
Kate

Weeks flew by, and Aaron informed me he was leaving again. This time, his trip would not be one or two nights but an entire week. I decided to pack up the kids and spend some time at my mom's place. She might not be much more help than my husband, but she was, at the very least, a distraction. It also helped she actually wanted to spend time with me, a huge improvement over Aaron's attitude lately.

My tires crunched over the gravel driveway as I parked behind Mom's electric blue Mustang. Mom never answered the door. She freaked out about people trying to sell her things. I resolved myself to wrangling the boys, plus all our stuff, and hauling it in solo. Will shrieked and hid his head inside my skirt before I could put the baby carrier down. I groaned inwardly.

"Momma!" he shouted. "You promised you would put the dolls away before we arrived."

I patted my eldest son on the head. "It's fine, honey. They aren't real. Nana will put them away. I promise." I couldn't stop shuddering. The only thing in the world worse than clowns had to be my mother's collection of antique ventriloquist dummies. I swear they watched me as I shuffled the boys out of the front den and into the kitchen.

"Momma?" My mom hadn't answered either time I called, yet she sat at the kitchen table, clearly within earshot. Her eyes were red and puffy. She was absentmindedly drawing circles with her finger over the checkered tablecloth. Her hair was half done on one side and half a tangled, wet mess on the other. I gulped, wondering what could have happened. Perhaps a breakup with current husband number? Who knew? Usually, though, she was the one doing the breaking up and was often overly chipper and manic. I'd never seen her this devastated.

I opened a container of crackers for Will to distract him. The baby was sleeping, so I left him in his car seat while I approached the table. I gingerly patted my mother's shoulder to get her attention. She jumped a foot back, clearly in a world of pain. She hadn't noticed the commotion of my arrival.

"Oh, Momma," I whispered. "What happened? Is it Chloe? Did you hear something?"

"Kate," she cried brokenly. The sobs shook her tiny frame. She couldn't form words. Every time she started to speak, she collapsed into jagged gasps of air and mournful wails. Chills erupted down my spine.

I started to cry before the question could pass my lips. "Is Chloe dead?"

"What?" My question shocked my mother enough to speak coherently. "Chloe? No ... she just left."

I sank into the kitchen chair before my legs gave out. "She was here? What's going on?"

"I wasted all this time, and now he's dead." Lost and helpless, she dabbed her eyes with a tissue.

"Oh, Momma." I placed my hand over hers, trying to offer comfort. I hadn't gotten acquainted with her current husband Ben. Often there was little point, as her relationships rarely lasted more than a year. He seemed like a kind man, though. "What happened? Ben seemed so healthy."

"What are you talking about?" My mother stared at me with her brows scrunched tightly together.

I was at a loss. "Did Ben die?"

"No," she answered, staring at me strangely.

"Why do you keep asking if all these people are dead?"

I threw up my hands in exasperation. "I come in here to you crying. You just said he is dead. Who died?"

Her face crumpled as a few more tears slipped out. "Your father."

Vague memories of a man I hadn't seen since I was five ran through my mind. "I thought you never heard from him again or knew where he was?" It was hard to keep the accusation out of my voice. I remember my father as warm and always there with the hugs until he simply vanished completely. My mother was tight-lipped and told me next to nothing about him, claiming it was for the best. I should have fought harder to see him, but I wasn't one to buck authority. Mom always shot me down the minute I asked about him.

"Mommy." Will's little voice wobbled as he pulled at my sleeve. "You okay?"

"Yes, honey." I pulled out my iPad and handed it to him. His favorite game would keep him busy for at least twenty minutes. Glancing over his head at my mother, I wanted to demand she start talking. Once Will was happy and squealing at his game, my mother nodded to herself as if she had formed a plan.

"Please, Momma," I whined, worried she was going to keep me in the dark. "Tell me what happened?"

A breathy sigh escaped her lips. "That's a more loaded question than you could ever realize. I want to start by saying I'm sorry. I truly thought I was doing right by my girls. Chloe showed me how living in the dark about who—no—what you are wasn't fair to you. Chloe knows everything now, it's only fair you do too."

A million and one questions formed about the "what I am" comment, but I bit my lip, waiting to see what she would say next.

"Your father was my true mate," she announced

as if it had meaning. I tried not to groan. If this was another of her new age wisdom concepts, I was going to pull out my hair.

"I guess poor Ben then," I replied sarcastically, surprising both my mother and myself.

"Ben's human. He could never be a mate to me. Because you and me and your sister ... we are Wa'ya. We're not human, but shifters or, some might say, skin walkers."

Despite the serious tone in the room, a sharp, barking laugh escaped me. "Have you started day drinking? Taking any new meds?"

"I know I sound crazy. I've only myself to blame for it. Your sister was spitting mad at me for keeping the secret. It's why she *disappeared.* She found her true mate, he's helped her to be able to shift, and she's now an alpha of a pack." She spoke as if proud of the news she delivered.

"Stop. Just stop." I held up my hands. "I don't understand anything you're saying. Can we please talk about my father. You said he died?"

Her eyes shuttered at the reminder. "Yes," she whispered brokenly. "He drank himself to death because I was a selfish bitch." Another sob broke free, and she hunched over in her chair. "I will never get to see him again."

"When's the funeral?" I asked quietly.

"It already happened. He's been gone for years," she answered sadly. "No one contacted us because I'd asked them not to."

"Why would you do that?"

"It's a rather long story, baby." She grimaced. "I'm not sure you'll believe it either."

"I may not," I admitted. "But I'd like to hear it anyway." My mother was right. The "not being human" thing was a bit more than I could blindly accept.

"I was born as part of a pack of wolf shifters," My mother spoke robotically. Her bizarre confession spilling from her lips in an oddly dull tome. "I was shiftless. A problem happening more and more with the women in the packs. My parents were embarrassed about my state and wanted me gone. As soon I was able I took off with my best friend Valentina. She's an alpha and always looked out for me. She found her mate when we were just eighteen. I loved her, but I was also bitterly jealous. Without being able to shift, I could never feel pack or mate bonds, and I wanted that more than anything."

She covered her face with her hands when her composure broke. Even though I was seriously worried she was having a mental breakdown, I stayed silent, waiting for her to continue. "Then I met JT, your father. He told me I was his mate. He was so certain. I was attracted to him, and I thought of him often, but I couldn't feel the mate bonds like he did. I tried to make it work. I did." She looked at me beseechingly. "But I was an outcast among the Wa'ya. Not in the way they treated me but in the way I didn't feel like I belonged. Every month they would shift for three days around the full moon and I would stay back at the house, alone, usually crying and feeling sorry for myself. I didn't want that life for my girls, so I left. Better to raise you as human since it was clear you were shiftless too. I thought if you never knew any better, there would be nothing to feel the loss of." She shrugged before more tears spilled down her cheeks. "Except now there's a cure and your sister is an actual alpha with a pack of her own, and my chance of experiencing that died with your father."

"Are you saying Chloe changes into a wolf every month and runs about with a group of guys in the wilderness?" I tried to tamper the incredulousness in my tone, but I wasn't a strong enough actor to pull it off.

"And this is why I never wanted to tell you." Her mouth pinched into a tight frown like it did when I was little, and she planned on scolding me. "Believe it or don't. I haven't lied."

A long silence followed. Part of me wanted to pack up the kids and head directly back home. Had to be the only sane choice in this situation. My mother had officially lost it.

"Prove it," I demanded instead. With my own dull gray life, this vibrant story had my mind racing. A small kernel inside me wondered *What if?*

Chapter Five
Kate

My mother didn't exactly offer proof of her insane ramblings, but she did give me the phone number of the woman named Valentina. She claimed this woman was still the alpha female of her former pack and would be more than happy to speak with me. If Valentina was the head of some weird cult, I wasn't sure I wanted to get sucked in. I wanted to speak with Chloe, but she didn't answer any of my texts or voicemails. I grew more frantic as weeks turned into a month, and still not a call from my sister. The contact for Valentina sat in my phone, the only possible source for answers. I broke down and dialed.

She picked up on the first ring. "Hello?"

"Hi," I squeaked. "Is this Valentina?"

"Yes." Her tone became a little less friendly. "May I ask what this is about?"

"Oh, I'm not trying to sell you anything," I assured her. "I got your number from my mother, Dianne. My name is Kate. I believe you know my sister Chloe?"

"Kate," she spoke my name with such warmth I could almost feel a hug through the phone. "It's amazing to hear from you! Your mother messaged me that she gave you my contact info."

"Ah, I suppose that makes my next few questions easier. My mother had some pretty crazy things to say to me. I haven't been able to process them. The first thing, though, is my sister. I'm worried about her and want to speak with her. Badly. Do you have a way to connect me?"

"I do." There was a momentary pause as if she was considering her options. "In fact, your sister and the guys will be here in four days. We're having a Thanksgiving celebration but on Saturday instead. You're welcome to join us. You can meet her in person then."

"That's very generous of you to invite me. I have two small children though ... "

"Bring them! I'm sure Chloe would love to see her nephews," she added.

I hadn't mentioned they were boys. I guess Valentina did know about me. It made this experience all the stranger when she added, "What about your husband? Will he want to join you?"

Want to join me? "No," I answered barely above a whisper. "I don't suppose he would."

I heard her exhaling over the phone. "Good. That's good. More time to be able to talk then."

Neither of us mentioned the outlandish things my mother insisted were true. I guess explaining how we weren't human was more of a face-to-face kinda conversation. She gave me her address and a time to arrive before I woodenly hung up the phone. I didn't remember saying I would come, but Valentina steered me in the direction. I just let her. It was better for me not to consider it a choice. I would go just to make sure Chloe was truly alright. If she was actually happy. I realized after I hung up I should have pressed her for a number my sister could be reached at.

Maybe bringing the boys was a mistake? I guess I could ask Mary or my mom to watch them. It was a couple hours' drive to the address Valentina gave me. Was taking them dangerous? Or was I being paranoid? Visions of a crazy cult howling at the moon danced through my head.

My phone buzzed, and it was an "unknown caller." Potential spam would get an immediate "to voicemail," but something told me I should answer. "Hello?"

"Hey, Sis." Chloe's voice floated over the line as if she'd never gone missing.

"Oh. My. God," I answered. "Why have you been avoiding me? I've been going crazy thinking someone made off with your body!"

She chuckled weakly after clearing her throat. "I'm sorry. My life got pretty crazy. Didn't Mom tell you I was fine? I went to see her last month."

"Mom told me you are a werewolf, and you have a pack," drawled, waiting for her to snort.

"I'm not a werewolf," she refuted with a sigh. "I can't imagine she said I was."

"Oh, she made it sound much more mystical. You magically turn into a wolf and run wild in the wilderness three days a month." I chuckled.

"Damn it, I was mad at Mom for keeping this all a secret from me, but now I'm having a hard time wanting to tell you about it. Valentina called. I don't think you should come to the pack party. It's better for you to stay away from all this. You have the perfect life. This will just confuse things."

The "perfect life" comment was a gut punch, but the idea of my sister also wanting to keep me in the dark was burning me up. "Chloe, I just want to know what's going on. I want to see you. You missed Tommy's birthday party. Don't you want us in your life?" I couldn't suppress the cry-hiccup at the end of my plea. My husband no longer wanted me, and now neither did my sister.

"Kate, I promise that isn't it!" Chloe exclaimed. "I'm sorry about the party. I should have been there for you. I'm afraid of what all this craziness will do to you. It's been a real mind-bending experience for me, and I'm still coming to terms with it."

"Are you saying this is a real thing! You can't be serious?" I pressed her to give me a straight answer. "Do you need me to send help? Are they controlling you in any way?"

"I know everything you're thinking right now," Chloe replied calmly. "I know how crazy I sound. It took me a long time to come to terms with it. No, I have not joined a cult. No, I'm not on drugs. No, I haven't been hypnotized. There's something different about us, Kate. But for you, there doesn't have to be. Just stay away and you can keep on living your life. Nothing has to change. If you come and meet the packs, something might."

It was hard for me to fight against my big sister. It went against my nature to confront things head-on. *Something might change.* It didn't sound scary at all. "I'm coming. I'm bringing the boys," I responded firmly, wondering if she would push harder knowing the kids were coming. She would never put them in danger. Her reaction would tell me in no uncertain terms if it was safe.

Chloe sighed. "I understand. I'd probably want to do the same thing. Just please think about it before you come. It might change things for you. Things you cannot change back."

To me, that sounded more hopeful than my sister had wanted it to be. A change sounded like a necessity. A hand to grasp onto while I'm drowning. "I'll meet you Saturday."

"Okay, Sis. See you then. Love ya."

My entire body relaxed now things were settled. "Love you too."

Chapter Six
Kate

Months ago my husband had shown concern when Chloe went missing, actually checking in with me regularly to see if I'd spoken with her. When I showed him the "note" she left, he'd agreed with me, it didn't sound like something my sister would do. After coming home from my mom's, confused as all hell, I decided to say nothing, having no idea what I would say, but now I had to come up with something to explain my absence for the visit.

I rehearsed a few times in my head before making my way to the garage. Deer hunting season had officially started, and my husband was prepping his equipment before a few trips planned with his buddies began, The task of cleaning his gun was keeping him in a relaxed state. It seemed as good as an opportunity as any I would get.

"Aaron?" My hesitant whisper reached him.

His shoulders bunched before he set down the gun and looked up at me. "Yes?"

I plastered on a smile, fervently hoping it looked natural and not as fragile as cracked glass. "Great news. Chloe finally called me."

His usually dull eyes sparkled slightly with interest. "Oh? So, everything is fine?"

I nodded emphatically, keeping the smile fixed in place. "She really and truly fell head over heels for some guy. Can you believe it?"

He huffed out a less than amused laugh. "I guess anything is possible. She's wild enough to jump in the deep end in any situation."

I tried not to bristle over his comment. "She has a passionate personality," I rationalized it away rather than engage him further on my sister's personality. "Anyway, she's having a get together the Saturday after Thanksgiving and wants me to come and meet him."

He breathed out slowly while his gaze assessed me. "And you expect me to join you?"

"No," I dissuaded him. "I can take the boys for a visit and give you a free day to watch football. I know there are some big rivalry games you wouldn't want to miss."

I expected relief and then dismissal, instead he narrowed his eyes and questioned me further. "Just Chloe and the boyfriend?"

I swallowed. The action sounded loud in my ears. "Funny you should ask. It will be his family too."

His eyebrows rose. "That is a big step for your wayward sister."

"I know, right? I'll have to see it to believe it."

"Me too," he replied sarcastically.

I held my breath hoping he didn't want to come. "I'll be sure to tell you all about it."

"I rather not have you talk my ear off about your sister's love life," he groaned. "A day without you and those noisy boys bothering me is all I'm interested in. Just share you phone location in case you get lost or do something stupid."

I ground my teeth a few seconds before I responded. "I think I can handle driving to dinner and back without causing you any inconvenience."

He waved a hand shooing me back toward the door. "Then it's all settled then."

If I was my sister, I would lash back, tell him off for good measure, and storm away. But I was me. Meek. More afraid of being alone than being unhappy. Aaron resumed his cleaning as if I was no longer in the room. The tantalizing idea of something drastically changing to alter my life was just a few days and one long car ride away kept. I could keep it together until then.

Usually the days flew by. Juggling my business and two small kids kept me on my toes. When I woke on Saturday it had felt like each day was a marathon before I reached this finish line. With a spring finally back in my step I got ready. Today I would get some answers. I timed the car ride to nap time, hoping I wouldn't have a screaming baby and grouchy toddler for two hours in the car. Locating a podcast with the most soothing voice, I set off, butterflies tumbling around my stomach the entire way.

The address Valentina gave me was off the beaten path for sure, but once I arrived to the private road, I found it quite lovely. The neighborhood appeared ideal, surrounded on one side by farmland and the other butted up against the forest. The massive house at the end of the cul-de-sac was my destination. Chloe was waiting for me, sitting on a porch swing with a tall and chiseled guy.

She hurried down the steps when I parked to help me with the boys. I gave her a fierce hug while searching for any signs of distress. She looked better than I did. Chloe was always the beautiful and confident sister.

"Hey." She smiled while rubbing my back. "You made it here no problem?"

"Yes," I replied. "The boys just woke up a few miles back. It was a quiet trip."

"Kate. This is Raff." Chloe gestured to the dark-haired man glued to her side.

I reached out my hand to shake, but he pulled me in for a firm and strangely comforting hug. "Kate, I'm glad you're here."

"T-thank you," I stammered. His affection and warmth genuine.

"Everyone is dying to meet you. Would it be overwhelming for the boys if they come out to say hello? Or should we start it off small?" Raff's gaze pierced through me as if he could read my mind.

"They're not shy. It should be fine," I assured him, touched he was considerate enough to ask.

Raff whistled loudly, and Chloe slapped him across the chest. "That was right in my ear," she groused playfully.

Fascinated, I watched them together. She was clearly taken with him, something I thought was an improbability with my sister and men. A large group of people exited the house and joined us around my car.

First, I met both of Raff's parents Valentina and Austin, although neither looked old enough to have grown children. Valentina quickly stole the baby from my arms. I couldn't protest in the slightest. A bubbly and energetic woman, she was visibly excited to hold the baby, more than my own mother ever was. Both the boys took to her instantly. It also helped she had treats at the ready for Will and a toy for Tommy he immediately jammed into his mouth. Austin was intimidating, but he delivered the same comforting hug as his son.

"This sounds strange, of course." Chloe glanced at me almost sheepishly as she gestured to a group of guys huddled behind her. "But this is my pack."

My eyes may have bugged out of my head. I was even more overwhelmed meeting all these men in her life. *How exactly does this work? Is she with them all?* The idea both shocked and aroused me.

"This ox of a man is Tate," Chloe spoke fondly. A man nearly six feet five lumbered over and smiled sweetly. He acted the epitome of the gentle giant trope.

"This is Raff's brother, Rollin. You'll meet all the siblings inside. He has five more." She emphasized the five extra brothers with wide eyes. Poor Valentina, she must have the patience of a saint. As a mom of two boys, I couldn't wrap my head around having seven.

The hottest man I'd ever seen who wasn't on the big screen gave me a hug and a wink. "Always more brothers to meet, but I'm the best one," Rollin joked. Or maybe it wasn't a joke? He was too pretty to be real. I nodded wordlessly.

Next was a wiry, tatted-up man named Weylin. He shoved Roland to the side with an audible groan over his antics. "I can clearly see the resemblance to your big sis. You both have the same face shape," he observed kindly. I might resemble my sister, but she oozed sexuality. I oozed overwhelmed mom vibes.

"And this sweet guy here is Lowe." Chloe ruffled his hair, and the young man blushed under her attention.

"I know it was a long drive," Lowe spoke softly. "I'm happy to help out with the kids, too, if Valentina doesn't monopolize them." He shot Chloe a mischievous smirk. "I could use the practice."

My eyes went as round as saucers as I stared back at my sister. "Wait! What?"

Chloe rolled her eyes. "Don't listen to them. It's a bit of a joke."

"Okay," I replied uncertainly. This was getting stranger and stranger. I wanted to see Chloe in this new life, though. Make sure she was doing well and find out if there was an entirely new world out there I knew nothing about.

My sister had the guys take my things inside. She slung her arm over my shoulder and leaned in to talk with me before we entered. "This is going to be a weird day on a lot of fronts. First, everything will be new to you. Valentina and I spoke. When you want to talk we can set up a time and sit down. Both of us will answer any questions you have. You can't tell any of this to Aaron. He's an outsider, and this is a big secret. Are you going to have a problem with that?"

I watched her chew at her lip until it must have stung. She probably believed I told my husband everything. *Isn't that what happy, well-adjusted couples do?* "It's not going to be a problem. I doubt he'd believe me anyway."

She nodded, clearly relieved. "I do have to warn you. We have another pack coming today. That in itself isn't unusual, but this pack was on the outs with Austin's pack. They're coming for a fresh start. A lot of misconceived notions and old prejudices might spring up. I'm glad you came early enough to have time here before they arrived."

That made me a bit jittery. I only wanted to find out what was going on, not be here for any altercations. "Will there be v-violence?" I stammered.

Chloe gave my shoulder a tight squeeze. "More likely just some male posturing. Nothing us gals can't handle. I got you."

I believed her. Chloe never let anyone mess with me. At least the ones I told her about. My sister was the overprotective sort, and I was careful to say if anyone had been unkind to me. It was why I never mentioned my imperfect marriage to her, or things about my husband that would have her seeing red. I knew the minute she learned about Aaron's cheating and general lack of presence in our marriage, she would do something drastic. I hadn't been prepared for drastic before, but I was starting to suspect I was now.

Chapter Seven
Kate

The house was strangely familiar. I kept having these intense déjà vu moments. It was comfortable and safe here. I never felt safe in a new place. Ever. It helped that everyone was great with my boys. I guess I should've been nervous about them not being at my side the entire day, but listening to their constant giggles and happy ramblings made me content. I never had to ask for help with them. In fact, I barely watched them. They were well cared for and soaked up the attention like sponges. Lowe prepared a bottle for Tommy before his second nap. Raff set up the pack and play with the monitor in a quiet bedroom away from all the noise. All the while, I sat, enjoying the appetizers and the company. Raff's family was open and welcoming. When I tried to help with dinner in the kitchen, I was shooed away and told to sit back and relax. Relaxing. A thing I couldn't ever remember doing.

Valentina joined me on the couch. "The turkey needs at least another hour. Do you want to talk now or after dinner?"

"Oh," I replied uncertainly. As if sensing my unease from across the room, Chloe honed in on us and hurried over.

"I told her talking was up to her," Chloe rudely snapped at Valentina.

"Chloe, she was being kind." I gasped at her attitude.

Valentina chuckled. "It's alright, Kate. Your sister's being protective. She's right. It's your choice to talk."

It felt like the right time with them both here. "Yes, I want to know everything."

Chloe appeared devastated. "Are you sure?"

I nodded.

Valentina patted my knee. "Let's go into the office."

It'd been such a nice day. I hoped it wouldn't end with me grabbing the kids and running for the hills. There was a love seat and chairs in the office she instructed us to head to. This put me more at ease than if Valentina sat behind the massive maplewood desk dominating the room. I would have felt like I'd been sent to the principal's office then or, worse, a job interview.

Chloe perched beside me on the love seat. She chewed her bottom lip nervously and looked like she would rather be anywhere else. I tittered at her. "You're kind of freaking me out more."

On this rare occasion, my sister looked sheepish. "I'm sorry. I just didn't take this well. I'm worried about how you'll handle it. I'm sure Mom told you some stuff, but this is a lot to take in."

"Let's just pull off the Band-Aid." I gulped.

Chloe looked to Valentina to take the lead. She reached over, grabbed a photo album, and handed it to me. "For starters, you've been here before. Actually, you were born here." She flipped a few pages with images of my mom, Chloe as a baby, and a man I assumed was my father. Mom never kept or gave either of us any images of who our dads were. She settled on a picture of my mom holding me in a rocking chair. The same man had toddler Chloe on his lap.

I glanced up at my sister. "But we don't have the same dad." The statement was laced with questions.

"Truth bomb number one," Chloe muttered. "We did have the same dad. Mom lied to us about it. Among so many other major things."

"Huh." I took it in. "I always thought maybe having different dads was why we acted so differently."

"I do believe Dianne meant well!" Valentina interjected. "I disagreed. It ended our friendship. She thought it was best you both forgot about him."

"And that ended with him drinking himself to death in a deep depression and neither of us getting to know him." Chloe frowned. "Truth bomb number two."

"Mom had claimed my father died," I responded with a matching frown. "She was sobbing uncontrollably when I got to her place. It was hard to understand everything. I thought all my life that he didn't want me." The realization was a slap to the face. I was currently with a man that made me feel unwanted. An older man I agreed to marry after two months of dating. My daddy issues were so obvious I couldn't pretend otherwise. I wanted to ask why she would put us through it, but I knew it would be a question only our mother could answer. I stared at my sister. "What's the next truth bomb?"

"We're not human." She shrugged. I waited for the punch line, but a tense silence followed her statement. It was beyond strange for my practical sister to make such a bizarre statement.

"It's true, Kate," she continued, trying to work around my disbelief. "We come from a race of shifters called Wa'ya. Our kind turn into wolves three days around the full moon. We stop being men and women. We become our other half, the wolf. I've shifted three times now and only have the faintest memories of what it's like when we're animals."

"How do you know it's real and not some drug-induced vision?" I questioned.

"Because they showed me video proof. Even

experiencing it, I struggled to believe it. But when I watched it on film, I stopped denying," Chloe spoke gently, as if fearful I was going to bolt.

I flipped through the pages of the album, studying pictures of me as a child here in this very house. No wonder it had felt familiar. I took a calming breath. "Why haven't I shifted?"

Valentina took over the conversation. "For over fifty years, we've experienced fewer and fewer female births. On top of that, girls would come of age and never shift. It affected all our kind from all over the world. My husband discovered a genetic marker causing the issue and invented a serum—"

"That can kill you!" Chloe angrily interjected.

Valentina kept her composure. "It's true, the first subjects died."

"A crazy, painful death," my sister added ominously.

"But," Valentina started with a challenge in her tone. "Since your sister, we've found the key to success. If a true mate match is found, the serum works. In the last few months, we have had four successful trials."

"True mates?" I questioned. "Is Raff yours then?"

Chloe's angry expression was replaced with something soft and wistful. "He is."

"How can you know?" I asked breathlessly. This all sounded like a fairy tale.

"Because our kind has tangible bonds." She tapped her chest. "I don't mean feelings of love. A mate bond goes beyond. The other bond is a pack bond. I also feel the emotions of all those in my pack. We can pick each other up when we are sad, lend each other courage, and calm each other when upset." She smiled ruefully. "Right now, they are flooding me with happy, calm emotions, understanding how I didn't want you involved in this."

"Does this mean I have a mate?" My heart beat wildly at the thought.

"That right there is why I didn't want you knowing," Chloe lamented. "I don't want you to doubt your marriage."

"But do I?"

Valentina patted my knee kindly. "There's no way to know for sure. There could be someone out there. You could have a mate but never meet. Or there isn't anyone. Many of our kind marry and have families without fate stepping in."

"What else?" I pushed.

Chloe stared at me critically. "You're taking this far better than I did."

I shook my head. "I'm not sure I'm processing it. I just don't want to walk out of here if there are things I don't know. Any other bombs?"

My sister sucked on her lip. "Not any that aren't painful."

I chuckled dryly. "More painful than what you've told me?"

"I guess I should say harmful," she stated, appearing wrung out. "Some truths are just daggers."

"Our father dying from depression sliced fairly deep, even if I hardly knew him," I countered.

"Infertility," she replied baldly.

I flinched. That was a hurtful subject. I was broken and unable to have children. There was a part of me that believed Aaron resented me for it. It had been a tough couple of years for our marriage while we'd been trying. Our sex life turned into more of a chore than anything passionate. He had hardly touched me since. The cheating started when the doctors announced I was the one with the faulty equipment. I never protested or called him out because of guilt.

"You're most likely not infertile like the doctors told you. We can only procreate with our kind." Chloe tried to be gentle. She was right. Some truths hurt more than others.

"And Mom knew about this?" I ground out. I had zero regrets about my beautiful boys. I was meant to be their mother. It was those years of injecting myself with fertility drugs that made me an emotional mess I was angry about. It was the monthly failures and finding out I couldn't do this thing so many women around me could do without even trying. Knowing my own mother watched me suffer and thought it was better to keep silent than spare me the years of pain was more than a dagger. It was a machete.

Chloe leaned over and pulled me in for a hug. I resisted at first, stiff in my anger, but quickly crumpled till the tears started falling. "How could she keep this from us?"

"I know, honey. I was mad for you. But look at your life? You have two amazing kids and a man who loves you."

"No matter what, those boys are my world. Being able to have biological children doesn't change that ever." I stayed silent about the husband part. No need to lay salt on the wound.

"I was the mess," she added. "Jumping from guy to guy just like Mom. Never finding anything resembling a home. This news is eye-opening for sure, but for you, it doesn't have to be life-changing." She stressed the last part, still believing I was living this ideal life. Now, I was the one holding on to a secret.

"I want to be a part of your life," I stated firmly.

"I want that, too," Chloe agreed. "More than anything."

A soft knock on the door to the office stopped us. Valentina raised her voice. "Come in."

It was the sweet young man Lowe who made a bottle for Tommy. "Sorry to interrupt ladies, but Akela and her pack were spotted on the street rolling up."

Valentina pressed her lips together. "The street this time? Not my rose bushes?"

It was Chloe's turn to act the calm one. "Remember. You're going to try for Akela," she cajoled. "We spent time with them last month. She's clearly happy. Her only fear is her family will reject her."

Valentina huffed. "I guess seeing is believing. I do want to see her happy with her own pack. I'd never reject her for being with her mate."

We exited the office together. I caught a glimpse of another group outside on the large wraparound porch before Chloe recommended I stay inside for the initial meeting of this new pack. Agreeing, I beelined it for the den. I had enough to process without adding "watching an awkward and maybe hostile meeting" to my list. From my glance at the monitor, Tommy was clearly still sleeping. I hunkered down on the floor with Will and opened up his train set. Building the track was a good distraction from the noise outside. A few raised voices floated our way, but for the most part, the conversation was quiet.

Lowe was the first to step back inside. After he checked on the turkey, he spotted me and headed over. "I had a set just like that as a kid," he addressed Will, but was grinning at me.

Will was in his zone. Chatting away at the trains and making explosive noises when they crashed. "Everything going okay?" I whispered.

Lowe groaned and rolled his eyes. "It will be."

"Who is Akela?" I asked.

"Akela is Raff's cousin," he answered.

"And there's family drama?" I guessed.

"Not really. Her fated mate comes from a pack Austin doesn't approve of. Miles is nothing like his former pack, though. He can't be held accountable for his parents' actions." Lowe turned toward the windows near the porch. "Akela held him off for years because she was afraid her parents and Austin would shun them. They just need to work their stuff out. This family dinner is a good start."

The front door opened. A stream of people entered. I hadn't been here long, but it was obvious who the newcomers were. The men had to duck to enter the threshold of the house. They resembled professional basketball or football players, with their extreme height and athletic builds, just less friendly. A striking, tall blonde entered with them. She would have been hard to miss before. Like a runway model, she strutted in. Compared to her, I was a complete frump.

The biggest man of the group had his arm draped over Akela. He was daring anyone with his eyes to dispute his right to be at her side. I guessed this must be Miles. Behind him was a younger man dressed like an eighties punk rocker whispering to the least intimidating man in their group, a nerdy, techy type. Then, three more massive guys squeezed through the door.

One was smiling and chatting with ease had long black hair and Native American features. I was drawn to the other two men with crashing magnets. They walked in side by side, as different as possible. A pale man with marble white skin covered in inky black tats, short cropped blond hair, and almost colorless gray eyes that peered menacingly around the room. He was the type to see a threat in every situation. His companion had perfectly unblemished ebony skin, bulging biceps, and was scowling fiercely as he argued loudly with Rollin about a car part. His perfectly symmetrical features accompanied bone structure quite possibly pressed by an artist's hands. Aside from his gargantuan size, he was simply stunning.

Everyone passed around drinks. The low hum of conversation settled in the kitchen and living room. Being a bit more tucked away in the den area, they had passed me by, but Chloe spotted me, waved, and gave me a reassuring smirk. I smiled back, not wanting her to suspect I felt out of place. My lips froze as I spotted a devastatingly bright grin. The lovely dark-skinned man and the techy guy headed right over to me, mistaking my smile for my sister to one sent to them in welcome.

"What do we have here?" I was startled by the deep, rumbly voice of the beautiful man. "You weren't present at the welcome party out front." He sucked on his bottom lip, his eyes of burnt gold twinkling. "I would have remembered."

The fine hair on the back of my neck raised as tingles spread down my spine. "I'm just visiting," I squeaked, signaling my nerves.

"Not a member of Austin's pack?" He fixated upon me. "I don't think I've seen you before at the summer gatherings."

"You wouldn't have. I'm Kate, Chloe's sister." I was curious to see his reaction to me being an outsider. If anything, the knowledge had him instantly flustered.

"Ah." He exhaled loudly while rubbing the back of his neck. "This is Kyle." He pointed to the nerdy dude who saluted me. "I'm Caius. I don't suppose she mentioned me?"

My eyebrows shot up. "My sister? Should she have? I only recently met all her pack."

"Oh." He grimaced. "Full disclosure, I kidnapped

her once. But I hadn't wanted to. According to her, it's water under the bridge now."

"What?" I gasped, thinking about her ramshackle apartment.

"Welp." He chuckled nervously and glanced at Will, who continued to ignore us. "It wasn't her first kidnapping, after all. If she could fall in love with Raff after he kidnapped her, then I guess forgiving our pack wasn't too much of a stretch."

My eyes must have bulged out of my head because he gawped around. "Oh shit! You didn't know any of that." He held up his hands in surrender. "I'm sorry. When you said pack, I just thought you knew the story."

Kyle snickered. "Way to go, man. That might be a record for pissing someone off."

I inhaled, not realizing I'd been holding my breath. "I'm not upset," I clarified. "It was kind of an information dump today. Your pack's arrival put a pin in things before we finished. Although, I'm not sure she would have shared that tidbit. Might be too hard to explain."

Caius crouched down and held out his hand. "Can we just start over?" he pleaded. "I'm Caius."

I fidgeted at his outstretched hand. "Sure, why not? I'm Kate." When I placed my hand in his, heat coiled low in my stomach. He was even more striking up close. The image of me leaning forward and biting his plump lower lip played on repeat. His eyes dilated the longer our hands were clasped, the pupils blowing out and eclipsing the dark gold.

"Sweet Kate." His voice rumbled over me, curling my toes.

The moment was interrupted by my sister and the blonde runway model. "Kate," my sister called. "I want you to meet my friend Akela."

"It's great to meet you, Kate!" Akela beamed before she twisted her lips in a scowl. "Caius, you are behaving yourself?"

I bristled at her tone, wanting to defend him. "He's been the perfect gentleman."

"Caius?" Akela snorted. "I'm sad I wasn't around to see it."

"I can be a good boy, Alpha," Caius replied too sweetly, causing Kyle to choke and cough.

My shoulders settled as I realized they were teasing each other.

"Valentina wanted me to announce dinner is ready." Lowe entered the den. "It's buffet style, but the table is set in the main dining room for us all."

"Thanks, Lowe." Chloe ruffled the young man's hair. He blushed beet red under her praise. It was then he noticed me watching. "Oh, Kate. I can watch Will so you can get your plate."

"I don't mind going towards the end." I was fussed over enough.

Lowe arched his brows knowingly. "You're our guest."

"I'm hungry, Mommy." Will tugged at my sleeve.

"Sure thing, honey. I'll make you up a plate. Do you want to come with me or stay here until it's time to go to the table?"

"Trains," my son answered abruptly.

"Hey, little man." Kyle caught his attention as he sat cross-legged on the floor. "Which are your favorite?"

Will took that as an invitation to load up Kyle's lap with various train cars. "I'll hang with the little dude and bring him to you when you are settled," he offered.

I glanced at my sister, unsure if this guy could be

trusted. Both Akela and she gazed fondly at Kyle as if he was an adorable toddler. I guess that meant he was harmless. Lowe realized his job duties as a good host were being filled and headed back to help with the food. The women encouraged me to follow them as they walked to the buffet. Caius was left standing. He observed Kyle with a slightly puzzled frown. "I didn't know you liked kids."

Kyle jerked his head back as his eyes went wide. "I'm an omega."

Caius chuckled. "You're such a complete computer geek, I often forget you're an omega."

What the heck is an omega?

Caius extended his hand out to me to help me stand. "Thanks," I whispered shyly.

A grin split his face. "Sure thing, sweet Kate."

I scolded myself for being delighted at his words.

"Do you know where the bathroom is around here?" he asked.

I nodded dumbly without answering for a few beats. He raised his eyebrows, waiting for me to find my tongue. "Down there," I blurted out.

He winked at me. "See you soon."

Being a married woman and a mother, I shouldn't have butterflies because a man winked at me. Even if said man could ignite the room with his hotness, I needed to get a hold of myself!

Chapter Eight
Kate

Akela waved me over. Making a beeline to her, I left behind the impure thoughts circling my mind. Handing me a plate, she jerked her thumb at the man beside her. He was easily the biggest man in the room. His inky markings peeked up from under the cuff of his shirt. His hands were as large as the plate he cradled. "This giant brute here is Miles," she spoke affectionately. The man turned to nod at me. His entire figure was imposing, but his expression when he faced Akela was all warmth. It made him appear *almost* approachable.

"Are you related to Tate?" He reminded me of Chloe's gentle giant pack mate, only scarier.

Light flooded into his dark eyes. "He's my little brother."

Suddenly, I was curious why there was such a tense atmosphere between the families. It appears they were all somewhat related. I held my tongue. Best not to ask until a more private moment. "This spread is amazing," I quipped instead.

"Yup," Miles popped his *P*. "Fancy spread for the fancy pack."

Akela shot him a glare. "Don't start," she hissed.

He rolled his eyes as he placed a delicate puff pastry layered with asparagus on his plate. "Yes, dear," he replied with only a hint of sarcasm.

I was struggling to manage the two plates and the heavy ladle in front of me. "Allow me," came a dulcet drawl. A pale hand shot out and took the ladle from my fingers. "A lot or a little?"

"A little on both please," I answered with a

tremble.

He was the pale one from Akela's pack. I'd yet to discover his name. Ice-blue eyes settled on me, along with the weight of his appraisal. Accompanying me down the entire buffet, he graciously put what I wanted on my plates. Few words were spoken. He was an intense, silent type. I desperately wanted him to talk again. That soft voice was the most soothing sound I'd ever heard. Reaching the end of the table, I was a little at a loss for where to go. The man put his free hand on the small of my back to help guide me. I almost dropped my plates in shock. Not because he touched me but because I had a surge of lust jolt through me at the sensation. My panties dampened. I gulped and gawped at him. His gaze held a matching intensity.

What the hell is my problem? I was in a dry spell, for sure. My cheating husband obviously preferred female company other than my own. Not being an overly sexual person, I took Aaron's dismissiveness of me as inevitable. I wasn't passionate with him, nor was I thinking about jumping his bones from the slightest weight of his hand on my body. Yet I could've just stood there, basking in Luke's captivating stare, while I was just fantasizing about Caius mere moments ago.

Propelling me toward the table with light pressure on my spine, I followed him, at a loss for words. I'd gone my entire marriage not feeling as turned on as I was this very moment. Was this because what they said was true? Not being human meant I'd never experience passion with regular men? Had being who I was doomed my marriage to a loveless one from the start?

My quiet companion pulled back a chair for me and seated himself beside me. I put Will's plate to my right. It was a massive formal dining room. The table could easily hold over thirty people. Yet it still felt lived in and not stuffy. The table and chairs were hand-crafted wood, and the cushions on the seats made with pretty needlework. Overall, it had an elegant farmhouse vibe, just expanded to cover a large group.

"I'm ... " I faltered when he stared icily at me. I licked my lips to get back the moisture. He watched my mouth. His Adam's apple bobbed up and down when his breathing became labored.

"Kate," I finally choked. "I'm Kate."

"Luke." His soft voice slithered around me. He pulled my hand to his mouth and pressed a faint kiss just above my pulse point. "Is that short for Kathrine?"

I shook my head. "Katrina."

"Katrina," he breathed out my name like a prayer. "What a beautiful name. It suits you."

Everything about Luke felt magnified. A single benign compliment ratcheted up my emotions to touching the sublime.

"Thank you," I answered, breathless.

A high-pitched toddler giggle broke up our staring contest. "Special delivery!" Kyle jogged up with Will perched on his shoulder. He settled my son down next to me. "Alright, buddy." He ruffled Will's hair. "Save me a seat now while I get some grub."

Valentina, Austin, Chloe, Raff, Akela, and Miles were at the far end of the table. Austin gave a quick toast and thanks to the cooks of the feast while the remaining people settled in. Caius claimed the seat next to Will, but my son didn't notice as he stared at Luke suspiciously.

"Who's dat?" my toddler sputtered with a mouth full of food.

"Luke," the man in question answered. "Please to meet you, young sir."

Will had brought two trains to the dinner table. "You like to play trains, too?" he asked, holding one up.

The question was heavy with the potential for Luke to be dismissed entirely.

Luke nodded his lips lifting higher on one side.

Kyle made it back last, didn't miss a beat when his seat was stolen, and squeezed in next to the punk rock dude. Conversation was stilted at first. Everyone kept to the weather until a fierce debate started about Alabama football vs Clemson. Caius was more of a University of Tennessee fan, but apparently, they hadn't had a stellar season, so he was begrudgingly willing to root for Alabama if they made the playoffs.

While Caius was loud and easily offensive with his harsh jokes, Luke was a silent presence at my side. I kept making furtive glances his way and was never disappointed. He kept his attention centered solely on me, and something about being the center of his attention had me preening.

Wailing erupted from the baby monitor, and I sprang up. All eyes at the table shifted to me. "Tommy's up. I'll go get him."

Chloe stood too. "You haven't finished eating. I'm done. I'll grab him. I've gotten hardly any time with my nephew."

Grateful for the reprieve, I settled back in my seat and ate until I was stuffed. Miles might have been sulky, but he was right. Everything had been much fancier than I was used to. It was also the best meal I think I'd ever eaten. Will, a picky toddler, only touched the turkey and a plain slice of crusty French bread. Not liking to throw away the food I put on his plate, I ate my portion and then his. Never had I been more appreciative of flowy dresses. Pants would have inflicted massive torture with the waistband digging into my inflated belly.

****

After dinner, Valentina directed us to go to the

game room. It was too cold to enjoy the outdoors. A blustering wind was whipping the leaves around the backyard. I watched them floating like little ghosts from the large bay windows. The game room had a pool table, a dart board, a ping pong table, and a massive TV with gaming consoles. With all those sons, they most likely needed a space to keep them occupied during the winter months.

Chloe and Valentina were playing with my boys when I returned from the bathroom. "It's nice to have help with them," I confessed. "I often feel overwhelmed watching both and juggling work. Today has been a real treat."

Chloe blew a razzberry on Tommy's tummy, causing him to squeal with joy. "Doesn't Aaron help?"

"Hah," I snorted. "Not in the least." Chloe gasped at my frankness. After a day of seeing what a family that supports you looked like, I didn't have it in me to pretend Aaron was the perfect spouse.

"Well," Valentina added sweetly. "You ever want to bring these angels here and have some time for yourself, you just have to ask. It'll be good practice for when your sister and Raff start their family."

"That is the second time I've heard about practicing!" I exclaimed, doing a double take at my sister's heated cheeks. "Are you planning to start a family?"

"Planning?" My sister looked like she had swallowed something sour. "Not really. A few tidbits we hadn't gotten to yet, sis. Apparently, we don't have regular cycles but go into heat once a year."

My eyes comically bulged at the idea.

"Yup, heat! Like dogs. Alphas are very fertile the first time they create the pack bonds," she continued, "and birth control isn't as effective in wolf form."

It was hard for me to understand not wanting children since I worked so hard to be a mother, but no one should just stumble into it. "That's terrible, Chloe. I know you never wanted kids."

My sister scrunched up her face and sighed. "Well ... I do. It's just everything is happening quickly. It's hard to adjust. I'm strangely excited by the idea of starting a family now the bonds are in place. It feels right. My logical side, though, keeps cautioning me to slow down. But the Wa'ya side of me is new. That side wants to grow my pack."

Valentina had an eager glint in her eyes. "Maybe, Kate, now you know about us, that is, you can convince your sister to set a date for the wedding! Mating rituals are simply beautiful."

Chloe threw up her hands. "See?" She gestured to the other woman. "Three months, and everyone acts like I've had years to adjust."

Valentina gave a mock pout. "He's my eldest boy. You know you secretly want to. Kate, tell her what fun we would have planning a party."

A giggle slipped out. "I can try, but convincing my sister to do anything she doesn't want to is an impossible task."

"Very alpha of her," Valentina teased. "But seriously, my dear. With your pack bonds as solid as they are, do you truly find a wedding to be a big commitment? Can you imagine your life without him now that you can feel him inside your soul?"

A dreamy expression flitted over Chloe's features. "No," she admitted.

Embarrassingly, I jolted with jealousy. I wondered what it would be like to feel a soul connection to someone. "Do you mind watching the boys some more? I think I'll go get a coffee before I have to hit the road."

"Take your time," my sister replied. "Valentina and I got you covered."

Chapter Nine
Kate

I entered the industrial restaurant-sized kitchen. They had a fancy coffee maker I couldn't possibly operate. I was relieved after spotting an already brewed pot. Walking in, I assumed the kitchen was deserted, but Caius strolled in from another entrance. He made a beeline for the coffee before I could. A predatory gleam entered his expression when he noticed me walking toward the mugs, giving me pause.

"Would you like me to pour you a cup?" he asked, luring me over and holding it out to me. "It's good. Creamer is in the fridge if you need some."

"Thanks," I spoke shyly. I gingerly took the offering from his hands, brushing his fingers. The innocent act felt deliciously scandalous. The way he devoured me with his eyes, when I sharply inhaled, created naughty images in my brain. Images of me catching my breath as he thrust deeply inside me. *I'm clearly attention starved.*

To distract myself, I took pains fixing my coffee just how I liked it. Leaning against the counter to take a sip, I peered over the rim at him. Caius took that as an invitation to come closer. His shoulder brushed against mine as we both slouched back to drink. "Come here often?" he joked.

"Ugh," I grimaced. "Truly terrible."

His grin slipped as he nibbled on his plump bottom lip. "Sweet Kate," he murmured, eyes glowing with mischief. "I want to do terrible things to you."

"Oh?" My entire body tingled. The image of us alone, bodies pressed together, lips fused, sparked through my mind. One look at him, and my brain jumped to sex.

"Tell me you want that too?" He pressed in close, his pant legs brushed against my dress.

"Oh," I repeated more somberly. "I'm married."

The answer didn't cut down on his smolder in the slightest. "I know. But why should it matter?"

Why indeed?

He lifted the cup from my hand and set it down. Facing me, he rested his hands on either side of me on the countertop, effectively pinning me in. It felt like a loose embrace. I could escape if needed, but did I truly want to? Heat emanated from his body, which was tantalizingly close. If I tipped forward, our lips would meet.

My mouth went dry, and my heart pounded. The woodsy scent of his cologne mixed with the coffee we were drinking enticed me. His eyes, two large dark pools, studied me. I should step away, but I couldn't. My body came alive as if it just discovered electricity.

"Sweet Kate," he whispered over my lips. "I need to kiss you."

Any protest I might have had formed died when he leaned in. I wasn't able to stop myself from arching towards him. His lips were warm and soft, and without thinking, I opened my mouth wider, licking and teasing his tongue. His hand reached up to circle around the back of my neck, keeping me in place while his thumb caressed my jawline. "Hmm, taste even sweeter than I imagined."

The words made me flush. It was wonderful to feel desired. For the past three years, I'd barely been touched. He kissed me again. When his tongue invaded my mouth, I rested my hands across his chest. I was mindless with desire. Not thinking about what I was doing or where I was. I didn't push him away as my brain was telling me to. My body demanded more. My fingers skated over his pectorals as they flexed at my touch. So badly did I want to feel him without the layers of clothing between us. Flesh pressed against flesh. Seeing the perfection of his smooth dark skin under my hand, I wondered if it felt as silky as it looked. I fixated on the gun metal buttons of his shirt, wishing I had the nerve to tear them off.

"Do you feel it too? Do you know what you are to me?" he whispered against my lips.

My heart jackhammered. Dizzy with lust, I pulled back to look at him fully. "What?" I dared to ask.

"You're my mate, sweet Kate."

Before I could even process what he said or utter a single word, Luke stormed into the kitchen. "Damn it, Caius! I can't believe you would do that shit again!"

I winced at the implication this was an act on Caius's part. I'd been ready to fall for it, desperately depressed by my life to accept this man's words. Hoping my insane reaction to a stranger meant something more than me being lonely.

"Getting thrown out of one pack for it wasn't enough for you to learn your lesson!" Luke's angry retort was accompanied by him dragging Caius away from me. "You trying to start a war? We just made nice with Austin's pack."

Caius scowled at Luke and shoved him away. "You don't know what you are talking about!"

"Like hell I don't," Luke clipped. The anger in his eyes caused me to shiver. "I will end you before I let you pull that shit with someone else. Mate bonds are sacred. Not something you lie about to get in a beautiful woman's pants."

A pained sound escaped me. I covered my mouth

with my hand. Was this his usual game? The naïve new girl was easy pickings?

Caius folded his arms, displaying those massive biceps. "What's up with you, cockblocker?" he sneered. "Were you hoping to jack off in the corner while you watched?"

The callous way he spoke made my stomach drop. It took everything in me not to cry on the spot.

"You fucker!" Luke roared. He shoved Caius's shoulder and punched him in the face. Hard.

Caius's head swung to the side, blood spurting from his nose. A fraction later, he launched at Luke. They both fell to the floor, pummeling and rolling around. I screamed when they hit the kitchen table and a pile of plates clattered to the ground. Neither man stopped fighting though.

Miles and Raff both ran into the room. Miles grabbed Caius, and Raff pulled Luke away. Both men struggled, wanting to continue the fight. The kitchen flooded with people. If I could have fallen through the floor rather than see everyone gape at me in the middle of this fight, I would have. I hated being the center of attention, especially for everyone to be here to witness my foolishness.

"Calm down now!" Miles growled out. It was like a light switch. Both men went limp, the fight knocked right out of them. "What the hell is this about?"

Luke wiped at his bloody mouth with the back of his hand. Staring daggers at Caius, he spoke. "Caius is up to his old tricks."

Caius shook his head. His breathing was labored as he held his right ribs. "Fuck you."

"Explain yourselves," Akela demanded as she entered the fray.

Caius glanced at me quickly before his focus

landed on the floor. "It's personal."

"He told Kate he was her mate," Luke outed him.

Gasps were heard throughout the kitchen. Miles groaned. "Not this again, man."

"It's not like that." Caius shrugged off Mile's grip on his shoulder.

Akela glanced at me uncomfortably pity in her eyes. My stomach soured. I was on the verge of tears, not sure if I was going to cry or fall sick first.

"Cut it out, asshole!" Luke shot out. "I know your history. It's an ugly lie."

I could hardly breathe. "I need to get home!" Turning, I searched for my sister and found her walking toward my side. She scoured my face and body for any signs of injury, but the pain wasn't on the surface. The humiliation of it all after such a wonderful day was the worst part. "Help me get my things," I requested in a painful whisper.

I could tell she was upset for me. Her hands were balled into fists as she glared at the men still being contained. Her lips were pursed, probably to keep herself from yelling. She gave me a terse nod, placed a hand on my shoulder, and steered me away from the scene. I heard Austin speak before I left the kitchen.

"I think it's time your pack left, too, Miles," he growled.

Miles gave a grunt of acknowledgment. I didn't turn back to see what anyone's expression was. Feeling guilty and stupid, I couldn't face it if anyone resented me for the ruined evening. Chloe was a calm presence by my side, pushing me out of the room and up the stairs where Tommy's pack and play was set up.

"Lowe's got the boys in the living room. Let's get you packed up. I'm sorry this happened. I was right. It's better if you just stayed away from this craziness," she bemoaned.

"Please don't shove me away," I begged brokenly. I might be mortified, but I didn't want to be shut out. "As crazy as everything is, I still want to understand. I want to be part of this with you."

"Oh, Kate." She pulled me in for a hug. "It's just ... I don't want you getting hurt."

A jagged little cry escaped me. "At least I felt something. I've been numb for a while now. Today felt like taking a full breath. Up until these last few minutes, it was one of the best days I've had in years."

Chloe studied my face, and for the first time, she understood me. "I hadn't realized you weren't happy." A tear slid down her cheek. "I'm here. You can tell me anything. Whatever you need, I got you."

I shook myself out of my melancholy. Not mentally ready to confront the sad truth of my life, I pacified her. "I'm fine. I didn't mean to make it sound dire, but I would like to talk more. When can we get together?"

"The change is coming soon," she answered apologetically. "Maybe in a little over a week? I can come see you."

I packed away every sprouting emotion. The idea I was part of something completely unheard of. The feeling of comfort and safety being with these families inspired. My body flowered with desire for the first time ever. Even if it was to some jerk playing a prank on me, it was a heady mixture. It was too much and suddenly not enough. I would process it all later. For now, I had a long drive with tired kids, I had orders to fill in the morning for my business, and a cheating husband to go home to and pretend everything was alright.

Chapter Ten
Kate

It was bedtime when I put the kids in the car, making it super late when I finally arrived home. They were completely out. The lights were on inside the house prompting me to text Aaron, I needed help carrying Will inside. We only had room in the garage for one car. Aaron had the more expensive car and, therefore, got the spot. It was a point of contention for me, tonight being a perfect example. If the kids were safe in the garage, I could carry one inside and go back for the other. Leaving my son sleeping in a parked car on the street, even if it was only for a few minutes, felt wrong. Our front door faced away from where I parked. I worried he would wake up all alone and be scared. Or worse, someone would see him in the car and judge me as an unfit mom. As much as I berated myself for it, appearance was important to me. I hungered for approval like a teacher's pet with my arm raised, begging to be picked. The idea of being seen as a bad mom was worse than knowing my husband was a cheater. I know, I have issues.

Just as I was about to wake Will and have him walk in with me, Aaron appeared. "Jesus," he blew on his hands clasped in front of his face. "It's cold out. Why are you back this late?"

"It was a two-hour drive." My lips pressed together. He never truly listened to me.

"To your sister's apartment," he scoffed. "Since when?"

Case in fucking point! "My sister's apartment?" I ground out through clenched teeth. "You mean the one she went missing from months ago and does not live in anymore?" I reached into the car and unclicked the baby carrier. I handed the baby to Aaron and crawled over the seat to reach Will.

"What?" Aaron appeared perplexed as if I hadn't told him how worried I'd been for an entire month or shown him the strange letter that was left behind. "I thought she just hooked up with some guy and came back."

Admittedly, I hadn't told him everything, having been asked to keep the fantastical information a secret. I wasn't even guilty about having no plans to convey what I found out about myself today. You should be able to tell your spouse everything, but ours was a marriage built on secrets and deception.

The one thing I had claimed was I'd be gone all day. "I went to meet Raff's family," I explained as patiently as I could while wrestling my toddler out of the seat belt and securing his limp body in my arms. I cursed when I realized I hadn't put a pull-up diaper on him before the car ride. I just wanted to leave as quickly as I could after that scene in the kitchen. He was still dry now, but he wouldn't make it through the night. Potty training during the day was mission accomplished. Nighttime? We were nowhere close. Maybe I could change him on his bed without waking him?

"What were they like?" he sneered. "Bunch of hillbillies?"

"No." My tone was sharp. "Raff's father is a scientist. Raff is an engineer."

Aaron hoisted the baby carrier from the ground where I had set it down. "Your sister did always like the college boys. Guess I thought maybe the one to sweep her off her feet would be different."

Following my husband inside, I got the kids squared away. Will had such an exciting day, he was sleeping like the dead. He didn't even make a sound when I put his pajamas on. Entering our room, I rubbed along my lower spine at my aching back. I just wanted to wash my face, brush my teeth, and climb into bed. It was an emotionally exhausting day.

I kissed another man.

If I was being completely honest with myself, I didn't regret it. Humiliated at being played? Yes. But for a brief, passionate moment, I was wanted. I'd felt sexy. My husband, usually completely fine with ignoring me, decided tonight was the time he would play twenty questions.

"Tell me more about this family. Seems pretty soon for you to meet the folks of your sister's boyfriend isn't it? Or does the apple not far fall from the tree and Chloe is starting to play marriage hopscotch like your mother?"

It was hard to look at my husband. I should be able to come home to the man I married and confess all about what I learned about my family. Instead, it was simply better to just lie outright. "You guess it." I shook my head with a forced grin, playing at not taking offense at his jab at my mother. "She fell hard. There was talk about a wedding."

His eyebrows shot up above his bangs. "Truly? Your sister always seemed more like a player than the settle-down type."

"She had a goofy love face on the entire day," I stated offhandedly. "This might be the real deal."

"Where do they live?"

"Tennessee." I was purposely vague.

He scowled at my short response. "Where in Tennessee? Nashville?"

"No big city. They live near farmlands." I felt strangely protective.

"Cattle?" he guessed.

"No, looked like corn to me." I was wondering where this was all going.

"How big is the family?"

I snorted. "What's with all the questions? Since when are you interested in Chloe's love life? You said not to bother you about it before and you didn't even want to come with me."

He shrugged it off. "Bored today," he clipped. He reached forward and pulled me over to him by the waistband of my jeans. His finger dipped inside, touching the skin of my stomach. Usually, this small show of affection would have pleased me, proof he still might want me. Tonight, my skin crawled. Thoughts of how he most likely spent his day crept in. His latest girl had been texting nonstop last night. The chance he was alone watching football all day? Slim to none.

"Well, I'm tired." I stepped back, retreating to the bathroom. "I'm going to get ready for bed."

Aaron was relentless tonight, though, following me in and standing by the sink while I brushed my teeth. "Is Chloe living with him then?"

"Yup," I answered with a toothbrush wedged in my mouth.

"Just the two of them?" he probed.

I spit out the toothpaste. "That's a weird question."

"Is it?" he huffed. "They could be living with his parents or roommates."

I rinsed and dried my mouth. Something about his conversation felt strange. "Do you have a thing for my sister?" I asked.

Aaron scoffed. "Your imagination!" He shook his head in disbelief. "I've never shown any inclination of having a thing for your sister. I was just curious about whom my wife and kids spent an entire day with. Is that a crime?"

"Not if you truly cared," I mumbled.

"Of course I care," he snipped. "What the hell kind of comment is that?"

"I didn't mean anything by it," I answered placatingly.

"Whatever." He stormed out.

I should have gone after him and smoothed it over. He was only asking innocent questions. I couldn't muster up the desire smooth the waters, so I washed my face and put on some night cream. I hoped by the time I entered the bedroom, Aaron would have either calmed down or gone back into the living room watching TV. I just wanted to get to sleep.

I found him with his hand in my purse, pulling out my cell phone. "What are you doing?" I asked calmly.

I watched as he opened Google Maps and clicked on my last search. He tossed the phone back in my bag after. He didn't look at me, didn't give me an answer, just strolled out of the room. I stood there, dumbfounded, wondering about his strange behavior. Could he be suspecting me of the same thing I knew he was doing? Did he think I was cheating? The idea was prosperous. Except ... I had kissed another man today. I touched my fingers to my lips with the memory. They still tingled. Not only had I kissed Caius, but I was aroused sitting next to Luke. Undressing, my gaze landed on the waxing moon. Its pale light reminded me of Luke's skin. I removed my dress and bra, exposing myself and thinking what it would be like to stand naked before him. He'd been so quiet, and yet his eyes had spoken to me. The way he attacked Caius felt protective, but there was a flavor of jealousy, too. Could Luke have wanted me like

I had desired him? Or was I just a pathetic, lonely housewife excited for any male attention?

Chapter Eleven
Luke

Controlling the impulse to follow her was impossible. I had to see for myself what her home life was like. From the minute I focused on her, I hadn't been able to calm my racing heart. She was the one.

I'd tried not to let my past make me believe I was cursed. When my entire family was slaughtered, I was away visiting relatives in Greenland. Many believed I was lucky to escape their fate. The loss was monumental. I didn't feel the least bit lucky. All I could feel was damned. How could I endure being forced to a life without a pack, without the ones I loved, without those bonds that made us more than single humans? When I met Miles, things changed. I became part of a brotherhood again, yet I still battled loneliness. It wasn't until Akela settled the pack bonds that I dared to hope for something better.

Meeting Kate was a nuclear explosion. How could fate be this cruel? Destiny set our paths to collide, only to hear she's married with children, unable to shift, and therefore unable to feel the full impact of the mating bond that shouted at me to claim her. I considered trying to speak with her about it. The idea of just walking away set my teeth on edge. Then fucking Caius had to pull his famous line. Telling shiftless females you were their fated mate was deplorable. I thought getting the crap beat out of him by his last pack and left for dead would have taught him a lesson. How could I even speak to her about it now? She would already have been hard to convince, and now she was most likely jaded too.

I parked just down the road, shutting off my

lights early, hoping she wouldn't see me. She sat in the car for a bit. I wondered if her husband planned to come out and help her. I was glad he hadn't come to Austin's house today, but it made me wonder what kind of man he was. Watching her struggling with the infant car seat had me reaching for my own seat belt to leap out and help. Before I could, the front door opened. A tall, slightly graying man came out. Kate could not be more than mid-twenties, but her husband appeared to be around forty. There was no warm greeting. He didn't hug, kiss, or even say hello. He appeared bitter at being forced outside as he rubbed his hands for warmth. The man stood there like a passive observer while Kate placed the infant carrier in front of him to get him to assist and then went back to grab their toddler.

Kate was different with him. She was such a sweet thing at dinner, all smiles and blushes. Next to her husband, she wilted. Her shoulders were hunched in. Her face was resigned as she accepted his frigid demeanor. I was ashamed the entire scene made me inordinately pleased. If she was better off without him, then that eased my conscience. He didn't deserve her. I would give her everything.

Get a hold of yourself, man! Make sure you're not just seeing what you want to see.

I reached into the back seat to grab the black hoodie I'd stashed there. I didn't even give it a second thought as I jumped out for a closer look at what her domestic situation was like. Unable to get a decent view from any of the windows facing the street, I trotted around the house. The backyard wasn't fenced, allowing me easy access. The master bedroom and bathroom windows faced this direction. I spied Kate brushing her teeth while her husband towered over her, arms folded, with an unpleasant expression on his face. Everything about him made me want to throttle the shit out of him. Even better, he looked like the perfect place to stash a knife. Seeing another man with a stronger claim to your mate would make any Wa'ya stab-happy. There was something even more grotesque about Kate's husband, though. Something made me see red.

I watched him riffle through her things and pull out her cell. The idea struck, and I snapped a photo. He required further investigation. Something was off. Something was nagging at me. Kate entered the room. I couldn't help but focus on her. She was exquisite. There was an obvious family resemblance, yet where Chloe was like a siren luring a man into the depths, Kate had the face of an angel. Open expression. Guileless hazel eyes welcoming. Even with her face freshly washed and her hair in a messy bun, she was breathtaking.

Catching him red-handed, I waited to see if a fight would break out. Kate accepted the invasion of her privacy as if she didn't deserve better. Her husband left her alone in the room, wordlessly brushing by her as she stood puzzled and forlorn at his actions. Her shoulders tightened up, and her eyebrows drew together when she glanced at her purse. Kate raised her hand to her lips, a smile lifting up one side and she brushed her pointer finger over them.

I'd been angry seeing her with her husband, but I knew it wasn't him she was thinking of. The surge of jealousy was like an electric shock through my body. My hands clenched, and I wished I could pound Caius's face all over again. That he touched her was enough to set me an edge. That he made her smile, even slightly, made me unhinged. I had to take some deep breaths in through my mouth and out my nose to find my center.

Her last image of me was less than savory, bloodied, wailing on a man I considered a brother. What would she say the next time she saw me? Would those sweet smiles still come easily to her lips? Would there be fear? Would she perceive any side of this bond that made me unable to walk away from her?

Kate stood by the window, staring up above my hiding spot behind a tree. I stilled, not wanting to draw her attention. I stopped breathing entirely when she took off her dress and unclasped her bra. Her beautiful breasts were on display, as she was transfixed, in only a pair of black panties. A wistful longing owning her features. I should have left, but my feet were rooted to the spot. My dick grew uncomfortably hard wedged in my jeans. I wanted to paint those perky tits with my cum. The desire to mark her as mine caused me to adjust myself before I ejaculated in my pants like a horny teen.

I was grateful when she pulled on an oversized T-shirt, freeing me from the spell her naked body put me under. Her legs were toned, skin a milky cinnamon, even in winter. I stayed and watched her after she settled in bed and turned off the light. The fantasy of me entering through the window and sliding into bed with her played on repeat through my head.

Sweet dreams. I'll be seeing you soon, Katrina.

Chapter Twelve
Kate

I made Aaron his coffee to go while I cleaned up after breakfast. It was the Monday after the long holiday weekend. Thankfully, he was headed back to the office. Sunday had been even more tense and awkward after my late-night return on Saturday.

"Will you be home for dinner?" I asked. He'd been unusually quiet this morning, refusing to engage in any polite conversation. I wasn't sure what drove me to continue to try, except the silence grated on me.

He grabbed the coffee off the counter without a single word of thanks and stepped over a pile of Wills trains in the living room on his way to the front door. "Clean this place up," he barked. "It's a mess."

I ground my teeth, holding back any response. Our house was clean. It was a compulsion of mine to keep it so. I noticed he still refused to answer my question. "I need to know if I should prepare something. Otherwise, Will and I will just eat earlier."

He turned with his hand on the door and glared at me. "Can you manage something decent?"

I didn't understand why he was trying to get a rise out of me, but I refused. "What would you like?" I forced a smile.

He gave me a cool once-over, scouring my body, the house, and then back to my face. "Something different," he clipped.

The remark left me frozen. He glared for another second and then left the house. I didn't understand what I'd done to deserve it. It felt like such an impossible task to make him happy. I only snapped out of my stupor when Tommy started crying in his high chair, demanding to be put down.

It was to be a full day. The Black Friday sales from my online store needed to be packed and shipped out, I needed to update my website for the Christmas weeks ahead with different specials, and the worst task of all—making sure there was enough money to restock my inventory. Cooking, cleaning, and mothering were all squeezed into the mix. Expected. Taken for granted.

Mary would be coming over to watch the boys at ten, enabling me to drive my deliveries to UPS. I needed to move fast if I was going to get everything ready in time. The morning flew by in typical mom-of-young-kids style. Before Mary arrived, there was one diaper explosion, a toddler tantrum over not getting a special snack, and a gassy bout of crying followed by a copious amount of spit-up. I hadn't even gotten halfway through my packaging and nowhere near taking a shower when Mary knocked.

I opened the door, relieved to see a friendly face. She winced when she saw me. "Rough morning?"

"Living the dream," I replied sarcastically.

"You reek of spoiled milk. Go hop in the shower. I'll get the baby down for a nap." Mary winked at me.

"You're my guardian angel." I sighed.

"Lindsay only has a half day today. She can come by in the afternoon and help with your order prep," Mary offered.

"I can't pay her much." I chewed on my lower lip guiltily. "Maybe forty bucks?"

"That's plenty," Mary assured me. "She just needs to earn her own gas money for the week."

I broke the world record for the fastest shower, put dry shampoo in my hair, brushed it out, and dabbed on a little concealer and blush before declaring myself presentable. The packing went by much smoother with Mary helping with the kids. I got out the door to make my deliveries only thirty minutes later than planned.

The hair on the back of my neck tingled when I went to my car. I scanned my environment. I suspected I was being watched, yet I didn't see anyone. Scolding myself for my nerves, I loaded up the car with my packages.

The long line at UPS made me groan. It usually wasn't this bad on Mondays, but it came with the start of the holiday season. Luckily, I brought my portable cart with me. I wouldn't have to carry and hold everything while waiting in line. There were at least seven people in front of me, so I pulled out my phone to warn Mary I'd be away longer than expected.

"Hello, Katrina." A silky voice resonated through my entire body.

I turned, shocked to spot Luke standing behind me. I raised my hand to my chest. "Oh," I exclaimed. He was absolutely yummy. A gray-fitted, long-sleeved T-shirt showed off his muscular physique. Dark denim jeans were just snug enough to let you know he never skipped leg day. His pale blond hair was slicked back, revealing those icy blue eyes. The last thing I noticed after thoroughly checking him out? He wasn't holding any packages. "What are you doing here?"

"Got something to pick up." He jerked his chin toward the store.

"Do you live around here?" I asked, confused. I had no clue as to where Akela and Miles lived. Wouldn't Chloe have mentioned if we were neighbors?

"You look like a spring day in the middle of a winter storm." He gave me the once-over. His attention caused my body to heat up like summer.

"I'm a mess," I protested, patting down my

windswept hair.

"You're not," he stated firmly as he raised his hand to tuck a lock behind my ear. "You're perfection."

My mouth went dry as tingles from his touch raced down my spine. I glanced around self-consciously at the other people in line. His hand slid from my face over my neck and rested on my shoulder. I shivered from the delicious warmth radiating from his palm.

"Are you cold?" he asked while his eyes penetrated me. "I have a jacket in my car."

I had to swallow before I could speak. "I'm fine."

"Are you sure?" He stepped in closer.

What was with these Wa'ya men? Were there no personal boundaries in a pack? Two customers finished their transactions, but before I could move forward, Luke pushed the cart for me. "I've got it," I cut in, reaching for the handle.

"I interrupted you on your phone. Was there someone you were calling or texting? The least I can do is help you out." His slow drawl was slightly exotic. He didn't sound like a Southern man.

"I need to text my neighbor and tell her I'll be back a bit later." Taking advantage of his help, I shot out the text. Luke pushed my packages up one more spot in line before I finished. "Where are you from?" My curiosity won out.

"Before I moved here, I lived in Alaska."

"You have an accent I can't quite place, though," I probed.

"I was born in Greenland. We moved to the States when I was ten. I spoke Greenlandic and Danish before I learned English," he answered with a glint in his eyes. "My father was a huge fan of John Wayne. I learned to speak by listening to many of his movies. I've been told my accent is a bit unique."

"I like it! I-I mean… " I was a bit embarrassed at my confession. "Your voice is soothing."

His eyes lit up. "Glad to hear it."

"Next!" the lady at the counter shouted. With a surge of disappointment, I realized it was my turn. Luke came up to the counter with me and insisted on unloading my cart.

"You don't have to," I protested. "You'll miss your turn." I pointed at the other register as a lady was handed her receipt.

He smiled at me as he bit his lower lip. "You are too adorable. I don't mind. There's no place I'd rather be."

As if I was in a drunken stupor, I handed the lady my card to pay. For the entire process, Luke was silent beside me. A warm grin lit up his face. "Here, let me carry that out for you." He folded up my cart and hoisted it up.

It was pointless to stop him as he escorted me to my car. He appeared determined. When he dropped is hand to the center of my back, my core exploded with heat. His hand remained, a comforting presence, only leaving once we reached the car, and my trunk sprang open. Setting the cart inside, he closed the trunk and faced me. We stared at each other for a beat as if neither of us were ready to walk away.

"I'd like to give you my number." It wasn't a question. He held out his hand for my phone. I unlocked it and handed it over without any hesitation or thought of Aaron. Luke typed in his contact and texted himself. His phone buzzed in response. "If you ever want to talk. To find out more about us. I'd be happy to tell you our histories."

"Really?" I asked wistfully.

He nodded solemnly. "More than happy."

"Thanks," I replied, suddenly breathless.

He leaned in, and I sucked in a breath, causing him to shift his trajectory from my lips to my cheek. He kissed me softly and whispered in my ear, "Talk soon, Katrina."

He walked to his car and drove away before I got my head on straight and turned on my ignition. It wasn't until I was halfway home when I remembered he never picked up a package.

Chapter Thirteen
Luke

I decided to make the trek up to the cabin earlier than the rest of the guys. The full moon was two nights away, but I needed to speak with our omega Kyle. Watching Kate these past two days, I went full stalker, but I had to see her. An unsatiated hunger compelled me. Just the briefest of contact unleashed something raw inside me. Now that I had her number, I felt more at ease. I wasn't sure she'd answer my calls or texts, but I had to hear her voice and see her again.

The cabin was over a hundred miles from the shop where we worked, but it was over two hundred from Kate's home. With a large section of dirt road, this was going to take me at least four hours to get there. I needed to let my alpha know where the hell I disappeared to. Miles was usually tolerant of my activities, but he disapproved of me shirking my duties. Plugging in my cell, I called him.

"Hey, man." His deep voice vibrated my speakers. "You good?"

His concern pleased me. Many alphas would usually go directly to pissed off if you flaked on them, but Miles was a good man. He genuinely cared about how we were doing and feeling. I wouldn't have wanted to join his pack otherwise. I'd been a lone wolf too long. Set in my ways, so to speak. It took an adjustment to acknowledge Miles as leader. For a beta, I wasn't very subservient. "I'm sorry about skipping work. I'd something I had to do. I'm heading up to the cabin now. I'll see you all tomorrow?"

"A dangerous something or a personal

something?" His voice was churned up gravel.

It wasn't unusual for me to go missing for days at a time. The safety of the pack and my need for revenge had me unexpectantly on the road a couple of times a year. Never had I ditched my pack for a girl. The former Miles was supportive, but I wasn't sure what his reaction would be this. "Personal."

"We need to talk about that fight before the shift," he spoke firmly.

A wave of anger still coursed through me when I thought about Caius claiming my mate as his own. "Only if Caius is prepared to admit it was a crappy thing to do."

I could hear Miles sighing. "I think we also need to address your reaction," he paused. "And the feelings we all sensed through the pack bond."

Fuck me! "Tomorrow," I agreed gruffly.

"Yeah, see you tomorrow." He ended the call.

I didn't feel ready to discuss the mate bond suddenly rising and bespelling me. Pack bonds made it impossible to keep secrets. Strong emotions bubbled to the top and spilled over to your packmates. Finding a book I was eager to listen to for the remainder of the drive, I attempted to distract myself from obsessing over Kate. It didn't work. When I wasn't thinking about seeing her again, I was thinking about how I would convince my alphas to allow me to bring her into the pack. I knew Chloe told Akela she wanted Kate kept away from all our drama, especially after the fiasco with Caius. Fate had stepped in, though. Now that I knew my mate existed, how could I walk away? She was married to an asshat who clearly didn't deserve her. It was why I needed Kyle's help.

****

It was late afternoon before I finally arrived at the cabin, taking way longer than it should have, having stopped for lunch a couple hours back. Kyle wasn't on the main floor of the house when I walked in. He had a set up in the attic with his home office and bedroom combined. Out of all of us, including our alphas, Kyle had the biggest space here. Considering he was the only one who lived and worked at the house full time, it was fair. The cabin was great for our wolf side, but it was remote and hard to get to. We were trying to spend way more time here though now Akela had solidified our pack bonds. The mechanic shop Miles owned, and many of us worked at, was our main source of income. It was too far from the cabin for us to move. We were still trying to find a place we could all be together for more than just five days a month. Wa'ya flourished in community environments. The bonds sent a discordant note when we were apart for too long. We all worried about our omega staying isolated from us and could feel his relief when we returned.

"Kyle!" I called.

"Up here!" he shouted back.

His room smelled skunky. I crinkled my nose. "Why do you smoke pot in the house? Your room reeks."

He chuckled, not caring about my complaint. "Hey man, good to see you. What brings you up a day early?"

"I want to see what we can find about Kate's husband."

"*Why*?" he drawled.

"I got bad vibes from him. He doesn't treat her right," I grumbled.

Kyle coughed in surprise. "Wait! Is that what you've been doing? Stalking Chloe's little sister?"

I ignored his question. "I have his name and photo."

"Bro, I'm a web designer, not a hacker. What

exactly do you think I can do for you?" Kyle turned to me, perplexed.

I rolled my eyes. "You've helped me with databases to look up public information before. Criminal records kind of stuff."

"What is this about?" he asked pointedly.

"I told you. I despise the guy." I crossed my arms over my chest.

"And it has nothing to do with the fact that Kate is your mate?" he hedged.

I glared at him. "I never claimed she was."

He took the opportunity to roll his eyes at *me*. "You went apeshit on Caius. We all felt the huge spike of possessiveness. As soon as she drove home, you went MIA on us. You've been stalking her for two solid days. What else could it be?"

"Fuck, man." I scrubbed my face and plopped down on the ottoman by his computer desk. "Can you help me or not?"

"I'm always here for you, Luke," he replied honestly.

I sighed with relief as I handed over the contact info I'd gathered and texted him the photo I'd taken. Despite Kyle saying he wasn't a hacker, he was still way more computer savvy than I was. He had info up on Aaron almost instantly. Only problem, none of it was helpful.

"He's clean, man. At least from what I can see. Mainly just a LinkedIn profile, no police record, background check has a speeding ticket, but that's it." Kyle patted my knee. "Sorry."

"It would have made it easier to pull her away if he was a confirmed bad guy," I admitted. "But he's still an asshole, and she deserves better. I just need to talk with Akela. She'll know if it's time for Kate."

"That's what alpha females do," he agreed with a wan smile. "In the meantime, let's go downstairs and get a beer. I'm sure we can find at least one movie we can agree on watching tonight."

I chuckled dryly. Kyle and I were on the opposite spectrum for entertainment. I was all mob movies, and he was strictly rom-coms. "It's worth a try, I guess."

Chapter Fourteen
Kate

The next morning was one of those rare end-of-November warm days. I decided to enjoy it by packing up the kids and taking them to the park. Answering emails from my cell phone while they played was easy. I deposited Tommy in the sandbox with a slight grimace before I unpacked his toys. He loved nothing better than to play in the sand with his buckets and shovels, but I usually found sand in his diaper for a few days after. Kid was a dirt eater. I was a bit more of a germ freak with Will, and would never let him put anything from the ground into his mouth. When there were two little ones to manage, though, you had to shrug off grubby hands in mouths as inevitable.

"Try not to eat the sand," I crooned. The baby gurgled up at me happily as I sat on the bench near him. He wasn't quite walking yet, no need to chase him. Will, on the other hand, was a runner. This park was my favorite. It had a gate surrounding it that was hard for little fingers to open. Will could run wild from the swings to the slides, and I didn't need to worry about him running into the street. One of the things they don't tell you as a new mom is how often you need to sprint to save your child from danger. With two high-energy boys, I practically needed to stretch before any outing.

I responded to a few inquiries about orders when a text from an unknown number came in.
Hey this is Akela.
I got your number from Valentina.
Are you home?
I would like to talk.

I frowned at the message.

Sorry I took the kids to the park.

She must have been waiting for me, for her message popped up instantly.

The one down the street from your house?
I'm in the neighborhood.

She had my number and knew where I lived. First Luke and now Akela. Did their pack live around here? I hesitated. She sent another text before I could answer.

It's important.

I immediately thought about my sister. Maybe Akela had something to tell me. Chloe did say they were friends.

Yes. I'm down the street.

Akela didn't text back. Five minutes later, I spotted her driving into the parking lot. She stepped out of her SUV, looking entirely out of place in suburbia. It was easier to envision her with wings on her back walking down the runway for Victoria's Secret than pushing a stroller at the park. Unconsciously, I sat up straighter and brushed off the goldfish cracker crumbs on my leggings.

"Hey!" She gave a friendly wave and plopped down on the bench beside me. "What a beautiful warm day. You have the right idea being outside."

Did she track me down to talk about the weather? "The boys haven't had any outside playtime," I finished lamely, dying to get to the meat of why she was here.

Akela stretched like a cat before assessing me. Her smile was replaced with a more severe expression. "I'm sorry about what happened at Valentina's."

My eyes bulged. "You didn't have to hunt me down and apologize in person. You didn't do anything wrong."

"Ugh," she groaned. "Your sister is probably

never going to speak to me again for doing this, but we need to talk."

"Oh?" I titled my head, perplexed at her discomfort.

"There's a role female alphas have in packs. I've learned quite recently ignoring my instincts is detrimental to my pack's happiness. I pushed Miles away for years, thinking my family would no longer associate with me if I was with him. If I'd followed my gut sooner, years of unhappiness could have been prevented," she confided.

"I'm sorry to hear it," I spoke with sympathy, yet still crazy confused. "But what does it have to do with me?"

"Everything is telling me to come to you. I'm not sure how much you learned about us yet?" She searched my face to see if I was following.

Clearly, I wasn't. "Chloe claimed she has a bond with her pack now. She can sense them. You change into wolves three days a month and go into heat once a year. That's about it." I summed it up quickly, wanting her to get to the point of this meeting.

"Oh good," she breathed out. "You at least know the groundwork. As an alpha female, once the bonds are in place, my main role is bringing individuals into our pack, either by finding new Wa'ya to join or ... " She regarded me pointedly. "Finding mates for my current pack members."

Her words brought Caius to mind. His mouth against mine. The electricity I felt as his body pressed up against me. His skin was so incredibly flawless and smooth that I had the urge to lick him like a popsicle. "But I thought he was lying?" My cheeks flushed.

Akela scrunched her brow. "Luke lied to you?"

Did she just say Luke? "Caius," I gulped. "Why

would you say Luke?"

A painful sigh escaped Akela. "Caius has a bad reputation as a womanizer. His last pack beat him and left him for dead for using the 'you are my fated mate' line on a few shiftless women." She cringed. "I'm not sure why he told you that. I truly thought that shit was behind him."

Her words sank like lead in my stomach. "It's fine," I lied. "None of it matters. I'm married."

"And that is what I came here to talk about." Akela turned to face me on the bench, tucking her left leg under her. "How is it?"

"My marriage?" I asked, even more perplexed.

"Yes," she nodded. "Are you happy? Is he good to you? Content?"

I snorted, incredulous. "I don't even know you. We met once. Why would I have this conversation with you?"

"I get it. I do. But the instinct in me? It's telling me to press this conversation with you." She patted a hand over her chest. "It's telling me to find out if you're okay."

"I'm fine," I clipped.

She rested her hand gently on my shoulder. "But are you? Truly? Is everything okay?"

I shook my head in denial, having difficulty getting the words out.

"Because, I don't think it is," she stated solemnly.

My nose tingled as I fought back tears. I looked up, trying to force them back. "No," I broke down. "I haven't been okay for some time now." A few traitorous tears slipped free. I wiped them from my cheeks in anger. "I don't understand what my life has to do with you or with Luke."

Her eyes were pools of sympathy. "I have this

strong sense of connection for the two of you. I felt it singing through the bond when he sat beside you at dinner. What did you feel?"

"He's nice, I guess." This entire conversation was surreal.

"Nice?" She pursed her lips. "Well, if that is all you felt, maybe I'm off base."

The memory of Luke's icy, intense stare penetrating me to my core zinged through me. After the Caius debacle, how could I be expected to admit to having any feelings? "How can I tell you I felt a connection? I just met him. We talked." I shrugged.

"That's fair," she agreed. "Would you want to spend more time to see if it could be more?"

"I have kids. I have a life. I'm not sure what you are asking of me?" I squeaked, my anxiety spiking.

"I know this all sounds crazy. But …" She bit her lip. "When you're in the wrong life, and you've lived it for so long, you might feel like you have to stay the course. It might feel like you made a commitment you can't walk away from. I understand. For years, I thought I needed to deny my relationship with Miles. I fought being with him because I thought it would upset my family. I buried my instincts. I buried the me that deserved happiness in order to do what I thought was right." She exhaled loudly. "Kate, what are your instincts telling you? Is this life the one that will bring you joy? Or are you here for the wrong reasons?"

Little detonations blasted at my heart. My husband was cruel and no longer desired me. I was raising these kids on my own. Aaron didn't support my company. If it wasn't for my wonderful boys, there would be nothing left for me. "I have a family," I uttered barely above a whisper.

"Families are made in many ways. Wa'ya know

this even more than humans. The family you create, the family you choose, is often the strongest."

I stayed silent, unable to dispute her words, yet unable to accept them yet, either.

She patted my knee encouragingly. "I have to head up to our cabin for the change. We're going to have a party for Abel's birthday in two weeks. Please come. Bring the boys and come."

My head felt heavy as my temples throbbed. I should say no. It was the sensible thing to do. "You have my number," I replied instead. "Text when and where."

Akela's shoulders dropped as the tension left her body with my acceptance. "That's good. Thank you, Kate."

Chapter Fifteen
Kate

I was shocked to see Aaron home in the middle of the day. He often worked late hours and was seldom around before seven. A year ago, I would've been excited to see him. I would've believed he came home to spend time with his family, having just brought Tommy home from the hospital. He didn't even take a week off work for the event. Our new son became entirely my own responsibility. Now, I wasn't even sure why he agreed to the second adoption process. He only ever held Tommy when I placed him directly in his arms. He barely interacted with Will. Our eldest sensed this distance, too. He went quiet when Aaron was home. Nothing made me sadder than seeing his sweet face deflate instead of getting excited when his father entered the room. No love existed between us. Our relationship had become more like estranged roommates than even ex-lovers. Maybe Akela was right. Maybe it wasn't worth pretending anymore. Keeping up the act of a perfect family was exhausting.

"Where were you? I thought you had customers to help today?" He asked, more disinterested than upset.

"It was such a nice day out," I replied a bit defensively. "The kids deserved to enjoy the sunshine."

"You've been out playing then?" he asked derisively. He pointed to the kitchen. "There are dishes in the sink still. Before you goof off, you could at least keep the house clean."

"I was going to clean up at nap time." He made me feel small when he addressed me like an errant child. Taking the children out wasn't goofing off!

"I haven't seen a deposit in the checking account this week. I thought you sent out orders?" He circled me like a drill sergeant at boot camp.

I lifted my chin. "I needed the money for supplies. I can't fulfill my Christmas orders if I don't get the ingredients to make more."

"Your little company is barely covering expenses lately. If you're spread too thin and can't handle the housework around here, maybe you should give up the hobby," he sneered.

My eyes watered at the rebuke. I couldn't get ahead with my company because he never allowed me to invest back into it. "December sales should be better," I answered softly.

"Maybe you need a real job." The rebuke hit me like a slap.

"What job could I do where I could still have the flexibility to watch the kids? I may not make six figures, but I bring in money. If I had a job away from the house, we would give it all back in daycare costs." I tried to state the facts calmly. I didn't want to get emotional. It would make him even more displeased with me.

"Whatever," he huffed. "Sometimes you're so useless."

I stared at my shoes and willed myself not to cry. It would be better to let it go. Nothing I had to say would change his mind. I'd been trying to please him for years. It was only recently that I wondered why I was trying as hard as I was.

Staring at the floor, I noticed his suitcase was resting by the sofa. "Are you going on another trip?"

"Are you planning on hassling me about work again? Work that ACTUALLY pays the bills around here?" He towered over me as he released his sharp words.

"I was just asking, Aaron." I steeled myself before looking up at him. "Why are you angry at me?"

He sucked on his teeth. "I'm not in the habit of having to repeat myself," he huffed.

"You're in a mood. I'm going to put the kids down for a nap." I turned. He grabbed my arm in a bruising hold.

"Don't you fucking walk away from me." His voice took on a dangerous edge.

I swallowed nervously, my body frozen. He didn't use that tone often, but it terrified me when he did. "I'm sorry," I squeaked. I braced for what would come next.

He yanked me closer. I could feel his hot breath against my face as spittle flew. "You're just lucky I need to get out the door. I don't like this attitude, though." He shoved me hard. I crashed into the side of the coffee table. My glass tray of candles shattered at the impact. Shards of glass pierced my arm and hip. I whimpered, attempting to pull a large piece out of my palm.

"Clean all this up before I get back!" he yelled as he reached down and jerked his suitcase into the air. I flinched and shielded my face in case he planned to swing it at me. "Oh, relax," he snorted. "Don't be such a damn baby."

He strode out the door without a single glance at our boys. They were crying from the commotion, faces red and agitated. I tried to hold it together as I found the rest of the pieces of glass in me. Nothing was too deep to need stitches. The cuts burned like hell, though. It was important to stop the bleeding quickly and get the boys settled. Only then would I let myself fall apart. Aaron would feel bad later about this. He always did. I'm not sure what I did today to make him this mad. It felt like the time between his rages was getting shorter and shorter. He used to make it up to me with grand gestures. Things would get a lot better after and I foolishly believed him when he claimed it was the last time.

He couldn't control himself. It was always shoving and pushing. He never hit me. This time wouldn't have been as bad if it hadn't been for the glass on the table. He might not have even noticed I was cut. Surely, if he'd seen the blood, he would have apologized right away? Or maybe not.

Hot, fat tears slid down my cheeks. I didn't know what the right thing to do was. The idea of leaving him filtered through my mind. I squashed it quickly when a terrifying thought hit me. He could take my boys from me. Even though he never acted like he wanted them, he always mentioned it after any fight. Scarring me with social services taking the boys away if I told anyone what happened. I hadn't considered it a threat since the idea of leaving or telling hadn't occurred to me. Until right this moment. Aaron was spiteful enough to ensure if I left him, he would make sure it was a battle to keep the boys. He delighted in having power over me. He held all the cards.

I slapped some Band-Aids on and rocked the baby to sleep with a bottle while I read to Will. Once they'd settled down and were sleeping quietly, I went back to the living room and started cleaning up the mess. It wasn't until I threw away all the glass and wax pieces from the candles that I slumped to the floor in front of the trash can and sobbed. Loud. Ugly. Heart-wrenching. Sobs.

Chapter Sixteen
Luke

We usually hung around for a few days together after a change if we could swing it with work schedules. Pack bonding time was even more special for us since we didn't all live together like most packs. This time, all I could think about was driving and seeing Kate. As soon as we made the half-naked dirty trek back to the cabin, I called first shower.

Waking up naked in the wintertime after a shift was my least favorite part of being a Wa'ya. Even with our increased resistance to the weather, walking barefoot in the frost-covered mud was brutal. A hot breakfast surrounded by pack after the change was usually one of my favorite things. We sat around, going through pots of coffee and trying to piece together what might have occurred over the last three days while we were walking on our wild sides. If Akela was in a generous mood, she would bake her mouth-watering monkey bread for us. As a new pack, it was important to create rituals. My plan, though, was to split shortly after. It would only be to lurk and watch my Katrina from afar, but it was all I wanted to do with my next two days off.

Awkward was the best way to describe the day before the change. Miles forced us to sit and talk. Caius promised me he would stay away from Kate, yet he acted hurt instead of apologetic about the whole thing. The bond whispering betrayal instead of remorse. When Akela joined us as a pack, we'd adjusted some living arrangements, and Caius was now my roommate in our little cabin. Neither of us had much space apart from each other to let our heads cool from the fight. I'd admit I was still harboring a grudge. Much preferring my role as stalker to that of pissed-off roommate, I wasn't going to stick around long.

Out of the shower, I started packing my duffel bag. Caius caught me in the act. "Where are you off to in such a hurry?" He rested his back against the doorframe and crossed his arms over his chest.

I gave him a cool stare. He hurt my mate with his lies. Seeing her embarrassed and running away from us was like a gunshot wound. It was hard to move past. I was hesitant to share information about her with him.

"You just met her, man. The obsession is a bit intense," he snorted, guessing at my intended destination. "Well, considering everything about you is intense, call it more intense." His lips twisted up to reveal his polished white teeth. Vaguely, I wondered if he would be less pretty if I punched a few out. It couldn't hurt to test out the theory. Trial and error, right?

Staying silent was best, not wanting to confirm his assumption I was going to see Kate. Aggressively zipping up my bag, I tossed it in a chair. I made to leave the room, but Caius continued to block the way out.

"Clearly, we still have some shit to work out," he huffed.

"Fuck off," I cursed, pushing past him.

He stepped up toe to toe with me. "I don't take orders from you." His face twisted with a snarl.

My hands curled into fists. Caius and I were even in height, but he had me by a solid thirty pounds in muscle bulk. Being a gray wolf, he was naturally bigger. I was deadlier. Maybe it's time I reminded him. He needed to stay out of my way, or I would ensure it.

"What is going on?" Akela's calm voice had us taking a step back. She assessed both of us, lips pressed tightly together. "Breakfast is ready. Come sit and eat.

Cooler heads after full stomachs."

I strode into the kitchen and plopped into a chair like a sullen teen. Miles was stuffing his face with bacon and chuckled dryly at my performance. "Still nipping at each other, I see."

Akela attempted to sit but he yanked her into his lap. She rolled her eyes at his manhandling and stole the bacon from his fingers. My stomach rumbled as I piled my plate. We most likely ate as wolves, yet whenever we came back to our human forms, we were famished. The change was a calorie burn. I took a huge bite of a bagel slathered in cream cheese to avoid talking. Caius took a page out of my book, too, as he crammed scrambled eggs into his mouth.

Kyle was the last to sit, bringing a skillet of breakfast potatoes with him. "Is this still about Kate?" he questioned with a frown. Kyle never liked it if any of us fought.

"I don't want to talk about it," I cried in unison with Caius. We both glared at each other.

"Ha!" Abel cackled. "Jinks. You both owe me a coke."

"You've stolen enough of my stuff over the years," Caius sneered. "I don't owe you shit."

"All the hostility this morning," Xan, ever the calm peacemaker, raised his hands for us all to chill.

I gulped down my coffee and threw my napkin on the table. "I've somewhere to be."

"Bullshit, stalker," Caius called me out.

"You two need to work this out," Miles stated firmly.

"There is nothing to say," I countered.

Miles was about to press further when Akela placed a hand on his chest, stopping him.

"Luke. Don't think we don't know where you are

headed to. I do think you should go and see her," Akela ordered. "Caius. You and I need to have a talk."

I was grateful our alpha was letting me leave, as well as keeping Caius away from my mate. "I'll see you back in the shop in two days," I addressed Miles, wanting him to know I hadn't forgotten about the busy week ahead.

Miles gave me a nod. With his permission secured, I bolted out the door.

****

I was only able to relax when her home was in view. Parking the car a few houses down, I sat and watched. It was late afternoon, and with the days getting shorter, it would be dark soon. She hadn't come outside yet, and I didn't see much movement in the windows. My urge to see her gnawed at me. I would take a closer look once it got darker.

Her husband drove up, forcing me to duck down to avoid notice. My view of the garage door and his activities was solid. He parked and unpacked a suitcase and an oversized bag, most likely golf. He looked the type.

I guess he'd been away, too. Grinding my teeth, I fretted over not knowing much about the guy. There was no way he could be good enough for her. Convincing her of that was my only mission. What she needed most was me. It was written in fate. If it wasn't for her boys, I would just throw her over my shoulder and ply her with multiple orgasms until she realized no human man could ever compare.

There was a muffled sound coming from the house. I rolled down my window to see if I could hear. It was still too light out to get close enough. My blood pressure skyrocketed when I realized it was shouting. I could hear an angry male voice, but I couldn't make out his words. I was halfway out the door, ready to pound his ass, when the jerk in question stormed back out into the garage and got in his car. He peeled out of the driveway and tore off down the quiet residential street. A few faces peered from windows as the neighbors tried to understand the commotion. I couldn't wait another minute to exit my car. I needed to check on her. Now.

There would be no playing off that I was just in the neighborhood. Showing up at her front door would definitely be showing my stalker hand. I didn't care. I needed to be sure she was alright. With purposeful strides, I flew up her porch and pressed on the doorbell. At first, no one answered. I rang again. I wasn't leaving till I had eyes on her. On the third ring, she finally came to the door.

Kate tentatively opened it, her eyes wide when she recognized me. "Luke?" Her voice was wobbly. "What are you doing here?" She frantically looked up and down the street.

"He's gone," I stated sourly. "Are you alright? I heard shouting."

Little Will appeared at the doorway and peered at me. His eyes were red-rimmed as if he'd been crying. He hugged his mother's leg while sniffling.

"Now isn't such a great time," she spoke softly, giving Will a pat on the head.

"Invite me in," I requested. Maybe demanded.

"I thought that was a vampire thing?" A note of teasing from her made me feel a bit more at ease.

I didn't wait for the words. I slipped inside her home and closed the door behind me. The house opened up to a living room first, and I could see the baby bouncing in a walker. There were toy cars and a half-made race track on the floor. I walked over and started construction. Looking at Will, I attempted cheerful.

"What are we building? Circle shape or a crazy track?"

Will peeked from behind Kate's legs, not yet ready to speak. "I prefer crazy myself. You'll tell me if I'm doing it wrong?" I rambled on while continuing to build a looping track. Kate watched me almost as warily as her son. Eventually, the lure of the toys won Will over. He examined the track once I finished my masterpiece and happily started putting the cars down.

Kate waited till his attention was off us. "Why are you here?" she whispered.

"I had to see you," I answered honestly.

She licked her lips. Her knee was bouncing like a jackhammer as she perched on the couch. "Aaron could come back any minute." Her voice held a scared, nervous twinge that caused me to grit my teeth.

I got up from the floor and sat beside her on the sofa. My leg barely brushed against hers, causing her to jump away. It wasn't for propriety's sake or even fear of me. I saw her wince in pain. "What's wrong?" My voice dipped.

Knee bouncing was accompanied by hand wringing. "I have a cut there."

I observed her closer. When I first entered the house, all I saw was how lovely she was. Now, I was fixated on the ring of bruises around her wrist and the Band-Aids on her arms covering what looked like large gashes. "That motherfucker!" I shouted.

Will flinched and stopped playing with his cars, looking at me with worry.

Kate's brows lowered. I could tell I roused the mamma bear, and she was going to scold me. *Shit, I didn't want to scare the kid.* I was too angry to calm down, though, but for Kate, I would try.

"How long has shit like this been going on?" I questioned in the calmest voice I could muster.

Kate reached behind her on a chair for a sweater and covered herself up. "It was an accident. I fell."

"How fucking original." I couldn't help the glare. "Don't make excuses for him."

"I'm not," she quavered.

I got in her face. "Let me see all of it."

"What?" she squeaked, pulling further away.

"A bracelet of bruises around your wrist tells a more compelling story than the lies spilling from your lips." Human laws be damned if that motherfucker was beating on her, I'd make sure today he would breathe his last breath. "I want the truth."

Chapter Seventeen
Kate

Luke was furious with me. Everything about him, from his incredibly pale hair and eyes to the laser-focused attention he placed on me, felt extreme. "I'm sorry." I apologized, unclear as to why it was always my go-to with men.

"Don't fucking apologize to me either," he growled.

I jerked my head at Will. "Stop cussing. You're making him anxious."

"Typical omega. Won't lift a finger to take care of herself but will attack the lion to save her cub." He shook his head as if I was a lost cause.

"What did you call me?" I narrowed my eyes at him.

"I'm guessing your sister didn't tell you." His anger deflated as he regarded me.

I folded my arms across my chest. "What?" I lashed out.

"You're an omega."

I sighed dramatically. "What's an omega?"

"We all have roles in the pack depending on our other half. Even though yours is dormant, we can still sense what you would be as a wolf." He looked uncomfortable relaying the information like a dad having to tell his daughter about menstruation.

"And that role would be ... " I trailed off, waiting for him to complete the sentence.

"I think we've gotten off topic. We need to be addressing my desire to kill your husband," Luke rumbled.

"Tell me what an omega is," I deflected, worried about how thrilled and flattered I was hearing he was willing to commit violence for me.

"Omegas are the pack caregivers." The resigned tilt of his lips displayed how unhappy he was that my ploy of distracting him was working.

"Well, that doesn't sound horrible. Chloe said she takes care of her pack, but I thought they called her an alpha." I hated that everything was still foreign and strange.

"Alphas are the most dominant members of a pack. Simply speaking, they're in charge. They lead. We follow," he explained.

"Are you an omega too?" I asked, intrigued in spite of being miffed at his gruffness.

He shook his head. "I'm a beta. We're like the assistants, so to speak. We're usually more levelheaded, good at being the peacemakers and counselors. Xan is the other beta in our pack. Then there are gammas and omegas. Gammas are a pack's front line of defense. Good soldiers but need a general. They often act without thinking and have impulse issues. Both Abel and Caius are perfect examples." He barked. "Abel's is a total klepto."

"And Caius?" His eyes narrowed when that name left my lips.

"Caius has a hard time keeping it in his pants. He's a manwhore. I would say impulse control has never been his thing." The frosty demeanor returned, making me shiver slightly.

"How do omegas take care of everyone then?" I asked quietly.

"Omegas are hot-wired to love kids. I've never met an omega that didn't want to sit down and play with them."

"Kyle." I smiled, remembering the younger man being incredibly sweet to Will. "What else," I was eager to know everything. "Why did you say typical omega?"

Luke glared at the bandages partially hidden beneath my sweater. "Omega's are people pleasers," he frowned. "They worry more about others than themselves. They're submissive, and if partnered with the wrong mate, don't defend themselves."

"Aaron is not my mate. He's my husband." The bite was back in my tone.

A fire sailed through Luke. "No, he most certainly is NOT your mate. I am."

I can't deny the tingles that shot up through my spine at his possessive tone. Heat flooded my core, and my clit throbbed like it had a heartbeat. Simultaneously, I remembered Caius and a wash of cold settled over me. "I might have heard that one before."

Luke leaned forward, solemn. "Katrina." My name poured from his mouth like warm chocolate. "On some level, you must realize you're mine."

The fine hairs on my neck raised. I shifted, restless and on edge. "I know no such thing."

A devilish smirk graced his face. "I think you do. Your body is telling me things you're not."

"I think you should leave now," I spoke through firmly pressed lips.

"Not gonna happen," he scoffed. "I need to have a chat with that piece of shit husband of yours."

"What!" I bolted upright. "No, you can't."

"Fine," he stared at me sternly. His acceptance made me relax for a fraction of a second before he continued. "Then pack up yours and the boy's stuff. You're coming with me."

I was flabbergasted. "I will do no such thing! I hardly know you!"

"Well, those are your two options. I'm giving you the choice. I wait here and assess the danger of the situation or you come with me where I know you'll be safest." The infuriating man acted like I had to obey him.

"This is my home. I can call the police." I jutted out my chin and tried to keep my body from shaking.

His eyes darkened. "Will you now?" He leaned further back on the couch, appearing to get comfortable.

I was bluffing, of course. I'm not sure what I would say to the police, let alone my husband when he did return. "You need to leave," I pleaded. "Aaron will be confused and upset to see you here. I don't want to have to deal with him. His trip apparently didn't go as expected, and he's in a foul mood."

"I'm not playing with you, Katrina. I physically can't leave you here, knowing he could hurt you. Don't ask me to. I want to give you a life where I deny you nothing. Let's not start it off like this."

His presumptuous statement had my mouth dropping open. "Are you for real?"

"Baby, what I feel for you is the most real thing I have ever felt in my entire life," His serious tone amplified his words.

How could I not be affected by hearing it? I'd been living with a man who barely tolerated me, and here was this stranger telling me I was his everything. After years of feeling like nothing, it was a heady mix. I shook my head. "This won't end well."

"Ending well is my specialty." The playful light was back.

"No, you don't understand. I have to think of my kids. Aaron could try to take them from me. I can't risk that." Tears welled in my eyes and splashed down my cheeks in hot rivulets.

I could hear him grinding at his teeth. A distraught panic was on his face as he watched me cry. He pinched his eyes closed and breathed out. "A compromise then. I don't like how angry he looked when he left here. Text him your sister called and asked to see you. Make up some story about her being upset. I'll go with you to Chloe's. Give him time to settle down. Give me time as well."

It was asking a great deal. I have own my business. I didn't have a boss to report to, but it meant I worked 24/7. I would fall even farther behind if I left. The image of my husband slamming open the front door like an angry animal earlier kept me from outright refusing. Aaron had been even more angry than when he left on his trip, taking out the brunt of his frustrations by shouting obscenities at me. I'd expected an apology about shoving me into the table. Instead, he'd been instantly volatile. Maybe a break was safest.

"I'll get ready, but you need to leave." He tried to protest, but I held up a finger to silence him. "All hell will break loose if he returns, sees me packing, and you are in our house. I'll meet you at the supermarket down the street in the parking lot." His stubborn expression told me he was debating the merit of my plan. "It's my best offer," I added.

"Alright," he agreed. I released the breath I was holding. "But if you're not there in one hour, I'm coming right back."

I nodded. "Deal."

Chapter Eighteen
Kate

Luke left, and I started second-guessing myself, big time. How could I pack up myself and the kids, leave my home, and get in a car with him? I contemplated calling my sister and talking with her. A part of me was afraid this would be a reason for her to push me away more. She would think she was protecting me, but instead, I felt left behind. Stuck in a life I'd gotten used to but wasn't healthy. I looked at my watch for like the tenth time since Luke left. It had been twenty minutes, and I still was stuck with one foot on the bottom stair, my hand on the railing and a ton of indecision about what the hell I should do.

"Fuck it," I muttered before I took the stairs two at a time. If I was going to do this, I wanted to be gone before Aaron came back. He stormed out, upset about his ruined trip and still pissed at me for no obvious reason. I didn't want to get into another argument. I'd text him when I got on the road. Based on his behavior lately, it could be a day or two before he even came home. He was probably at his current girlfriend's place.

Starting in the baby's room, I tossed in a suitcase all the things I would need for about three days. It was almost December, and the nights were cold. I needed to pack more bulky items than I would have liked for a quick getaway. I filled the duffel before even going into Will's room. Dropping the bag on the top of the stairs, I sprinted down the hall to grab another one. Will required slightly less change of clothes since I didn't have to worry about diaper blowouts now that he was potty trained. What space I had left though, I filled with toys and books to keep him occupied.

Starting in my room on the third bag, I heard the dreaded sound of the front door opening and then slamming shut. Ice blanketed me. I winced, hearing heavy footsteps on the stairs, knowing the evidence of my packing was on full display.

"Kate!" Aaron yelled out.

I shook my shoulders, trying to relax. I needed to sell this. "I'm in the bedroom."

He stomped inside, swinging the door wide. I couldn't stop the flinch I made when the wood banged against the wall. "What the fuck is going on?" he demanded.

You can do this. I turned to face him, acting nervous and frantic. "My sister just called. There's been an accident, and she needs me. I'm taking the boys, so it won't interfere with your work. I should be back in a few days."

The angry expression marring his face morphed into one of intrigue. "What kind of accident?"

"She wasn't able to go into detail. We were on for only a few minutes. She begged me to come quickly." I would have to put something more concrete together when I got back. "She never asks for help from me. I couldn't deny her."

Aaron sat on the edge of the bed and watched while I continued packing. He hadn't forbidden me to go. I took it as encouragement. "Should you be taking the kids?" he asked.

"She assumed I would and didn't say otherwise." I clenched my jaw worried my story was sounding suspicious. "Would you be able to watch them if they stayed here?" I knew the answer, but it was a hand I could win. "That would be a huge help, I'm sure."

He frowned. "No, Kate," he condescended. "I

can't not go to work this week and watch the kids because your sister got hysterical."

I bit my tongue as I was about to defend Chloe. She was the toughest person I knew. The woman was not weak, and no one would describe her as hysterical. "I understand," I replied sweetly. "I'll make do."

"And what about me?" There was an ugliness to his tone that caused me to freeze.

"You?" I asked, confused.

"What if I need something. What if I need you?" He watched my face too closely for my liking. I refrained from the eye roll I wanted to perform.

"Do you?" I stilled and stared back. "Do you need me?"

The moment hung between us. Seconds ticked by, and my heart squeezed.

"No," he answered. "I don't suppose I do." The words were meant to be cruel. To hurt. Crazy enough, I barely felt it. I'd grown immune to the multiple times he attempted to pierce me. "But make sure to leave your phone on just in case." He stood from the bed and headed out the door. Stopping at the threshold, he glanced back. "Give Chloe my love."

I scowled at the door when he was gone. I resumed my packing with zero guilt and a renewed sense of purpose. If there was a way to leave him and make sure I had sole custody of the children, I had to do it. This was no longer a marriage. It was a prison.

****

Luke was lounging against his car when I drove into the parking lot. I rolled down my window as I parked beside him. "I guess I'll follow you there?" I asked, scanning the parking lot with dread, not wanting any of my neighbors to spot me.

"How about I drive?" He leaned in the open

window. I could smell the mint from his gum.

"What about your car? They might tow it if you leave it here," I cautioned.

"Abel and Xan are on their way to get it for me. I would have offered to drive you in my car, but you have the car seats strapped in." He stood and looked at me expectantly, waiting for me to move to the passenger side.

I unbuckled my seat with a huff. "I can drive if you tell me where we're going," I offered, yet at the same time, I was still complying with his request and exiting the car.

"You look worn out, Katrina. It's a long drive. I'd like for you to be comfortable," he spoke sincerely, and I almost welled up. I couldn't remember a time Aaron gave a crap about how exhausted I was.

"Okay," I answered with a half-smile. My body brushed up against his when I stood from the car. My libido lit up like a Christmas tree from the brief contact. Luke's fingers stretched to caress the back of my hand as I walked by. His eyes heated with a hungry expression that in no way made me think of food.

How am I going to make it hours sitting next to him?

We got on the highway without me managing to combust. Luke kept the conversation light, mindful that we had an inquisitive toddler in the back seat. I noticed that around others he was virtually silent. With just the two of us, he was incredibly easy to talk to. A boring, dull car ride flew by with good company. We talked about favorite foods, movies, and books. I never once felt anxious or awkward. Before I was even aware, we were pulling up to my sister's home.

As I stepped out of the car, Chloe flew out the door. "Kate?" She searched me from head to toe. "Is everything alright?"

It was unusual for my sister to be frantic, usually more of our mother's thing. "I'm fine. Sorry for the surprise visit, but Luke was insistent."

The rest of her pack spilled out the door. Raff looked worried as well. "Was your pack attacked?" he asked.

"Oh god," Chloe's eyes went as wide as saucers. "Is Akela okay?"

Luke appeared as mystified as I was by their reaction. "Attacked?" Concern coated his voice. "No, we had an uneventful change. Did something happen?"

Lowe came forward and offered to take the boys inside for me. I nodded, too concerned to be shy about accepting his help.

Raff's jaw tensed. "A pack of wolves were slaughtered a few miles from my father's territory."

I gasped before Raff could correct my assumption.

"Not Wa'ya," he assured me. "But the timing for the slaughter coinciding with our change is worrisome."

Luke's expression went frosty. "You think we have hunters looking for us here?"

"I'm not ruling it out. We haven't had a close encounter like that since before I was born. Most of our packs stay where they should be fully protected," Raff spoke grimly.

"When there's an organization out there hell-bent on eradicating our kind, no place is truly safe," Luke was solemn.

"Miles told me your previous pack was targeted." Raff's alarmed demeanor was catching. His fellow pack mates hung on Luke's words.

"Targeted and eradicated," Luke spit the words out as if they tasted bitter.

"Oh, Luke!" I exclaimed. "You lost your

family?"

He nodded curtly. "What steps have been taken to ensure the pack's safety?" he addressed Raff.

"My father's lab and research are government-funded. He called in reinforcements to help secure the area from any trespassers."

"And what about here?" Luke looked around as if he could see people hiding in the trees. "If they know about your father, they may know about your pack too."

Raff wore a contemplative frown. "We haven't been here long, only a few months. My pack were nomadic before this, making us much harder to track. This territory is new, but I believe it to be secure."

"I've spent years tracking the Order. They're crafty. I can scout your woods out and search for their usual surveillance methods while I'm here."

Raff seemed grateful. "Take Rollin with you. He's our best tracker and can show you around our territory. I appreciate the offer."

"Why are you here?" Chloe pressed.

Luke stared at me grimly. "I couldn't leave your sister alone with that asshat she married."

"What?" Chloe was even more alarmed. "Why?"

"It was nothing," I assured her.

"He abuses her," Luke stated baldly.

"They were accidents!" I protested.

Luke threw up his hands in exasperation. "Case in point. She's still defending the fact she is cut up and bruised. Can't leave her with him when she's completely willing to remain a victim."

"That's not fair," I hissed. My blood pressure was boiling at being seen as weak and sad.

"Oh, Kate." Chloe covered her mouth, looking utterly crestfallen. "I had no idea. Why didn't I know this?" she berated herself.

"He's making it sound worse than it is. Aaron has a temper," I admitted. "Things haven't been great. But it's not all the time."

Tate, the gentle giant of Chloe's pack, looked ready to tear off heads. "There's no excuse for picking on someone weaker. That's predatory behavior."

"So, you left him?" Chloe asked hopefully.

"She should," Luke muttered.

"I can't," I answered firmly. "The kids. He could try to take my boys. I can't just pack up and leave without a plan."

"That's no excuse to stay," Chloe admonished me. "If he's violent to you, he could be the same to the boys one day. Then how would you feel?"

"This entire conversation has gotten out of hand! He barely looks at our kids, let alone lays a hand on them." My words had the opposite effect I was trying to attain. Chloe was even more horrified. "Can we please go inside? It's freezing out here, and I'm done being interrogated." I folded my arms over my chest as I fought back the tears of humiliation. My sister saw me as a negligent mother when my entire world was those boys' happiness. I was mortified. I was hurt. I was worried she might be right.

A warm hand rested on the back of my neck, softly messaging my tense muscles. "It will all be alright," Luke soothed me. "Let's get you in the house."

I let him tuck me against his chest and was able to relax with the comforting weight of his chin on my head. I didn't miss the look Chloe gave Luke over my shoulder. It was a thank you and a warning all in one.

Chapter Nineteen
Luke

I must admit, I underestimated Rollin the first time I met him. He looked like a bulked up Austin Butler. I assumed he was an empty-headed pretty boy who relied on his looks more than his brains to get by. The man was smart, though. Most of Raff's pack were college boys. That was unusual for shifters, as school was difficult when you had unexplained absences all the time. Rollin took education further than the others. Besides his engineering background, he had a passion for botany. I knew a great deal of what lived and grew in the forest from firsthand knowledge, but Rollin brought new light to every tree, bird, and insect.

We scoured the forest for the telltale signs of surveillance equipment. Rollin's in-depth knowledge made it easier to spot any fake plants that might be camouflaged as cameras. We spent almost the entire day walking miles around their territory, yet we found nothing. As the sun began to set, I agreed to head back. Raff's territory wasn't close to his father's. Kate and the kids would be safe here.

"Whelp." I stretched out my shoulders. "Looks like you're still undetected."

Rollin agreed. "How worried should we be? I never met anyone who had run-ins with an organization dedicated to our extinction until we met you."

I had to clear my throat before I could speak. The grief and rage of the past sat heavy with me. "The Order's main base of operations has always been Europe or Russia. They were the boogeyman my parents would threaten me with as a child to not stray too far from home. The past twenty years, though, they've been targeting the states. I uncovered over a dozen satellite offices. And that's just me stumbling upon them. There must be close to a hundred."

"Jeez." Rollin scrubbed his sandy blond hair. "How did they find your family?"

"God, I wish I knew," I groaned. "I was away at the time. The particulars are lost to me. Over the last six years, I tried to find out as much as I could. The assholes I found never gave me much." I abruptly stopped speaking. Our alliance with Raff's pack was new. I didn't know them well enough to trust them with all my secrets.

He clapped my shoulder. "Well, man, I hope those fuckers are no longer breathing. I know my brother isn't the warm and fuzzy type, but we all appreciate your willingness to help us out."

"Enough to put in a good word for me with Chloe?" I searched his face.

His eyebrows scrunched together. "You want to join our pack?"

It was my turn to be confused. "No," I stated politely but firmly. "It's Kate. She's my mate. Akela had mentioned Chloe would resist Kate wanting to join our pack."

Rollin blew out a surprised breath. "Does Kate want to? Chloe will most certainly have something to say about it," he winced, confirming my suspicion. "She was pissed about what happened with Caius." He looked at me meaningfully, asking without asking what the deal was.

"I'm still pissed about that," I conceded. As much as I was upset with my packmate, I didn't want to air our dirty laundry by broadcasting his prior transgressions.

"You punched him when he claimed Kate was his mate. Why?" Rollin halted our walk to give me the stare-down.

"Because I knew from the moment I saw her she was mine."

"Maybe you're both her mates." He shrugged. "It wouldn't be the first time a bond formed between more than two people."

I grunted noncommittally in response. Internally, my world was slightly rocked. It had never, even for a fraction of a second, occurred to me that Caius might not have been lying. As soon as I considered it, I dismissed it. He hadn't defended himself. He hadn't tried to see her again or plead his case. If it was the real deal, he would be as compelled to be around her as I was. Wouldn't he?

****

As we entered the house, all thoughts of Caius fled. Kate was sitting in the living room, the kids playing on the floor with Raff and Chloe. She jumped up at the sight of me and ran over. Her hand resting on my arm, concern lining her brows. Her touch was enough to warm me up from the frigid temperatures outside.

"Is everything alright? You were gone all day." She bit her wonderfully plump lip. All I could do was fixate on it. The ability to speak left me.

Rollin answered for the both of us. "We have the all clear. Luke was super helpful in showing me what to look for." He directed this part to Raff. "I think we should continue to monitor."

"Agreed," he grumbled. The ire of the situation was not settling well with the alpha inside him. "Better to be safe. We'll need to do the rounds again tomorrow."

Rollin nodded. "I'm freezing my balls off. Do I have time for a shower before dinner?"

"In honor of our guest's arrival, Lowe is making something special. You got time, but don't take too long. We won't wait for you," Raff chided his brother before he addressed me. "I assume you'll be staying with us for a bit, too?"

"I would appreciate the hospitality, alpha," I answered humbly, even though I had no intention of leaving Kate.

"Rollin can show you to one of the spare rooms," he dismissed me.

The differences between Raff's pack and ours were captured in that sentence. We had a homey little cabin tucked away in the woods where we doubled and sometimes tripled up. They had more than one spare room. Muttering my thanks, I grabbed the backpack I kept stored in my car. As a shifter, I had to keep a change of clothes with me routinely. As a man who knew what it was like to be hunted, I always kept a week's worth of essentials in my trunk.

Rollin opened a door down a massive, long hallway, and I stepped inside my designated room. It was fairly utilitarian. They hadn't been here long and it showed in the lack of décor. The room had a bed, an end table, and a small standing dresser. Fine for me. I was used to less. Dropping my pack on the bed, I fished out some clothes. My pants were wet from tracking through the forest, and I was shivering slightly. As Rollin mentioned, a hot shower sounded like heaven.

The bedroom even had an adjoining bathroom, so I wouldn't need to traipse through the hallway in search of one. When I was down to my underwear, my door pushed open. I turned to see a startled and open-mouthed Kate.

"Hello, Katrina," I practically purred as her gaze devoured me. She clearly hadn't expected to find me almost naked, but she wasn't apologizing or leaving the room either. Her eyes trailed down my torso. I could almost feel their caress. "Please come in."

"No." She shook her head frantically. "I didn't mean to ... " She trailed off as she continued to stare at me unabashedly.

I couldn't pass the opportunity up to entice my mate. I prowled forward, yanked her into the room, and closed the door. She gave this tiny, surprised squeal like a little chipmunk. Smirking, I wanted her to make all sorts of squeals and moans. Placing an arm against the doorframe, my other circled the back of her neck. Her entire body went rigid. I could sense it wasn't in fear. Even though her pulse jumped and her pupils dilated, she leaned closer to me and didn't pull away. The magnetic pull of our mate bond had her nipples pebbling and back arching to reach me.

"Do you want to be my good girl, Katrina?" I purred in her ear.

A shocked, shaky breath was my only response.

"I think you very much want to be my good little girl." My lips brushed against her cheek as my hands circled her waist. Being an omega, she was a tiny thing compared to me. I toyed with the idea of picking her up and fucking her against the wall. I bet I could get her to make all kinds of wonderful noises then.

"I-I was," she stammered. "Dinner, um ... ready soon."

"Soon? That means there's still time." My carnal message had her licking her lips. She darted a glance at the closed door but didn't deny me.

I held out my hand. Without any hesitation, she placed hers on top. She followed mindlessly as I tugged her toward the bathroom. "Beautiful," I praised. "Such a sweet, good girl for me." It wasn't until I'd closed the bathroom door and turned on the shower that she blinked and took stock of where she was.

"What are you doing?" The first hint of nerves

appeared in her voice.

I decided not to answer directly. Making her skittish was the last thing I desired. Her body wanted all the things I planned to do to her. It was her brain trying to talk her out of it. Approaching her slowly, like one would a cornered animal, I attempted to soften my gaze from predatory to mesmerizing. I rubbed a hand over the Norse runes inked over my chest that she had been studying. Like a fish attracted to a lure she looked where I pointed. "This is the motto of my family. Roughly translated, it means, give of the soul." Drawing her hand up, covering it with mine, I ran it down my chest till it rested in the center. "I plan to give you that and more, Katrina."

I held her gaze as I inched closer. Hovering my lips over hers, willing her to close the distance, needing her to show she wanted me as desperately as I did her, I waited. My girl didn't disappoint. The first light flutter of her lips against mine was all the assurance I needed. Threading my fingers in her hair, I tilted her head slightly to devour her mouth. She was all sweetness. I wanted to taste all of her. Parched. A man in the desert dying of thirst. When I broke away, we were both panting for air, hearts racing.

Like a kid on Christmas, I unbuttoned her blouse with little finesse. She had on a pretty pink push-up bra. My mouth watered, seeing her rosy pebbled nipples poking at the sheer fabric. I bent down and sucked one in my mouth hard. Kate's hiss turned into a moan when I rolled my tongue over the soft peaks. I flicked the back closure of the bra open, and her glorious mounds sprang free. "Look how soft and receptive you are to my touch."

She shuddered at my words. Tilting toward me, she thrust her breast further into my hands. Images of my dick sliding between them, cum dripping around down her throat, had my balls tightening. Her tight leggings were a bit more difficult to maneuver around, but Kate was eager to help. Relief washed over me when it was clear she was letting this intense desire between us take her places rather than resist it. I'd never sympathized with my alpha Miles more, knowing his mate kept him at arm's length for years. If Kate flat out rejected me, I wasn't sure how I'd manage to keep standing.

I turned the shower on. She arched a brow at me. "Why are we getting in the shower?"

"I desperately want to hear more of your moans," I answered, causing her to gulp. "But I don't want to share those sounds with anyone else. This is for us."

Chapter Twenty
Kate

I should have balked at all this, yet from the minute I walked in to see Luke in his boxer briefs, pale skin covered in black rune-like markings, I was in a trance. This had to be a dream. My body was doing things, and I was watching from afar. My role a silent observer to my ruination. The minute he called me a good girl, he owned me. I didn't even know I would like hearing such an endearment. Now, I practically panted, wanting to please him enough to praise me again.

Lacking any modesty or finesses, I shimmied out of my leggings, hopping about from foot to foot till I could get them off. He steadied me with a large hand while turning on the shower. "Why are we getting in the shower?" I didn't have anything with me in his room. No makeup or hair products, no change of clothes. Getting wet would be a real inconvenience, not to mention making it obvious we showered together.

"I desperately want to hear more of your moans," he rumbled. My inner thighs clenched. "But I don't want to share the sound with anyone else. This is for us."

His deep baritone was enough to start me gushing. I was embarrassingly wet. To hell with any reservations I may have had. A shower was exactly what I needed right now. I chewed on my lip while toying with the waistband of my panties. Underwear was the last thing either of us had on, like we were playing a game of truth or dare to see who would go first. Glancing at the steaming water in the shower, I hesitated. "Is this a good idea?"

Luke picked dare instead of truth. He pulled off

his boxer briefs, his fully erect member springing free. It bopped almost playfully against his stomach. I zeroed in on the motion, staring unabashedly at his beautiful cock. I'd only ever seen Aaron's small, thin penis, barely longer than his balls. There was no comparison. Luke's reached past his navel. A thick mushroom head sitting on top of an impressive shaft. For the first time in my life, I had a wild desire to drop to my knees and worship it with my mouth.

"Fuck," Luke heaved. "I'm going to incinerate if you keep looking at me like that."

Flushing at having been caught starting, I managed to look away. The steam was fogging up the mirrors now, minimally reducing the temptation to keep ogling this man.

"None of that now," he tsked. Placing his finger under my chin, he forced me back in his direction. "I always want your eyes on me, sweetness. I've never felt more alive than when you're hungry for me."

I was having difficulty swallowing. Denials and refusals rose to my lips. Yet I never uttered them. I was embarrassed at how needy I was around him, but at the same time, I couldn't force a lie that would keep me with a shred of dignity.

"Your turn," he purred, staring down at my black panties. He licked his lips as if I was unveiling a succulent treat.

His desire fueled my confidence. I wanted him to see me, not just my naked body, but all of me. I spent my life trying to be the picture-perfect version of myself. Hoping everyone would believe the facade I constructed as a shield around my broken self. This strange desire to be seen by Luke was foreign to me. I never wanted anyone to see me as less than ideal, yet I wanted Luke to see my ugly. For him to view my desperation to belong, to see my goofy side, watch my freak flag wave, and not just accept it but adore it. I should be terrified to be exposed in such a way. It felt thrilling.

His eyes turned into molten pools, shooting an injection of desire into my system. My clit throbbed. Desperate to be touched, to be petted, to be loved. A lame attempt at being sexy had me almost falling over into the sink when I tried to remove my underwear with any grace. Hoping Luke would take my clumsiness for exuberance, I giggled nervously over my near fall. "Sorry," I squeaked, blushing profusely as he once again had to save me from falling over.

"Never apologize for taking your clothes off to me." He grinned wickedly and lifted me at the waist to carry me into the shower. I wrapped my legs around his torso. Our most intimate parts were touching. The bulbous head of his cock brushed directly against my core with every step he took. The electric tinge of pleasure shooting up my spine at the slightest touch from this man made me eager to experience anything he wanted to do to me.

Hot water splashed over us as he shut the door to the shower. Luke kept me in his arms. Bringing his lips to mine in a tentative kiss, completely at odds with the fact we were both already nude and grinding on each other. I licked at the seam of his lips, wanting to feel his tongue against mine. His entire body shuddered when our mouths opened, and our tongues finally danced.

"I know you can't feel the mate bond," he groaned. "But it's like a live wire sending shock waves into me. I want to take it slow. I want to savor you, but it has me crazy horny, like a teen about to bust his first nut. Tell me to stop, and I will."

"Please," I urged him. "Don't stop. I want to feel so badly."

After another hungry kiss, he set me down as if I was made of spun glass. Reaching for the bar of soap, I watched in fascination as he lathered it up between his strong hands. Luke went to work on sudsing up my body. First, he rubbed my arms, then my shoulders and back before lavishing attention on my breasts. My nipples were sensitive to the point of pain when he finally reached them. His thumb rolled around the stiff peaks as a moan slipped out of my lips.

His eyes lit up at the sound. Sadly, his hands left my body entirely. I started to protest the loss when he dropped to his knees before me. While the warm water rained down over us, he gently kissed my pussy. I shook at the light contact. In all our years of marriage, Aaron had never once offered to pleasure me orally, even though he insisted I keep myself shaved. He always wanted me to look like the pristine little doll, one he kept in a box all these years and rarely played with.

"Hold on to the sides of the shower," Luke rumbled, barely giving me time to comply before he lifted my left leg and threw it over his shoulder. I braced my hands against the tiled walls the minute he flattened his tongue and devoured me.

The spike of pleasure at the first suck was so intense I might have had an instant mini orgasm. "Oh my god!" I shouted, almost slipping to the floor.

Luke braced me with both his hands cupping my ass. He pulled me even closer. The combination of licking and sucking had me seeing spots dancing in the corner of my vision. I came harder than I had ever been able to before. Caressing myself was no comparison to what Luke could do with his tongue. They should pay this man to perform research and development on his mouth. The sex toy business would flourish if they were able to recreate his technique.

A smirk hung on his face when he gazed up at me. My thighs were still shaking from the aftermath of an explosive orgasm when he kissed me softly, almost reverently, one more time before he stood. My hands remained up, anchoring me. I wasn't sure if I was even capable of standing on my own. He fingered through my wet tresses. I wasn't cognizant he was washing my hair until the floral smell of the shampoo hit me.

Opening my eyes after he rinsed off the soap, I stared at him, perplexed. He was still tenting a massive erection, yet made no move to further engage in sexy time activities with me. He was fully fixated now on finishing up the shower. Maybe he was waiting for me to offer in kind?

I wrapped my hand around his shaft and pumped a few times. It was slick from all the soap running off us. He clenched his jaw as if he was in agony. He tilted his head back, his Adam's apple bobbing as he attempted to swallow. I felt incredibly sexy and powerful right up till the moment he stopped my hand with his own.

Ducking his head under the water a final time, he turned off the shower. My hand was still wrapped around his cock, held in place by his. The lustful expression disappeared when he turned solemn. "I think that's all we should do for now."

"What?" I asked while quickly removing my hand, a little hurt. "Why?"

I shivered as he opened the shower door and yanked two towels off the rack. He tucked one around his waist and proceeded to dry me with the other. "I can do that," I snapped, embarrassed over the rejection.

"It's not because I don't want to, Katrina." He wrapped the towel behind me and yanked me close. I thudded against his wet chest and had to lean back to see him. His icy blue eyes were trailing over me, an intense emotion trapped behind them.

"If we have sex, it will trigger the bond between us. Being shiftless, you will barely feel it," he lamented. "While I will have an insatiable need to be with you. To be near you all the time."

I went cold at his words. My body shivered from the combination of the cool air after the shower and the knowledge he didn't want to be close to me.

"I'm not saying it right," he groaned. "Until you're ready to believe me, believe you're my mate, we should wait. I want to be inside you badly, more than you can imagine. I also know what my life would be like if the bond formed fully and you were not with me. Wa'ya have died from not being with their fated mates."

I gasped in horror at the implication we could have tied ourselves together, and I wouldn't have felt it, and he would have suffered. The knowledge my father had drank himself to death when my mother rejected him, curbed any remaining lust. "But you want me?" I asked, showing my broken side. The side of me Aaron had made pathetic.

"Baby, if you agreed right now to go back and leave that shithead you married and go away with me, I would be the happiest man on earth. I'm all in." He kissed my forehead. "I need to wait till you are."

A heavy weight settled on my shoulders at his proclamation. I pulled back, and this time he let me go. My heart felt constricted as his lips pulled down into a sad frown. As if he had taken up residence inside my head, he uttered, "I know it's a lot to ask in such a short period of time. If you felt the bond, the choice would be as simple as breathing."

"Then how is what you're feeling real? You're telling me this mystical force is bringing us together. What about what we want?" A vivid image of Caius kissing me popped into my head. It made me feel both guilty and justified. Luke seemed like an amazing guy, and I was definitely attracted to him, but if he was meant to be my fate, why did I think of Caius at all?

"You weren't raised with our kind. I understand your reservations. Being a Wa'ya means trusting your instincts. Our feelings in this body are tangled with our emotions in our other form. I know, deep in my soul, we are meant to be together." His plea made me wince.

"It's too soon for you to ask anything completely life-altering of me." I was proud my voice trembled only a little while I stood my ground. "I'm still married. I still have two boys that I love more than anything in this world. Their happiness and welfare come first."

"I'm not going to push," he promised. "I'm not insisting you accept everything all at once. I'm willing to risk a lot to be with you. I just need to know you'll give us a chance. It's why I stopped us. I know you need time."

With the heady aftereffect of climaxing long gone, I sighed as reality flooded back in. "We should head down. Dinner must be ready by now."

****

My sister clearly wasn't happy with me. She'd repeatedly scowled in my direction as I sat at the table. Arriving at dinner with Luke was bad enough. Arriving with both of us freshly showered most likely alerted everyone to what we'd been doing. Blushing profusely, I could barely make eye contact with all these men. Catching my sister's gaze was even worse. I wasn't sure if she was pissed because I left her with my kids while I had considerably the best orgasm of my life or the fact I was getting any at all.

Chloe wasn't politely ignoring the obvious or smirking, making it obnoxiously clear my upstairs activity was not to be tolerated. She was glaring at Luke and then glancing questioningly at me while bouncing Tommy on her lap. When I got up to get a drink from the kitchen, I winced when I noticed her following. As soon as we were out of earshot of the others, I spun around, ready to defend myself. "Alright, out with it. Say what you need to say."

Her scowl morphed into a frown. "I'm worried about you."

Not knowing if this was about the bombshell Luke dropped earlier about my husband or the fact I clearly just spent time with Luke, I wasn't sure how to respond. "You don't need to worry. I'll figure it out."

"That is just the thing, Kate." Chloe pulled me further into the kitchen. "Too much is happening to you! I can't believe this about Aaron, and only a fool couldn't see the connection between you and Luke."

I'd been able to avoid the Aaron topic all day. Will's refusal to nap and the baby's painful, gassy afternoon had kept this conversation on the back burner.

"Does he hurt you?" My sister's penetrating stare gave me no place to retreat to.

"Sometimes," I whispered, ashamed of my weakness.

Her expression hardened. "I will fucking kill him."

"Chloe," I began sternly. "I need to think of the boys. I agree it's time to end things and move on. I just need to do it the right way. No big scenes."

"Is that what Luke is?" she questioned, still scrutinizing me. "You moving on?"

I flushed, remembering what we'd done upstairs. "He says I'm his mate."

The sound of my sister's teeth grinding set me on edge. "Didn't that jerk Caius say the same thing to you?"

"He wasn't a jerk," I protested hotly.

My sister was taken aback. "Wait a minute. Did you feel something for Caius?"

I was mortified to say. "Not really."

"And Luke? Do you feel a connection to him?" she pressed.

"No," I quickly denied before backpedaling. "Maybe? I don't know."

Chloe scoffed at me. "Look they're both hot, I don't blame you for having an attraction for them, but believing either is your mate is a dangerous thing. I told you about the serum. It can kill you. I know these guys better now. They can't fathom being as you are and not sensing pack bonds. I don't want them talking you into anything risky."

"Wow," I held up a hand to stop her. "I'm not planning on taking anything."

The relief my words created was evident. Her face relaxed, and her shoulders slumped. "Good." She nodded. "That's good. As much as I love the bonds with my pack, I'm not sure I would have taken the risk. You have your boys to think about. This shit can kill you if you're not with your fated mate, and if it does work, you would turn into a wolf every month. Lose. Lose. What would you do with the boys? If you're having feelings for both those guys, then the risk is even greater. With Raff, I felt my entire world shift and re-center around him. He invaded all my thoughts. The fact that you're not sure and doubting if you have feelings at all indicates neither is the one."

She was emphatic in her certainty, but her statement left me hollow. I did have feelings. Strong feelings. At the end of the day, though, it did come back to my boys. I needed to live a nice, long, healthy life and provide them with the loving care I promised both of their birthmothers I would provide. "I'm not going to do anything rash. I have the boys to think about."

My sister cringed. "I don't mean to scare you. I'm the worst sister in the world for how oblivious I was to your suffering. I'm not trying to stand in the way of your happiness. If leaving Aaron and being with Luke is what makes you smile again, then I support you. Just please don't rush into any huge decision about the serum."

I was grateful she didn't ask me to keep my distance from Luke. I'm not sure I could, but this I could promise her. "You have my word."

Rubbing her temples as if a migraine was coming on, Chloe asked the question I didn't have an answer for. "And what is the plan about Aaron?"

"I can't just disappear on him," I stated firmly. "I bought myself some time, but I will have to go back. If I up and leave, he can say I kidnapped the kids or any number of crazy things. I can spend one more day here before I head home. I'm not saying this to excuse his behavior in any way," I defended my actions, knowing my sister was going to scoff at me. "He's been rough, but he doesn't beat me, and he has never laid a hand on the boys. I'm not happy and ready to move on, but I'm not in fear of my life. I need to separate from him the right way. I imagine he most likely wants to, as well. We haven't even been intimate since before Tommy was born, and he has a girl he sees."

Eyes as wide as saucers, Chloe stared at me. "He's cheating on you too?"

I sighed, deflated at her pity. "I don't want to get into it. It used to bother me, but now I see it as a good thing. He probably stays with me because he feels obligated, but if I end it and tell him it's time to move on, I think he will be relieved. We both get what we want."

"Oh, Kate," she sobbed. "I totally failed you. I

knew I had been MIA before I met Raff, then I fell off the face of the earth and you dealt with this all alone. I'm incredibly sorry."

I sniffled in response. "Don't be. I didn't want anyone to know my little bubble wasn't perfect. I kept it all inside, not wanting to be our mom." I hiccupped. "And here I am, planning to leave my husband and lusting after not one but two men."

My sister pulled me into a fierce hug. "I'm here for you. Whatever you need."

I chewed on my thumb, looking at the door to the kitchen as if I could picture who was on the other side. He wanted me to show him I was willing to give us a chance. I could do it, but it would have to be on my terms. "I'm going to need your help with Luke. I need to go home and end things with Aaron, but I don't think Luke will let me."

My sister gave me a watery smile. "I'll call Akela."

Chapter Twenty-One
Luke

I watched Kate head up to her room with her sons. The desire to join her was incredibly strong. I wanted to be near her, feel her skin pressed against mine while our bodies adjusted to each other's rhythms, till our breaths aligned and hearts beat side by side. If only Kate could feel the mate bond and know there isn't a world where we're not together. Instead, I gazed at her with longing and remained still.

Chloe must have spoken to her at dinner. She came back more reserved and withdrawn, barely noticing me. After a taste of her passion upstairs, I was starving for more. At least tonight, I could fall asleep knowing she wasn't next to the asshole husband.

I was restless. Nights spent not in my own bed never ended well for me. It's the pillows. To start, I need a minimum of two, one firm on the bottom and a feather-thin one on top. Everything else in my life was low maintenance. It had to be. I lived like a nomad for many years. Then my thirties hit, and I couldn't sleep without the fucking perfect pillow combination. It would be humiliating if I ever confessed it out loud. So, it was a restless night. I would rather eat maggots than admit to another pack I need better pillows.

I finally fell asleep a little after four, causing me to sleep in. My alpha Akela surprised me when she knocked on my bedroom door just after eleven when I was still in bed. Clever Chloe knew I wouldn't bow down to any of her desires surrounding her sister Kate. Refusing my alpha? Now, that would be much harder.

Akela plopped on my bed as I scowled at her

suspiciously. "Moring, Alpha. What brings you around these parts?"

"I got a call," Akela peered at me shrewdly. "Kate's worried you're going to be a problem."

I jumped out of the bed frantically. "What?" My voice was louder than Akela expected, based on her wince. "Did she do something? Is she safe? What's going on?" I scrambled to find my discarded jeans and shirt. There was no embarrassment having Akela see me in my underwear sporting morning wood. The woman saw me naked every month and never battled an eyelash. We were pack.

"Slow your roll, Romeo." She chortled. The nerve of some women!

"Why the hell are you laughing?" I growled.

"Kate is fine. We had a talk downstairs. She's agreed to come for a longer visit with our pack. Get to know us." She emphasized the last part.

I paused my frantic dressing. "That sounds like a good thing," I added, confused. "Why are you freaking me out then?" *Is this Kate showing me there was a chance?*

"Well," she drawled. "She believes it's important to settle things with her husband first."

"No fucking way! The fuckwad hurts her!"

My alpha held up her hand to settle me. "I heard about that too. She assured us it would be best for her to speak with her husband and end things. She has the kids to think about. She can't run away with them without any word."

"I'm going with her then." I crossed my arms over my chest and tried to get my breathing under control. Everything was still manageable.

"Kate doesn't want that. She was adamant it would be best if her husband didn't expect another man.

Could get retaliatory. He might make things more difficult for her," Akela was still speaking calmly, but I could only see red.

"Kate needs to be protected."

"No one wants her facing an abusive husband alone," she agreed. " It just can't be you. Chloe will travel back with her."

"God dammit!" I yelled, frustrated. The bond was making me crazy at the idea of letting her walk into danger, yet Akela had made some valid points. If I could think rationally, I might even be able to agree with her. "I don't like it."

"I know." She stood from the bed and offered a sympathetic squeeze on my shoulder. "They're leaving soon. Go say your goodbyes, and don't be a dick."

"Hmph," I grunted, not sure I had the ability to honor her request. I refused to say goodbye, and I sure as shit wouldn't be happy about all this scheming taking place behind my back while I was struggling with a horribly lumpy pillow.

****

Kate was packing her car up when I walked outside. I'd almost missed her. The boys were already in their car seats, and Chloe ran back inside to get travel coffee mugs for the gals.

"Are you avoiding me, Katrina?" The words came out sterner than I'd wanted, flavored with the hurt I felt at her action.

Immediately, she focused on the floor. I could have cursed out loud at myself, but I worried it would upset her more. "I didn't think you would understand. I need to do this right. I can't just run away."

I made sure to gentle my voice. "The idea of him hurting you is eating me up. I don't mean to come across as overbearing. You've had enough of that shit. But I need to protect you." I rubbed my chest. Our mate bond was incomplete but still strong enough to tug at me, urging me to keep her from danger.

Watery eyes sprang up to greet mine. Her breath hitched twice before she composed herself to speak. "It's nice to hear. To know someone cares enough to look out for me."

"You'll let me come?" Hope surged.

She shook her head quickly. "No. It wouldn't end well."

I started to speak, to plead my case, but she stopped me with a butterfly light touch of her finger on my lips. "I do feel something for you. This isn't goodbye," she stated. "Akela invited me to hang out and get to know your pack. The situation is delicate. You need to trust me to handle it. I'm doing what you asked. Thinking about the chance we might have a future. It starts with you believing in me. He doesn't want me anymore. I think that's why he's been so angry. I'll tell him it's over and leave. Chloe will be with me."

There were a few times in my life I regretted not being an alpha. As a beta, I was naturally levelheaded. We were meant to be advisors to a pack. Alphas simply took what they wanted because what they wanted was usually the right thing. I had to reflect and consider all the sides. It felt wrong to let her out of my site, yet at the same time, I couldn't let her think I didn't trust her.

Taking her extended hand, I pulled her in and engulfed her in a hug. She was stiff at first, glancing at the boys in the car, but soon melted against me. I kissed the top of her head and took in her floral scent. "Every instinct I have is screaming at me to not let you go. Please be safe."

"I will," she muttered into my chest.

"And don't keep me waiting too long." I pulled

back to gaze upon her sweet face. "I'm usually a patient man, but not when it comes to you. We have unfinished business."

Her cheeks pinked at the innuendo. "I'll be seeing you soon," she stated firmly, her lips betraying a crooked smile.

Chloe returned from the house with travel mugs in hand. "You ready?" she addressed her sister.

"Yes," Kate replied, still maintaining eye contact with me. She mouthed the words "soon" at me, and I gave her a wink and a nod in understanding.

I was antsy watching them drive away. I would be heading back with Akela and Xan, but didn't think I could sit still yet for such a long drive. Returning to the house, I saw Xan, Tate, and Rollin in the kitchen. My pack mate took one look at me, made me a cup of coffee, and slid it across the counter with a sympathetic grimace.

"It's not a rejection, man," Xan spoke.

"I know. It's not great knowing she's heading back to the jerk." I shifted my focus to Rollin. "I got some energy to burn. Might take another turn in the woods. We covered a lot of ground yesterday, but can't be too careful."

"Thanks." He jerked his chin up at me. "I got an urgent call about a project. Heading out to our latest construction site today, so I can't go with you."

"I'll go," offered Tate.

"Me too," added Xan, chugging the last sips of his coffee. "Let me get my shoes. I could use a stretch before the long car ride."

Chapter Twenty-Two
Luke

I couldn't stop feeling on edge with Kate gone. If this was what a mate bond incomplete felt like, I was glad I didn't listen to my dick last night and succumb to Kate's charms. I could tell she was more than ready to have sex with me, thrilling as that idea was, having a one-sided mate bond where I pined after her to the point of obsession and she felt little enough to flee back home to her scumbag husband, wasn't something my rational mind wanted.

Tate's resemblance to his brother Miles was comforting to my Wa'ya side. He felt familiar even, like pack, though the sensitive, quiet man acted nothing like my domineering alpha. Having my packmate Xan by my side in the forest also settled me somewhat. The three of us walked and chatted through the woods, far less vigilantly than I had with Rollin yesterday. This was more in an effort to blow off the nervous energy plaguing me than anything else.

After about an hour of hiking, I felt calm enough to sit through the long car ride, while Akela would most likely tell me everything would work out like it should. She would pump the pack bonds with so much comforting reassurance I knew I would be numb to feeling anything else.

"You guys have a nice setup here," Xan told Tate.

Tate pointed to a series of small mountain ranges a few miles away. "There're quite a few caves with good shelter over there. Our wolves have marked them as their den. We usually wake up there. I'm grateful to have them. Waking up in the snow naked is my least favorite part of being a shifter."

We both chuckled in commiseration. Our wolves were far more resilient to the elements than we were right after a change. "We have an amazing lake near us that the pack does not stray far from."

"But," Xan added. "Not much shelter. Growing up in California, most don't think we get the extreme cold, but my former pack was in the high Sierras, and we would wake up buried in snow." He shivered at the thought. "This guy," he jerked his thumb at me. "He has zero reaction. Arctic wolves are made of ice."

"I feel the cold." I chuckled. "I'm just not as much of a baby about it."

Xan's dark eyes went wide at the insult. "Like hell, you say." He grinned as he shoved me forcefully.

"The truth hurts, buddy," I joked as I righted myself and leaned against a rather large tree. As I stood, a glimmer of light reflected in my eyes. Scanning the area, I spotted a man squatting in the coverings of some dense shrubs. His camouflage attire made him difficult to see. I was on immediate alert.

Xan and Tate noticed my silence and tense expression. Their heads swiveled to the hidden man. He watched us watch him for a second before he blinked and smiled. "Hey, fellas," he spoke amiably. "Mind keeping it down a bit? I'm bird watching, and you're scaring them off."

Tate's friendly demeanor vanished. "What kind of birds?"

The man, seeing we didn't plan on leaving him, stood from his hidey spot. He had binoculars around his neck and a notepad in his hands. "The Carolina Wren."

Tate's expression stayed frosty. "That's a pretty common bird. What brings you deep in the woods to view it?"

The man scrunched his brows, appearing confused. I noticed his hands shaking just a little, but that could be attributed to the crisp air or the fact three significantly larger men were scrutinizing him. He held up his notebook, flipping to a sketch of a round little bird with spotted wings and a long protruding beak. "I can see them in the suburbs, but my drawings are more inspired when I'm in nature." He cleared his throat as if to diffuse the tension. "I make stationery," he offered.

Tate took the offered sketchbook and flipped a few pages. It was indeed filled with images of birds. Handing back the book and scrubbing his neck, Tate glanced sheepishly around. "Sorry for the third degree, man. We heard there were poachers in these woods."

"Oh." The man appeared shocked and genuinely concerned. "That's terrible. Few people respect nature like they should."

Tate's shoulders dropped as he backed away placatingly. "We'll keep it down. Your drawings are good."

"Thanks," the man replied.

About done with all this nonsense, I reached for the switchblade in my back pocket and opened it while they were still chatting about drawings. Pretending to want to see images of a bird, I angled closer to the stranger. He was more relaxed now, acting pleased with the praise Tate was offering on his sketches. Gripping him roughly by his hair, I yanked him backward. Before he could even protest, my blade was buried deep in his neck as I slit his throat from ear to ear.

Blood sprayed, hitting Tate, who was standing in front of the man. The big guy jumped back. Mouth hanging open and eyes wide, he yelled at me. "Oh my god! What the fuck? Why did you do that? Are you insane?"

The adrenaline was still pumping through me. The man choking on his own blood. I dropped him to the ground and watched as the light left his eyes. "He's a part of the Order. This man is a hunter."

"How can you be sure?" Tate was pacing back in forth, alternating between rubbing at his temples and running his hands through his hair.

"I've been hunting these fuckers for almost a decade. This one is on my list. His face is embedded in my memory." I tilted my head at Xan. "Go check his stuff."

Xan hustled over, grabbing the sack stashed in the bushes and bringing it back. He crouched on the ground as he rustled through it. "Surveillance equipment." He dug to the bottom. "And two handguns. Loaded."

Tate couldn't bring himself to stop staring at the dead man at my feet. "You're certain? You killed him without even asking a single question. Why?"

"He was here to observe," I answered, drawing his attention back to me. "But not birds, man. This is their MO. Set up surveillance. Wait for the full moon. Hunt us down as wolves for sport." I spit on the lifeless face of the asshole. "They kill us without any remorse. Remember it. The last time I hesitated, they wiped out a pack in Nevada. Hunters don't deserve mercy from us. This is war."

A guilty thought gnawed at me. Was I bringing these fuckers out around these unsuspecting packs? It felt like too great of a coincidence. I went to Austin's pack territory, and signs of hunter followed. Then I came to Raff's, and here they are again. I know they know who I am. I probably killed as many of them over the years as they killed my family members. Were they watching me? If that was the case, why was my own pack not attacked? The only thing I could think of was we didn't live where we shifted, unlike Raff and Austin's packs. Except for our omega Kyle, who lived there full time, the rest of us lived a hundred miles away from the remote location.

I pulled out my phone to text Miles what happened and to make sure he checked in on Kyle. "Call Raff," I instructed Tate. "Your entire pack needs to search these woods to see if any equipment is up and recording you. The next shift will not be safe until you ensure it."

I listened as Tate relayed the message to his alpha, letting him know where we were and what they needed to do. Xan repacked the sack, mentally cataloging everything he saw. Undisturbed and stoic as usual, he glanced at me. "It's about a third full. He must have set some stuff up. Hopefully, nothing is turned on yet."

That would be a problem. It would cause a stir with the organization if he didn't return of course, but it would be worse for Raff's pack if what we did had been observed and recorded. Tate ended the call and glanced over at me.

"What do we do now?" he asked, turning green.

Xan and I stared at each other before answering Tate. This wasn't our first rodeo. "Now, we dispose of the body."

Chapter Twenty-three
Kate

I entered my house more than a little trepidatious. The boys were a nightmare on the car ride. The constant crying had only stopped about fifteen minutes ago when they both passed out. Chloe agreed to stay in the car with them but made me promise to text if she was needed.

Aaron was home. I could hear the TV on in the living room with some kind of detective story playing. Gingerly, I set my keys in the dish on the foyer table. My palms were sweaty. My stomach was tied in knots. I wasn't sure how to tackle this. The complete bravado on the car ride over imagining what I would say was gone. Now, I was second-guessing everything.

Was I making a mistake? This was the man I chose to marry, for better or worse. Maybe I should consider counseling before leaving him? Was I truly ready to dedicate my life to a completely new existence sight unseen? There was still a small part of me that wondered if this entire shifter thing was an elaborate brainwash. I mean seeing is believing, and so far, I had no proof.

"Kate?" Aaron called from the living room. "Is that you?"

"Yeah," I replied, my voice slightly tweaking. Shaking my head to clear it of all the negative thoughts circling, I walked into the living room. Surprisingly, Aaron wasn't alone. His boss was sitting across from him, packing up papers and equipment in a bag. "Mr. Anderson." I rung my hands seeing him.

Aaron's boss was never a warm man. A retired military general he was always serious and I could never shake the feeling he didn't like me. The elderly man gave me a curt nod. "Kate. Sorry to intrude. Aaron didn't expect you back today."

I shifted from foot to foot, feeling awkward in my own home, like a schoolgirl caught ditching. "I guess I could have called first."

Aaron hadn't greeted me. No hello. No asking about the boys. Definitely no hug or kiss. Squaring my shoulders, my nerves settled from his lack of warmth. Leaving this loveless abusive marriage was the right thing to do. "I'll leave you to your work. The boys are sleeping in the car. Chloe is outside with them. I just came in to pack up some things."

"Oh?" Aaron's lips pursed. "How long are you staying with Chloe?"

I pointed upstairs. "Why don't we talk after I pack? I had a few orders I need to ship out that came in while I was away." I left it vague, hoping he would assume my packing was simply for my company and not for the extended stay I planned on taking with Akela's pack.

My reference to orders seemed to do the trick. He dismissed me with a backward wave as if he could barely be bothered to care. I reasoned there wasn't much to worry about with Aaron. He might actually be excited I wanted to leave him. I think he only stayed this long out of fear I would try to take his house or half of his savings. I honestly couldn't care less about the money. While he should offer some support for our boys, I knew I could figure the rest out.

I took the stairs two at a time feeling I'd done this mad scramble to pack just a day ago. Pulling out my cell, I shot a text to my sister.

Aaron is home
His boss is over

I'm packing
We haven't spoken yet

I saw the dots pop up, knowing she was texting back as I headed to my bedroom. I wasn't lying about having orders. Handling my business while I was away was always difficult. I would need to have access to my things until I figured out where I planned to live. I knew my mom had space. She would freak out about me moving in with the boys, but she would be cool about me taking over an empty bedroom as an office slash storage space for my business.

My sister texted back.

Boys still sleeping
Shout if you need me

I processed the orders from my website first and brought them downstairs by the door in my mailing crate. Aaron's boss was heading out the door when I descended the stairs. "Oh, goodbye, Mr. Anderson."

His stare was cold while he quietly assessed me. "You take care of those boys now."

The sentence felt mildly insulting, stiffening my spine. "Of course I will," I answered shortly.

A slight frown formed before he shook Aaron's hand. "Talk soon."

"Yes, sir." Aaron held the door open for his boss but didn't shut it after he left. He peered at my car. "Your sister plan on coming in?"

"The boys are sleeping. They were cranky in the car and finally settled as we got off the highway. I'm afraid to wake them."

He grunted and closed the door. Spinning toward me, he peered into the crate I carried, seeing my packages for my business. "You came home just to mail out five orders?"

"Not exactly," I squeaked. I could feel my cheeks

heating under his gaze. Confrontation was not my forte.

With narrowed eyes, he questioned me. "Why are you acting so squirrely?"

"Aaron, this isn't working," I blurted.

He leaned against the front door, his expression cold. "What's not working?"

My nose stung as tears threatened to fall. The word mush bubbled out. "Us. It doesn't feel like you love me. We haven't had sex in over a year. I know you've been having affairs. I've seen the texts before your so-called work trips. You've been hurting me more often. I'm not sure why we're even together." I panted at the end of my rant, having not taken a breath.

"You're not acting like yourself, Kate. Are you feeling alright?"

My mouth gaped. "Did you not hear all the things I just said?"

"Is it your business?" He glanced down at me with a raised brow. "I knew it might be too much for you to handle and still be a stay-at-home mom."

"What?" I struggled to understand what was going on. It was like we were having two different conversations. "My business isn't the issue. My issue is you're having affairs, and I don't think you love me."

"It never bothered you before," he replied nonchalantly. No dispute of my statement.

The tears cascaded down. "Why would you think that?"

He shrugged as if our conversation held little interest for him. "I thought we had an understanding. I feel I've been clear."

I scrubbed my face with the back of my hand to blot my tears. "Explain it to me then."

Sighing, he rolled his eyes as if bored with my antics. "You always were such a needy girl. I've given you all the things you asked for. The white picket fence house in the suburbs, the family life, and allowed you to have a hobby that takes up way more of your time than it should. We play house, put on an act for the neighbors and your friends. In return, you cook, clean, and stay the fuck out of my business." The last line was uttered with such menace I stepped back.

"Oh my god, Aaron. That's terrible," I gulped. "Did you ever love me?"

His tongue jutted out and he wet his lips as he looked at me dismissively. "You were a hot piece of ass at nineteen, but since you had the kids ... you put zero effort in."

My breath hitched. It's true I used to put on makeup and wear dresses and heels, but what mom with two kids under three can pull that off every day?

"And the sex?" His face scrunched as if he smelled something noxious. "I guess it was fun in the beginning breaking you in, but let's face it, sex with you is boring as hell. Other women are the only thing keeping our marriage going."

A well of insecurity sprung up as he tore me down with his cruelty. "I think you've said enough." My tone was flat. I was in shock. *This is how he's felt our entire marriage?* "You don't want to be married to me. Fine. I feel the same."

"I'm not ending our marriage," he clarified.

My eyebrows jumped to my hairline. *He's got to be kidding me?* "Why not? Clearly, you don't even like me. I deserve more than this."

"No, you don't," he sneered. "You're being an ungrateful little bitch right now. This ... " he pointed around our house. "Is exactly what you asked for. Don't suggest otherwise. You get to pretend to be perfect to the outside world, show them you're better than mommy dearest could be, and I get someone who folds my laundry."

"You could hire a maid then," I hissed.

"You're such a drama queen. Why don't you spend a week with your sister? Calm the fuck down, and when you're ready to acknowledge this is what you signed up for, I'll be ready to hear your apology." He tilted his head to the side as if he was making me a reasonable offer.

My temples throbbed. Hearing I wasn't human was less confusing than my husband thinking we had some twisted living arrangement our entire marriage. "I will be packing up my things," I conceded, not wanting this to get any uglier. "I'll be back when I figure out where to move my inventory."

He nodded along as if we were in agreement. "That's right. Cool your heels for a bit. But I expect a change of attitude after."

I ground my teeth, holding back any angry retorts. He wasn't worth it. I would do what was best, and he would have to come around to it. In a small way, I couldn't even blame him for his perverse thinking. I never complained. I never called him out. I'd wanted to prove to myself I wasn't as flighty as my mother. This conversation was eye-opening. Devastating, but exactly what I needed to hear to move on without any regrets. I shifted the bin to my hip so I could open the door with a free hand. "Please move." Aaron was still blocking the exit with his body.

He pointed at me, a fraction away from my nose. "Only since you asked nicely." He moved to the side. No surprise, he didn't assist me by opening the door. I struggled to juggle the crate and get the door open. He silently watched. I kept my expression neutral. My only other options were to rage or cry. He wasn't worth either.

The door clicked shut behind me as soon as I cleared the entrance. I'd planned to pack up more things, but that would have to wait for when Aaron wasn't home. My neighbor Mary would tell me when the coast was clear. Chloe jumped out of the car when she saw my face.

"What did the jerk say?" She searched me with worried eyes.

"Not here," I choked, emotion clogging my throat. "Take me anywhere but here."

Chapter Twenty-Four
Kate

"I take it that went well?" Chloe asked dryly.

I snorted. "It was a trainwreck. He thinks we have some agreement where he can do his own thing, cheat on me with whomever he likes, and apparently, I'm his servant." I gritted my teeth to force the tears away. I didn't want Will to wake up and catch me sobbing.

"You're such a great mom and wife. He doesn't deserve you. I hope you know that." She clasped her hand over mine and gave me a tight squeeze.

"I wasn't ready to hear it before," I admitted. "But finding out about who we truly are has helped me."

"Truly?" Chloe shrilled.

"It makes this failure feel like less my fault in some way. Stupid. I know."

"It's not stupid. However you're feeling is warranted. Our kind are meant to live in packs. Without realizing it, you tried to create one with Aaron to fill the driving need inside you. Through my entire fucked-up situation, I learned to trust my instincts more. I never thought I could forgive Raff for taking away my choice." Her mouth puckered, and I could see a storm brewing. "There are days I still feel angry at his recklessness. Yet, I'm happy. For the first time in my life, I am content. I had to let go of my ideals as fully human to accept this. Pack bonds. Mate bonds. There's nothing like them the old Chloe would have understood."

"Does that mean you won't fight me then on taking Akela up on her offer to hang with her pack this week?" I hedged my question, truly curious if she changed her mind.

Her slight grimace before she answered gave me a clue that maybe she hadn't. "I still think you should come back with me. It's one thing to get to know them all, another to go right to living with them. I'm still your big sister. I worry."

I'd listed the reasons why staying with Akela and not my sister made the most sense. Akela was closer to my home, so I could travel back for my work things. Akela was also closer to our mom as well, making transferring my stuff all the easier. I would fore go mentioning I wanted to see where this thing with Luke might go, knowing my sister was worried a week with Mile's pack would have me taking the serum to turn me fully. I might be thinking about the big D injection a bit more than was healthy, but I had zero intentions on the serum.

"Do you trust Akela?" I was putting a great deal of trust in a woman I didn't know well myself. My sister's answer would solidify my choice.

Chloe breathed out in a huff. "With my life. Female alphas usually grate on each other and don't get along, but she felt like family to me from the start."

Grateful her confession would make convincing her to drive me to Akela's rather than back to her place easier, I was going to reply we should head to the address when Chloe's cell phone rang. She answered. I could see Raff's name on the car monitor.

"Are you safe?" he blurted out.

"Yes," Chloe raised her eyebrows at me while she spoke. "Everything alright?"

"Luke, Tate, and Xan came across a hunter. We found surveillance equipment in his bag and anchored to a few trees behind our home," Raff growled. "We need to compare what we found with what happened by my folks' place. We are all headed that way. Is Kate still with

147

you?"

"She is. Where should I take her and the boys?" Her skin had gone almost as white as milk hearing their home was in danger. I couldn't imagine how scary it would be to shift into a wolf and no longer have a sense of yourself. The fact that there were hunters out there when you were in such a delicate state must be terrifying.

"Head to Mile's garage. Akela left about an hour ago and might arrive at the same time as you. They have an extra apartment up there that's open Kate can use. Its either that or your mother's."

The idea of managing my erratic mother and dealing with my life falling apart was too much to process. "Let's go to Miles's garage," I offered.

"You sure?" Chloe looked torn. "Maybe Mom's will be safer. People are targeting us."

"You told me to trust my instincts. It feels right to go there," I replied with a bit more confidence than I felt.

"I'll call you when we get to the garage," Chloe spoke to Raff.

"Be safe, darlin'. We have some loose ends here to tidy up. I'll come by and collect you before we head to my folk's place."

"Sounds like a plan." She ended the call and turned to me. "I guess you're fully into our world now." She glanced at the review mirror, seeing my boys continue to sleep in their car seats.

I trusted Raff wouldn't send me to the garage unless he thought the boys wouldn't be in danger. Looking over my shoulder at their sweet faces, I actually felt more resolved. "I'm going to find a better life than this one, Chloe. For their sake, I won't settle for anything less again."

A genuine smile graced my sister's face. "As I said, better is what someone as incredible as you deserves."

Miles's mechanic shop wasn't too far from Austin and Valentina's pack territory. Most of his pack worked with him at the garage. When we pulled up, it was early afternoon, and there were two cars up on hydraulic lifts being worked on. Once we parked, the big man himself came out to greet us.

"Akela here?" My sister was gruff in her greeting, barely acknowledging the giant man.

"It's just going to be like that, is it?" Miles asked ruefully.

"So, Akela's not here then?" Chloe's tone remained cold.

"Not going to see your way into forgiving me? Raff kidnapped you, and you love him." He grinned cheekily.

"He didn't hold a gun to my head," she deadpanned.

I gasped, shooting glances back and forth between them.

"It wasn't loaded," Miles admitted.

"Somehow, that makes it worse," she muttered.

"I never did get the full story here," I interjected. "Feels like I'm playing catch up. Exactly how many people have kidnapped you? Or how many times? Care to enlighten me?"

My sister had the gall to look exasperated. "I guess twice. Miles here." Chloe jabbed a finger in his direction. "Carjacked me and then used me as a hostage exchange for Akela."

"Really?" Tendrils of fear started to creep in. Everyone was friendly at Valentina's house. I thought maybe what I had heard was simply a misunderstanding. Caius had joked about abducting my sister, but it had been a joke, right? Otherwise, what the heck was I doing here?

"It was a lapse in judgment. I was at the end of my rope," he replied sheepishly.

"Is that an apology?" Chloe placed both hands on her hips, glaring daggers.

"Have I not yet apologized?" Miles rubbed his chin, a devilish gleam in his eye.

Chloe spun from him to turn to me. "I change my mind. We should go to Mom's house."

"Don't get your panties in a bunch. Your sister and the boys will be safe and watched over. I promise you." Miles held up his hand like a boy scout taking an oath.

"Still not an apology," Chloe muttered. "At least the pretty boy apologized."

Miles was completely unfazed by her vitriol. "Alphas aren't known for apologies." He shrugged. "I can promise not to do it again if it will help you get over it."

"An apology would help me to get over it." Chloe was never one to back down.

"I'm sure it would." His eyes crinkled at the corners as if he was enjoying her ire. "But it got Akela to take me and my pack seriously for the first time in my life. I couldn't be happier with the outcome."

"Gah," Chloe cursed under her breath. "Why the hell do I find that tragically romantic? Fine. Water under the bridge." She jutted out her hand.

Miles chuckled while shaking it. I stood there, transfixed at the bizarre conversation. Shifters were weird. "Thank you for having me," I lamely uttered, uncomfortable with knowing kidnapping was apparently a common thing among the Wa'ya.

"I still have to clear out a few boxes from upstairs." He acted a bit put out. "A former pack mate lived there and hasn't shown his face to collect his things. Guess it's a good time to donate them. Come on. I'll show you the apartment."

Will woke up as I pulled him out of his car seat. Tommy started crying for a bottle. Chloe was a godsend, prepping one for me and feeding him while I carried a confused toddler up a flight of stairs.

"Where are we, Mommy?" he asked sleepily.

"We're still having an adventure. Staying here for a bit."

"I want to go home," he cried. I rubbed his back and shushed him as well as I could.

Miles opened the door to the apartment to let us in. "There are two bedrooms. I got you a pack and play for the baby. There are two twin beds in the guest room." He motioned towards the door.

"That was very kind of you." I felt like a homeless woman seeking shelter.

"For you, little guy," Miles soothed. "I found an entire trainset at the thrift store you might like." He pointed to a box sitting by the sofa in the living room. It was filled with Thomas the Train sets, Will's absolute favorite. My son's eyes went wide, and he squirmed to get down. He ran over to them, tears dried up, and homesickness pushed aside for now.

I blotted a stray tear at the sight. "Even more kind of you."

"I wanted to make sure you had an easy time settling in." He watched Will pull out the toys with a soft smile. "I sanitized them."

"Well damn." Chloe sat beside me while Tommy sucked away at his bottle. "Why did you have to go and do something thoughtful? I almost WANT to like you now."

"You got them?" I asked my sister. "I'll go back

down to the car and get my stuff." Everything felt surreal. I just needed to keep moving.

Chloe nodded at the same time Miles offered, "I'll help you."

We made a few trips until the car was unpacked. Miles brought my bags to what would be my room. I decided to unpack to become more settled. There were three boxes stacked by the door. Miles started to take them away. He came back for the second box while I was putting my clothes in the drawers. I sensed his presence directly behind me, but he didn't speak.

Peering over my shoulder to see if he needed anything, I gasped. It wasn't Miles. Caius stood over me. Dark eyes blazed with undecipherable emotions. I turned to face him, absentmindedly holding in my hands two pairs of lace thongs I'd been about to put away.

His gaze trailed slowly down my body to see what I held. Heat flared between us. "Are those for me?" he teased, thick pink tongue skating over his bottom lip.

I immediately thought about the scorching kiss we shared in the kitchen. How I swore I felt sparks when he touched me. "I was putting my things away," I explained the obvious.

He came close enough I could see the gold flecks in his brown eyes. His hand sprang forth as if of its own volition and brushed strands of my hair behind my ear. The touch was light. Gentle. Yet, I could feel it resonate throughout my body. Tingles started at the tips of my ears, traveled down my spine, and settled in my core. *How can one touch get me this aroused?*

"What are you doing here?" Suspicious of his motives and alarmed at my reaction to his presence, I threw the thongs in the drawer and slammed it shut. My frantic motion caused him to snap.

"Why wouldn't I be here? This is my pack. My

place of work. My home." He backed me up against the dresser, all softness gone from his demeanor. My heart pounded. Worry swirled in my gut. Had I left one bad situation to find another? Were these men dangerous?

"What's going on?" Akela's firm voice immediately relaxed me. I was overjoyed she finally arrived, I wondered if Luke was here too.

"Thought it might be good to establish some ground rules." Caius backed away, giving me my much-needed breathing room, yet his eyes still held mine as he spoke with his alpha.

"I hardly think that's necessary." There was a question in her tone. Her pale brows bunched in confusion as she assessed him.

Caius faced her, all charm and smoothness back in pace. "You're the alpha. I guess rules are more your thing?"

She scoffed at his antics, as if he was only teasing me. It hadn't felt that way. He'd gone from hot to frosty in under a minute. I wasn't sure if he was threatening me or lusting after me.

"Come on," Akela jerked her head toward the living room area. "I stopped and picked up lunch." She walked out, expecting to be followed.

I made it a few steps when I heard a drawer open. My jaw dropped at what I saw. Caius had reached into the dresser, pulled out a pair of my panties, and pocketed them! "Put those back," I hissed.

He walked by me, his arm grazing mine slowly. "I don't know what you're talking about." Stepping out of my room, he raised his voice. "Mmm, something smells good enough to eat."

My cheeks heated. He spoke to Akela about lunch, but I couldn't help feeling his words were meant for me.

Chapter Twenty-Five
Kate

"What's this one." Will giggled, pointing to a drawing in his book.

"That's an elephant dragon," I replied patiently, even though this book depicting dragons at the zoo was his favorite and one we read for bedtime often. Tonight, he was in a new room and a new bed. I wanted to make sure he had something predictable. Timmy was in his pack and play, half asleep, sucking on his thumb, oblivious to anything different.

"Do the voices!" Will demanded. I snuggled him, peppering kisses on his face while I recited the book from memory. His laughter filled my heart. I loved he could feel such joy over something so simple. The thing we lose most when we grow up is unfettered joy. I was lucky to experience it again through him.

Happy to humor my homesick toddler, I did all his favorite voices, then switched to a more soothing book to calm him down and get him to sleep. I read a few pages of a chapter book each night until his eyelids were too heavy, and he could no longer fight the inevitable.

Tiptoeing out of the room, I closed the door behind me. A soft knock at the front door alerted me I had a visitor. Forgetting to check the peephole, I flung open the door. Luke was on the other side. He rested against the doorframe. Akela had told me Miles had needed him at lunch. Much to my disappointment he'd spent the latter half of the day working in the shop, but must have come straight to me when he could. There was grease still on his hands his hair was mussed up as if he'd been brushing his bangs out of his way all day to see, and his mechanics jumpsuit was fully unzipped and tied at the waist. Only the bottoms remained intact, providing me with an unobscured view of his ink covered arms and chest. I watched as he wet his lips. He looked famished.

"Akela said you were here, but I needed to see for myself. You came," he growled.

I gulped before I could speak. "I came."

"You could have gone to your mom's, but you came to me instead. It has meaning." I felt the declaration in my bones. A claiming.

"It does." No part of me was able to deny it.

"You left him?" His stare was intense while he waited for my answer.

"I told him it was over." I left out the part where Aaron didn't believe me.

A slow, lazy smile settled over his lips. I couldn't resist licking my own. I might be hungry too. Starved for touch. Empty inside and needing to be filled. He breathed in and out twice, slow and heavy. I stopped breathing entirely, trapped and fascinated while his gaze lingered over me.

He pounced then. Springing forward from the entry and into the apartment, Luke picked me up by the waist and fused his mouth over mine. I wrapped my legs around his torso, my arms circling around his neck, and kissed him back as if he was a last meal. He nipped and sucked, alternating between delivering little bites over my lips and sucking on my tongue. I honest to god moaned directly into his mouth. This man could kiss. It made my entire experience with my husband a sad parody of what kissing could be.

"I missed you," Luke rumbled as he carried me to the sofa and sat us down. I remained straddling him. Throughout all the motion, we never stopped kissing, as if it had been a lifetime and not simply a day since we were together.

This new position had his erection pressed firmly against my swollen need. I couldn't resist grinding, the desire for more friction riding me. The action had Luke pulling his mouth away. I chased after his lips, needing them back. He gave me one hard, closed-mouth kiss, then turned his face to the side and panted.

"The bond is already singing inside me." He turned back to face me. "I want you, Katrina."

Gently, I glided my fingers over his brow. I knew what he was asking. This wasn't just sex. He wanted to know if I would consider this the start of a relationship. "I want you too."

His eyes scrunched closed, and he sighed. "Thank fuck," he replied. "I don't have the willpower to hold back again. Here or your bedroom?"

Perhaps I should have played it coyer and commented on his presumptions. All I could think about was seeing his naked body again. The bedroom shared a wall with the kids' room. The living room was the farthest away. "Here," I whispered over his lips while my hands made short work of his belt buckle.

"I should shower first," he offered, trying to still my hands.

"I don't mind you dirty." I could feel my cheeks heat at my forwardness, but I wanted this man like my lungs needed air.

He chuckled at my eagerness and aided me in opening his fly. His cock sprung out, and I was almost giddy, circling my hand around it. There was a bead of pre-cum at the tip, and I rubbed my thumb over it. Luke's hips shifted at the caress. His groan was deep, his body vibrating with the force of it. "You're going to be an addiction."

Pumping his shaft with a firm, slow stroke, I slid to the floor, landing on my knees. Hissed expletives busted from his lips when I took him in my mouth, I felt powerful, desired. I sucked on the head while fisting the base, proud I could manage without gagging. When he tunneled his fingers into my hair and praised me, I thought I was going to combust. My toes curled at the tingling sensation over my scalp as he kept me in place, where he needed me most.

"Such a good girl," he murmured. My back arched at the compliment. I loved hearing him moan. It was a far cry from the passive sex I had with Aaron. Luke would never call me boring. Wanting to continue until he came undone, I quickened my pace, but Luke had other plans. "I want to be inside you."

I popped him out of my mouth and gave a long, lingering, wet kiss over his crown. "But I was having fun," I playfully pouted.

A wild gleam entered his icy blue eyes. "Don't be a brat, or you won't get your treat." He stuck his finger under my chin and lifted my head. "Strip."

With my heart wildly beating out of my chest, I stood and stripped. Luke had seen me naked in the shower, but if his increased breathing and dilated eyes were any indication, he was more than excited to see me naked again. I wondered why I didn't feel awkward baring myself to him. Aaron hadn't been particularly interested in my body for such a long time I'd started to see myself as deficient. Standing in front of Luke, desire radiated off him and engulfed me. I was transformed from the not-as-hot sister to a succubus. Confident, I shimmied my panties down my legs and tossed them at him.

"Naughty minx." He chuckled. "Now come over here and ride my cock so I can suck on those pretty nipples."

I stumbled forward, eager and terrified at once. I

was doing this. I was leaving my cheating husband behind and starting something new with this man who called me his fated mate. This act would connect us. By agreeing to the sex, I knew Luke would expect me to commit. It was too fast, too reckless, and nothing the old me would have contemplated, but since discovering the truth about myself, I no longer cared what old Kate would do. She'd lead me wrong one too many times to be trusted. New Kate was going to embrace being a bit wild. I was going to fight for the love I deserved.

I sat astride him again, but this time with no barriers between us. My thighs tensed, tickled by the rougher hair on his legs. My breasts were at the perfect level for Luke to do what he'd promised. His hands scooped my right boob as his tongue stroked my hardening nipple. My core clenched at the sensation.

The gentle licks turned into a pinching bite. I hissed in surprise and then moaned as he soothed the ache with a powerful suck I felt zing to my core. My hands circled his neck and played with his short-cropped blond hair. A playful slap on my ass was delivered. "Get to work," he mumbled between sucks.

I mock glared at the demand until another smack made me shriek, which transformed into a giggle as his fingers danced up my spine. I raised myself, lining up my core directly over him. He shifted up, the tip penetrating me, and waited for me to complete the motion. I was crazy wet. My thighs sticky with desire. I slid down and fully sheathed him after only a few thrusts. He was wonderfully snug inside me, and at this angle, if I leaned forward, I could grind my clit over his abs.

"Yes, that's my girl." Luke grabbed both my ass cheeks and squeezed. "Take your pleasure, baby."

No more encouragement needed, I did as instructed. Eager, Luke met my movements with powerful upward thrusts of his own. Small beads of sweat formed on my brow as I struggled to keep quiet and not wake the boys. Desperately, I wanted to groan in appreciation of how amazing he felt underneath me. At that moment, I believed in the mate bond. It had to be real because the connection was otherworldly. His hard cock pounded relentlessly at my G-spot at just the right angle. In the relatively few climaxes I've had, never did I experience an orgasm without external stimulation. As the pressure built and built, I could tell it wouldn't be a problem with Luke.

"Oh god." The words slipped out of my clenched lips. Spots of fractured rainbows formed behind my eyes as little earthquakes of pleasure wracked my body until I couldn't hold back a cry. Sealing his lips to mine, Luke muffled my noises as the intensity of the orgasm mounted. My legs, no longer able to keep rhythm or hold me up, trembled as I collapsed against his chest.

"That might have been the single most beautiful thing I've ever seen," he whispered into my hair.

"I have no words," I panted, trying to catch my breath.

"Probably for the best, then," he joked as he stood, pulling out of me. "Lay over the couch. Show me that cute little butt of yours."

It thrilled me how demanding he was, made me want him to do all sorts of things to me. On trembling legs, I leaned over the couch, my head angled back to watch him watch me. "Like this?"

He was staring at my opening, stroking himself and smiling. "Just perfect," he crooned, lining up behind me. "Such a perfect girl." In one powerful thrust, he was sheathed inside me. I had to brace against the arm of the sofa to keep from falling over. "You ready?" he asked, taking only shallow thrusts, teasing my opening, as I regained my balance.

"Honestly"—I choked—"I'm not sure."

A dark chuckle followed my statement. "Your body is, though." Luke set a punishing, brutal pace, hitting that secret magic spot inside me over and over. I squirmed. The pleasure was bordering on discomfort, the mix bringing me to an even higher height.

Holy crap, I'm going to come again!

"That's it," he murmured as my walls squeeze him tighter. "Come for me, baby."

I pressed my face into the pillow to muffle my cries. Luke leaned forward, going impossibly deeper inside me. He wrapped his arm under my torso, and his clever fingers strummed my clit. It took barely more than a few strokes before I tumbled into another climax even stronger than the last. I was a boneless passive participant floating on a cloud of pleasure when I felt him finish inside me.

"Fuck," he grunted as his thrust grew sloppy and sporadic. He slumped forward, trailing kisses on my neck and upper back while he was pulsing inside me. I might have been content to pass out slumped over the side of the couch. Our coupling had taken everything out of me. I closed my eyes in a bubble of bliss.

"Let's get cleaned up and get to bed." He kissed my temple as he pulled away. I couldn't help the wince. "Too rough?" Concern laced his voice.

I shook my head. "It's been a while. I think I'm gonna feel that tomorrow."

I opened my eyes to see him staring at me adoringly. "Please don't hate me, but I love the sound of that. I promise to kiss it all better."

"Hmph," I snorted.

His face turned serious. "I'm glad you came."

"More than once," I answered cheekily.

"The brat is back, I see." His fingers danced along my rib cage. Slapping my hand over my mouth to cover my squeal, I danced away from him. "I'm glad you came," he began again, the meaning heavy between us. I came here for him.

"Me too," I replied softly, feeling vulnerable for the first time tonight.

He scooped me up and cradled me to his chest. "It's going to be alright, you know."

I squeezed my eyes tight wanting desperately to believe in the fantasy. "Is it?"

"Yes," he stated firmly. "I'll make sure of it."

Chapter Twenty-Six
Luke

The mate bond wrapped itself firmly around my heart. I couldn't lie—it killed me she didn't sense it like I did. I'd never given too much thought to the serum allowing Wa'ya shiftless females to shift. I'd been on the road looking for my family's killers and trying to find a new home. Then, with Miles, I just wanted us to have the pack bonds back. It felt greedy to want to have a mate bond, too.

Having it all was never an easy task. How could I ask her to take the serum without coming across as a selfish jerk? Was it even fair of me to think about? She didn't grow up in a pack. I knew her sister was still terrified of the change, seeing it as a loss of oneself and control. When you grow up as a shifter it's a part of who we are, never fully complete unless both sides can have the reigns at times. I believed it was why shiftless females couldn't sense pack bonds. Without their wolves coming out to play each month, the mystical side of our nature was subverted.

Would Kate want this life? Would it be fair to ask her to make any decision so soon after discovering what she was? I knew I wouldn't even consider it unless the danger of the Order wasn't lurking over our heads. I watched her sleep beside me, unable to venture into the dream world myself. Hearing she'd come to our pack instead of staying with her husband or going to her mother's home confirmed she did feel something. Why else agree to move in with people you just met unless you felt a connection?

A crash in the shop below had me jumping up,

almost waking Kate. I waited for my heart to stop pounding while I listened for any follow-up noises. Something heavy dropped. Loud footsteps accompanied the noise. Quietly springing out of bed, I threw on my boxer briefs and stuffed my feet into sneakers. Worried the garage might be getting robbed, I texted Miles. Hopefully he could check the cameras or call the police before I made it down to the shop. I tiptoed down the stairs, not wanting to alert the invader. Just before my hand reached the doorknob, my phone buzzed. It was a text from Miles.

Its Caius
He looks drunk
See what's going on

Tampering down the instant aggression I felt at seeing my packmate's name, I took a calming breath and opened the door. With grim satisfaction, I watched Caius attempt to stand. He must have fallen walking around in the dark. A tray of tools was knocked over, and the car jack was askew, looking like he stumbled right over it.

"Working in the dark tonight?" I shouted so he would know he was no longer alone.

"Shit!" I'd startled him. He slammed back down to one knee while trying to turn towards my voice.

He winced, covering his face when I flipped on the lights. With the cold, sterile lighting, Caius looked like shit. His eyes were bloodshot, his dark skin was sickly pale, and there was a mottling of bruises on his face. I admit I wasn't certain if they were from me or more recent activities. I rested my back against the door and folded my arms over my chest. "Piss someone else off?"

"Fuck off," he slurred.

Peering at him more closely, I pushed off from the door and took a few steps forward. The man reeked. The stench of stale beer and cigarettes permeated the room. "Damn, man." I fanned the air with my hand. "You reek of a dive bar." Caius's choppy, lurching movements confirmed Mile's theory. He was absolutely wasted, stumbling his way to a swivel chair by a desk. My face scrunched in concern. "Did you drive here?"

"Walked," he mumbled. "Now, fuck off."

Fine by me. I didn't need to waste a moment more with this loser. I huffed and turned to go.

"Wait!" he drunkenly bellowed.

Facing him, I watched his face morph from confusion to where he was to the realization he was speaking to me. His eyes narrowed, noticing my lack of clothing. "What are you doing here?"

Without meaning to, I glanced upward, where I hoped my beautiful mate was still sleeping.

"Ah." Something ugly slithered across his features, and the pack bond fizzled with jealousy. "Never mind." He dropped his head on the desk and closed his eyes, dismissing me.

I watched him for a beat while I rubbed a spot over my chest. The bonds had a discordant thrum I wasn't used to feeling. Caius's breathing slowed. He was most likely passed out. I dimmed the lights and left him there, taking the heavy wrongness of the pack bond up the stairs with me.

Chapter Twenty-Seven
Kate

I woke deliciously warm and boneless. Luke was wrapped around me like a weighted blanket. His leg tangled with mine, his arm slung over my torso, while his hand cradled my breast, and his face nuzzled in my neck. Aaron and I slept as far apart on the bed as we could. He complained my snoring kept him up at night. I never considered myself a cuddler, but waking up this morning changed every notion I had. I'd never slept better.

Usually, the sound of a crying baby jostled me awake. I panicked for a second, tensing, thinking I forgot to turn on the baby monitor in the room. Shifting to look at the nightstand, I relaxed when I saw the green light. The boys went to bed later than usual with all the travel, and I wanted to thank every deity known to man for the rare gift of getting to sleep in. My movement pulled Luke from his slumber. His lax arm tightened into a hug.

"Morning, beautiful," he mumbled groggily as he trailed soft kisses down the nape of my neck.

I stretched like a cat, nudging him for more attention. He rolled me to my back and sprang on top of me in a lightning-fast move. Giggles bubbled out of me like a shaken can of soda. The laughter died quickly, though, when I gazed at the rampant desire in his eyes. He settled between my thighs, his erection hot and heavy, teasing my folds. His hips thrust, rubbing his cock against my entrance, meeting little resistance.

"Mmmm, already wonderfully wet for me?" he crooned as he continued to rock.

I titled my head away self-consciously. "I should brush," I protested.

"Nothing about you could ever be less than

sweet," he answered, burying his tongue in my mouth and groaning to prove his point.

Who knew how much precious time we had left before the boys were up? No need to waste it! I kissed him back, happy for once to feel lusted after, gratified this man considered me sexy and was eager to be with me. It erased some of my normal hang-ups. I didn't have to act perfect for Luke to want me. He wanted me any way he could get me. It was freeing.

Luke gazed into my eyes with a silent question of consent. I eagerly shifted under him, lining myself up. He smirked as he tortured me with shallow thrusts, drawing out my wetness but doing little to satiate my need to feel him fill me. I tried to take what I wanted, shifting upward and reaching, but he refused to sink in fully.

I mean time is of the essence here? Does he know what a crazy morning it will be once those kids are up?

"Please hurry," I moan-whispered. "We may not have much time."

That evil little grin didn't leave his face. "The boys woke up over an hour and a half ago."

"What?" I exclaimed just as he pushed in forcibly, causing my breath to hitch.

He continued his slow, torturous movements. "Akela brought over a tandem stroller her mom had saved from when the twins were little. She took them for a walk and told me to meet her at their place."

It was hard to concentrate on his words when his languid pace was driving me crazy. I wiggled restlessly under him. "Why didn't you wake me?"

"You needed more sleep. You were worn out." He plied a sweet, chaste kiss on my lips. "I wanted to make sure you had plenty of energy for me." He winked.

"It's strange having other people take care of

them," I fretted.

"That's pack life. We share each other burdens."

What a wonderfully sweet and tender thing. Could it be that simple?

"Do you mind?" He paused his teasing to search my face. "I craved more time with you, and Akela was happy to watch them."

I circled the globes of his ass and squeezed. A huge smile stretched across my face. "More time with you is exactly what I need, but I still would like to request faster."

"Oh, is that so?" he mused, acting like he was contemplating the mysteries of the universe. "Well, I don't want to disappoint."

Luke's body could never disappoint me. It spoke to mine on a heightened level. Every caress was a balm to my soul, every nip broke me down on a cellular level, every kiss repaired my shattered pieces. I loved the woman I was when I was with him. He pistoned faster as requested, targeting the sweet spot that made my vision blur and toes curl. I raked my nails down his back, overcome in sensation as my climax crested too soon. It was almost sharp in its pleasure, jarring my body with its abruptness. "Oh, my god!" I screamed, unable to contain the overwhelming sensation.

"Not god, just your mate. That's the bond you feel tugging at you, exponentially growing your pleasure. I feel it, too. Let's try for one more, shall we?"

A feeble protest left my lips, but when Luke's tongue flicked over my pebbled nipple, I pushed in for more rather than pull away. The first orgasm had been built with speed. Luke clearly had different plans for the second.

His hot mouth devoured every inch of my skin he could reach. I never realized how turned on I could get from delicate nibbles on my earlobes or his tongue over my neck. An actual mewling sound erupted from me when he finally paid attention to my clit. My hips thrust on their own volition, demanding more friction. He was in a teasing mood, though. Keeping the pace slow. Shifting away from where I wanted him most to torture my ticklish belly button with his warm breath. I squirmed and almost jumped right off the bed when he slapped my pussy.

"Be still," he admonished.

I went ramrod straight, not wanting to disappoint. "Yes, sir," I whispered.

"Oh." He kissed my mouth. "I like that. Such a good girl to take direction so well."

I wordlessly nodded. Good girls get rewarded.

Lifting up my legs, he threw them over each shoulder. I lifted my ass off the mattress as I bared my opening to his hungry gaze. He grabbed his dick and rubbed it over my wetness. "So beautiful," he murmured, transfixed as he slotted himself at my opening.

"Please," I begged. He'd worked me up with his lingering kisses, and I was mindless in need.

"I got you, baby." He inched back inside, keeping his thrust shallow. I could do little but accept the pace he set. With my legs thrown over his wide shoulders and only my upper back on the bed, I had very little leverage. My one attempt at forcing him in deeper caused him to immediately still.

"Am I going to have to tie you up?" The sparkle in his eyes told me how excited the idea made him. I never considered it before, but I trusted Luke. Giving over control and having him take care of me in every way excited a dark part inside me.

"If you like," I responded breathily.

"I would like, but it will need to wait till we are at

my place for that kind of play."

Images of a sex dungeon popped into my head. Luke didn't seem like the playroom type of guy, but he was giving Dom vibes. I had no idea where Luke even lived. I was caught up in him, but I didn't know him.

He sank into me fully. "Where did you go, baby?" Seductively, he sucked on his thumb before bringing it to circle my clit.

Thoughts? I might have had thoughts. Now, there was only feeling. I flung my head back as my climax started to build. He filled me so beautifully. Hot velvet steal slid inside me while his thumb never faltered in its motion. I dug my heels into his back as my body shook. Little earthquakes of pleasure rattled me.

"Come with me, baby," he demanded, his deep baritone the final stimulant to propel my body to the pinnacle. Even though we were alone, I muffled my scream, biting on my first to ground me. His face scrunched, orgasm seizing him. I was little more than a spent rag doll while he finished inside me. Luke allowed my legs, overcooked noodles, to drop. Careful not to collapse on me, Luke rolled us to our side. He managed to stay buried deep inside me, softening slightly but not fully. "We aren't done yet." He kissed my hair. "That was round one. Be a good girl and stay right where you are. I'll be ready in a minute."

I hid my smile with my face buried under his chin, pressed against his chest. The feeling of his rapidly beating heart mirrored my own. "Not sure I believe you," I spoke as seriously as I was able.

"Oh, my sweet girl, you doubt me? Don't think I'm capable?" His guffaw shook us slightly.

"I've heard most men are one and done. Nothing to be ashamed of if you can't go twice." I had to press my lips together to keep the giggles in.

"Twice?" His hand circled around my throat as he lifted my chin up to greet him. "I have you all to myself in a bed with no interruptions. It's going to be a hell of a lot more than two times before I even consider letting you out of this room."

This time, I scoffed. "Oh, please." I rolled my eyes. "Girls can go multiple times but guys only got so much juice in the tank."

His eyes narrowed. "Is that so?"

"Medically speaking? Yes."

"And you are an expert on Wa'ya physique?" His brow arched.

"It can't be incredibly different. You're still a man. And men have limitations in that department." I smirked.

"Certain, are you?" I could feel Luke hardening inside me as we spoke. He emphasized the word *certain* with a hard thrust.

"Yup," I chirped, popping the P and grinning up at him. Clearly, he was capable of going again and I was more than eager for him to, but surely sexy time would come to an end after that.

Lessoned learned. Luke spent the next hour and a half proving me wrong.

Chapter Twenty-Eight
Luke

As much as I would have liked to keep Kate locked away in a room, naked and at my mercy, I could tell she was anxious to see her boys. I drove her to Miles's place, my hand resting on her thigh, her hand covering mine. Already, we were comfortable in each other's presence. Being with her was as easy as breathing.

As soon as we entered Miles's pad, I could tell the boys were excited to see her. I loved watching her with them. She was an amazing mom. Always anticipating their needs, creating structure in the day to help them deal with the changes happening, and crazy affectionate. My family was loving but not overly physical. Watching Kate ply the boys with kisses and hugs shouldn't have made me jealous, but in a sad way, it did. I didn't begrudge the little guys, it was more about knowing I would never be able to kiss or hug any of my family ever again. I wish I'd done more of that before I lost them.

Fucking Order.

The seriousness of these hunters in two pack territories was strumming through the pack bond. Miles had called us all to come over. Even Kyle drove in from the cabin. I could tell our alpha didn't feel we were safe unless he had eyes on us.

Akela and Kate sat on the floor with the kids, sharing a plate of nachos and talking animatedly about some Netflix show I'd never heard of. Caius was nursing a hangover as he reclined in the lazy boy. When I looked directly at him, his eyes were closed, yet I could swear I saw him watching Kate in my peripheral vision. Xan was with Abel in the kitchen whipping up lunch for themselves. Kyle was sitting at the kitchen table with Miles, going through the camera feeds at our properties, looking for anything out of the ordinary. I set down my own plate and joined them. Curious if they'd seen anything or if another set of eyes might find something they missed.

"How far back did you go?" I asked.

Kyle rubbed at his red-tinged eyes. "I've been watching for six hours now. Fast forwarding and freezing at any movement. Ninety-nine percent are animals alerting the camera to record. I've gone back three days. Nothing." He sighed as he arched his spine and stretched.

"I can take over for a bit," I offered.

Miles nodded, pushing his empty plate away. "Go get yourself some food," he instructed the omega. "Luke has a good eye for this stuff. Better than us."

Kyle didn't protest. The guy seemed worn out. The worry of being alone at the cabin and being responsible for our safety when we returned there was obviously plaguing him. I could feel it sitting oily and heavy in our connection. "Hey. We know about the bastards now. We got this. It's not all on you." Kyle was our computer guru and we did rely on him for all the techy stuff, but hunting the Order was my specialty.

The oily heaviness of worry receded slightly from the pack bond as his shoulders dropped after being bunched tight. "Thanks, man."

Miles patted my arm in silent appreciation as I took my seat and got to work viewing the camera footage.

"I'll need to head to Austins' tomorrow. He called an alpha meeting among packs to see how widespread this is," our alpha informed us.

"Is that wise? You all grouped together?" I

frowned.

"We're meeting at his lab. It's heavily guarded." He shrugged. "Can't think of a safer place, and this feels like it can't be a phone call type of talk."

"Will your father go?"

"Doubtful," Miles scoffed. "My mom would think it was a good thing. Another way to weed out the weak kind of bullshit."

I winced, thinking about any brief interactions I had with that woman over the years. She was terrifying in her hatred. She had yet to acknowledge Miles had found a mate and we were a pack. I worried for my alpha when the day came when she confronted him. She was hell-bent on having Miles return to his old pack and become alpha. Never mind the huge fact it would require him to kill the current alpha male, his own father. "Well, it's probably best then they aren't there. We need alliances and solidified packs, not inner fighting."

"Agreed. Can you handle the shop for the next two days? We have eight cars coming in."

I didn't want him to worry about anything but keeping our pack safe. "I can handle the workload. Xan and I can get an early start."

"And Caius?" Miles's voice was low enough not to alert the man pretending to be sleeping.

"What about him," I couldn't help but grumble.

"You gonna work with him all right? No fuss? No fights?"

I hated he reduced me to feeling like a scolded teen caught fighting at school. "Yes," I spat.

Miles snorted. "Glad to hear it." He stood from the table, leaving me to stare at the monitors as he joined the ladies in the living room. I glared at Caius, catching him looking at my mate under half-lidded eyes. I shook my head and focused on the screen.

I could get through the next two days at the garage. Caius just needed to work on his own cars and stay the hell away from mine.

Chapter Twenty-Nine
Kate

My neighbor Mary gave me the third degree when I called her. I felt terrible how freaked out she was over my absence. "I had to leave him," I quavered. "He said the most awful things to me."

"Of course you had to leave him!" Mary agreed. "I've been hinting for a year now you would be better off, but you weren't ready to hear it. I only wished you told me! My brain went to dark places. I started wondering if he was off burying your body."

"Oh gosh! I'm sorry, Mary. Nope! Nothing as extreme as murder. It was simply your average case of a man wanting all the cakes and a maid to clean up after he eats them," I joked.

"That expression isn't one I'm familiar with, but I get the gist." Mary gave me a courtesy chuckle. "What can I do to help? Do you need someone to watch the kids?"

"The boys are good, and I'm covered there. I could use your help doing a little spying?" I asked tentatively. "I need to head to the house on the regular to mail out orders and make sure Aaron isn't working from home on those days."

"Easy peasy lemon squeezy. You got it."

"I'm getting supplies delivered for my next batches. I need to get through December. January is always a slow month. I can transition my store then." Running the logistics through my head, I felt confident I could make it work. I would need to put a cap on orders coming in to be filled with only current inventory. It would be less sales than I could accomplish, but as I was a nomad currently it was all I could manage.

"And you're in a place you feel comfortable?" Mary pressed.

I'd deflected the first time she asked straight out where I was. Telling her I left my husband and was already with another man sounded extremely bad in my head.

"My sister's helping me out. I'm good. Promise."

"Alright, girl. I'll get my binoculars out and start my neighborhood watch." Mary was going to miss having me next door to her, but I could tell from the merriment in her voice she was happy I stood up for myself.

"You are seriously the best." My eyes watered in gratitude.

"Don't I know it," she sassed. "Text me when you need to. Code name 007."

"Sure thing, Mr. Bond. Love you, crazy woman."

"Right back at ya."

When we hung up, I couldn't help but be melancholy. Mary would always be my friend, but this was a new chapter in my life I wouldn't be able to share with her.

On to the next part of my plan for independence from Aaron, I texted Akela.

I know you gave me a place to stay and this might sound greedy to ask

Akela: You have me intrigued

Is there a space I can make my soap and candles?

Akela: As a matter of fact I have just the space!

I breathed out a relieved sigh. Traveling the long distance to and from my mother's house was less than ideal. Hopefully Akela's location would be close by. With a weight lifted, I decided to head down the stairs to the shop and see if the guys would like it if I made them lunch.

There must have been a spring in my step, or I'd been horribly noisy. All eyes turned my way when I slung open the door connecting the stairs to the garage. My bright grin dimmed a little at the scrutiny. Luke's gaze was filled with heat, Xan's was friendly, but Caius downright glared, making my voice falter.

"I was ... " Stopping myself from fidgeting like a nervous school girl, I plunged ahead. "I wanted to know if you were hungry? I was making lunch."

"We already have a pack omega," Caius muttered. "No need for you to play the role of one."

"What?" I asked, confused, still not fully understanding pack dynamics.

"Uncalled for, dude," Xan reprimanded while Luke took a menacing step towards Caius.

Emotions of rejection tumbled through me. "I don't want to start a fuss." Embarrassing tears threatened to spill when, just seconds before, I'd been giddy at my cleverness. It was foolish of me to expect to fit quickly into their lives. Luke and I had chemistry for sure, but they had a bond I would never compete with.

Caius scowled before resuming his work. Luke altered his course from intercepting his pack mate to comforting me. His long strides made it to the door before I could decide to bolt. "Thank you for the kind offer. We usually order from the food truck, but the selection is lackluster. A home-cooked lunch sounds amazing."

"You sure?" I couldn't help glancing at Caius.

Gentle fingers on my chin shifted my gaze back. "When should we come up?"

"Forty-five minutes?"

"Perfect." He grimaced slightly as his fingers left my face. "Damn it. I got you dirty."

Thinking about the wonderfully dirty things he'd done to me yesterday, I blushed. "I don't mind." Heat flooded his eyes. We might have been thinking the same thoughts. "Welp, see you soon then," I spoke barely above a whisper before turning and hightailing it up the stairs.

Will still watched his cartoons and Tommy happily jumped in his bouncy chair when I returned. Getting started on lunch, I opened the fridge and pulled out all the ingredients I needed to make a quick chili. Miles had the apartment more than adequately stocked for me. If I didn't cook for others, most of this food would go to waste.

Closing the door, I stifled a scream. Caius was only a foot away from me. "You startled me." I placed a hand over my racing heart.

"Sorry." His tone was soft.

"It's okay." I waved. "I just didn't hear you."

"No. I mean for earlier." His hand settled on my shoulder as he crowded me.

Straining my neck, I looked at his face. He appeared contrite, his perfectly chiseled features marred with a deep frown. Heat from his body was penetrating through me, causing goosebumps to trail up my arms. Suddenly, there wasn't enough oxygen in the room. "I'm sorry, too." I forced the words out. "I seem to be intruding."

His lips pinched tightly as he closed his eyes. "You're exactly where you should be." When he opened his eyes a world of emotions I could not decipher swam there.

My pulse jumped. "I am?"

Leaning even closer, he nodded. It reminded me of the moment he delivered a searing kiss in Valentina's kitchen. I should be running for the hills or contemplating Luke's reaction, but I stayed frozen.

He took a quick breath, shook himself, and pulled away. "Yup." The derisive note was back in his voice. "Omegas are best in the kitchen." Throwing those hurtful words at me, he strode away without looking back. He wanted me angry. Repeatedly taunting and pushing me in a manner that made no sense. Standing in the kitchen, staring at the door he walked out of, I had a revelation. Caius was at war with himself.

Chapter Thirty
Caius

What the hell am I doing?

Storming out of the apartment, I took the stairs two at a time, eager to get away. Distance. I needed distance. How the fuck was I going to be able to get that? Obviously, she was becoming a member of this pack. For the first time in my life, I had a real family, and I was being forced to leave. I couldn't stay as long as she was here.

The door banged open to the garage. Xan raised his brows, clearly wondering what my problem was. No time to talk, I made a beeline to the exit. Luke blocked my way.

"Where exactly are you going?" He folded his arms over his chest, pissed.

"Out." I continued to edge past him, but he grabbed my arm.

"You need to chill. We are a man down with Miles away and a shit ton of work to do." Contrary to his words of calm, Luke shoved me away from the door.

"Easy for you to say," I snapped. "You have everything now."

He glanced up as if able to peer through the ceiling. "Did you upset her?" he growled.

"Of course I did." A rough chortle tumbled from my lips. "Isn't that my specialty?"

Luke went eerily still, his vision piercing through my armor. "Why do you have to be an ass all the time? It doesn't have to be like this."

Xan, always playing the peacemaker, approached. "Settle, brothers. Let's break for lunch early and cool our heads."

"No, he's right." I jerked my head at Luke. "I can't seem to stop myself from playing the role of asshole."

The guilt rested heavy on my chest. I was a fuck up. There was no excuse I could even tell myself to make up for my past. I thought it was a clever game to get in a girl's pants. Tell them what they want to hear. Love them. Leave them. The irony wasn't lost on me. My life was a pathetic rendition of the boy who cried wolf. I finally find my true mate and no one believes me. Even worse? She has a better alternative in Luke.

"You're the better man," I spoke gruffly. Being alone was what I deserved. I was unworthy of having such a perfect mate. I couldn't live with the torture of seeing her every day. Watching her with another man. All the while thinking I'm scum.

Luke's stance shifted. The rage, always around in my presence these days, cooled. "If you need to take some time ... " He checked his watch. "Be back in an hour? I promised Miles we'd handle the workload."

Low blow. I owed Miles. He took me in when no pack would. "Time doesn't solve it. I'll finish out the week. Then I think it's time I moved on."

"Caius!" Xan flooded the bond. It wrapped around me like a comforting hug. "Leaving isn't the answer."

Luke's jaw ground tight while he assessed me. Being a lone wolf was a scary prospect. We were far more easy pickings without a pack. It would be the right thing to do, though. Kate and Luke deserved a life together where I wasn't a constant thorn in their side.

Not waiting for him to say anything else, I rolled up my sleeves and continued working on the carburetor. Keeping my back to them, I tried to focus on the job at hand. Through my peripheral, I noted both guys rubbing their chests. I refrained from doing the same, but it was hard. Like when you bit the inside of your cheek and couldn't stop prodding at it. My statement had started the process of fraying my bond with the pack. I would wait to sever it fully after I spoke with Miles. My alpha deserved a face-to-face.

"Lunch is ready!" Kate sweetly called. I ignored it. Not making a single sound and continuing working until the garage closed, I could get through this week. One job at a time. Isolate myself. Do the work. Stay away from Kate.

I had to.

Chapter Thirty-One
Kate

The past three days were tense. Everyone kept me away from the business with the hunters, but I knew the packs were frantic. Akela had found an office space open in the travel agency down the street. They were willing for me to have the space for free if I made gift baskets for big clients. It was a win-win for me since I also put my card in the baskets to get my business name out there. I felt guilty worrying about my company when the packs were worried about their lives, but the work kept me occupied and out of their way. I fretted the extra burden of helping me was distracting.

Luke was acting exceptionally on edge. I wasn't sure if it was from the blow-up with Caius or this Order I learned about. Luke seemed to take personal responsibility for the difficulties Austin and Raff's packs were facing. He was working himself ragged between driving to each pack and helping with surveillance to pulling long hours at the garage. We hadn't been able to spend another night together. I missed his warm body in my bed.

When he asked me out on a date night to get drinks with him, I couldn't say no. Kyle drove over to watch the boys for us while we were out. It was super kind of him. He was even patient with me as I went over for the hundredth time the bedtime routine and emergency numbers.

"I got ya, Kate." He winked at me while rubbing my back, gently pushing me out the door. "You have fun, lovebirds. I won't wait up."

Giggling at his insistence, I grabbed my purse and flew down the stairs to meet Luke. He'd just pulled up and was getting out of his car when I closed and locked the door behind me. "You didn't have to meet me outside. I was going to come up and get you, like a proper date." He eyed me appreciatively. I'd done my best to dress cute for him, given my limited wardrobe and not wanting to freeze out on a December night. The form-fitting sweater dress covered me completely but hugged my curves in just the right way.

Luke looked good enough to eat. I didn't mind him right after work greased up, looking all manly, but he cleaned up fine, too. A black button-up shirt tucked into dark denim jeans was the essence of the outfit, but the way he wore it had me questioning if we shouldn't just go right to his place.

He walked over to the passenger door and opened it for me. Stealing a kiss before I got in, he leaned in and whispered against my mouth. "I love the way you look at me."

"You are kinda beautiful." I blushed.

A warm chuckle accompanied a swat on my butt as I got into the car. "No one holds a candle to you, my mate."

Smiling to myself, I fastened the seatbelt as he made his way to the driver's side. It was a strange feeling to go out with a man to a bar. I married Aaron before I could even legally drink. This was an entirely new experience for me. I was grateful to be able to do this in a town far enough away from home. Hopefully no one I know would see us here. As much as things were over with my husband in my mind, my marriage was still legally intact. Being careful was important.

Pulling into a bar only a few blocks away from the garage, Luke grimaced as he turned off the ignition and put the car in park. "Sorry, it's not something fancier. I wanted to take you out for a nice meal, something to make you feel special."

"You make me feel special." My eyes misted a bit at the realization.

"I'm glad to hear it. Still, I owe you a nice dinner. This place is ... " He looked slightly pained as he chewed on his lower lip. "This is a necessity."

"Alright," I replied, mystified. "It doesn't matter to me where we go. I'm happy to spend time with you. Out. Like a real adult."

Walking in, I found the bar a bit divey but clean. They had good music playing, people were dancing, and the atmosphere was festive with cheap Christmas decorations. Luke's warm hand was splayed at the center of my back while he escorted me in. I was beaming at him until I noticed him fixating on someone.

Still in his mechanic's overalls, Caius sat forlorn at the bar. An empty shot glass and a half-drank beer were in front of him. The place wasn't too crowded, yet a woman sat on his right, ogling the beautiful man.

The girl on the stool next to him was desperate to get this attention, her low-cut blouse able to fully display the wares as she leaned in to speak. For the most part, Caius ignored her. Stoically sitting and nursing his beer as if she wasn't there. The scene still made my stomach churn.

"Maybe we should go to another bar?" I suggested to Luke.

"Come on." He ignored my idea. Hand in hand, he pulled me over to his pack mate.

Setting his beer down hard, Caius turned when he spotted us. Luckily, he wasn't drunk yet, or this might have been my first bar brawl. "You knew I was coming here," he accused. "Seriously? This is fucked up." Seeing some tension unfold, the woman next to him scooted away a few stools.

Still holding my hand, Luke walked directly up to Caius. I tugged gently, hoping he would get the hint and not ruin our date night with a confrontation. Resting his other hand on Caius's shoulder, Luke leaned in. "Let's get a booth in the back." He signaled to the bartender. "I'll get next round."

"What?" Caius was confused. That made two of us. "No. I'm good."

Luke shook his head. "I don't think you are, man. But I'm going to make it right." He pointed to an empty booth. "Have a drink with us. Hear me out."

Licking his plump bottom lip, Caius stared at me, searching for answers. I smiled weakly and shrugged, indicating I wasn't aware of what this was all about.

"Fuck it," Caius huffed. "Why not?" He downed the rest of his beer while we waited for fresh drinks.

Luke situated me between the two of them once we got to the booth. I didn't know what he was playing at, but I was getting agitated. I thought this was a date, but it was clear he had another motive for coming to this particular bar tonight. Was he worried I was cheating on him? Did he sense I still had strange feelings when Caius was around? Was he going to confront us? We all had a few sips in relative silence before I couldn't hold it in anymore. "What's all this about, Luke?"

With a solemn expression, Luke finished off his drink. "Caius is your mate," he blurted out quickly.

A sudden choking noise had me turning to Caius in concern. Clearly, Luke's announcement caught him off guard and swallowing had been too difficult. As soon as I could confirm he was still breathing, I glared at Luke. "So what? You had me, and it's over? You're passing me on?" If I wasn't sandwiched between the two of them, I would most certainly have stormed off.

"Never," he insisted vehemently. "You're my

mate too."

I jerked back. "I know I'm new to all this, but are you being serious with me?"

"What is this, Luke?" Caius's face was blank, making it impossible to tell what he was thinking.

"The bond was telling me, but I was too upset to listen. When you said you were willing to leave the pack, I knew. If she hadn't been your mate, you would have gotten over our fight and moved on. You're usually a grumpy bastard, but lately, it surpassed assholery even for you. You were hurting." Luke heaved out a sigh. "This?" He pointed to the three of us. "Is me working things out."

Fidgeting in my seat, I ping-ponged glances between the two of them. "More than one mate?"

"It's not common, but it happens," Luke answered. "What's important is how you feel about it."

"Are you saying I have to choose between you now?" I shifted nervously to Caius. "You haven't acted like you want to be with me."

Resting both elbows on the table, Caius scrubbed his face with his hands. "I don't deserve a mate. What they said about me is right. I used to tell girls the fated mate line to get laid before. It fucking came back to haunt me." He huffed..

My mouth opened in an *O*. I wasn't sure how to process this. Did Luke want me to date them and then pick? "I'm not interested in breaking up your pack by getting between the two of you."

"Oh, babe," Luke pushed my hair away to be able to see my face. "Choosing between two mates isn't our way. You have two mates. You have *two* mates."

My mouth opened even wider. "You mean have a relationship with *both* of you?"

Luke nodded. "Getting between us ... would be

incredibly sexy."

My face flamed, but so did my core at the image. Luke's milky skin, my cinnamon, and Caius's dark brown complexion all flushed together made a pretty picture in my mind. With a mouth devoid of moisture, I gulped down my vodka soda and wished I had a fan.

"Our girl likes the idea." Luke's voice was husky.

"H-h-how," I stuttered a few times before managing to get the words out. "How would it work?"

The smile gracing Luke's face showed all his teeth. "The better to eat you with," drawled the big bad wolf to Little Red Riding Hood. "Such a tight dress you're wearing, yet I didn't see any panty lines."

My brows scrunched together. "I'm wearing a thong."

"Caius, you should check on that. Make sure our girl isn't lying."

Caius settled his hand on my knee, my dress bunching up at the touch. "What do you say, Kate?" Caius whispered in my ear.

"You've been rather hot and cold with me." I frowned. "Is this something you want too?"

"More than breathing," he admitted.

Our booth was dark, and in the back, no one was looking at us. Not sure if this was the best or worst idea ever, I opened up my legs wider. Caius's entire face lit up. Pushing my dress to my knees, his hand trailed over the naked skin of my thighs till he found his destination. My lace thong was soaked as his index finger rolled over my clit and nudged the fabric to the side. "You were right. She does like the idea."

"Of course she does. She's our perfect girl," Luke praised.

I was panting as Caius fingered me under the table, and Luke pulled my face towards him and claimed my mouth. His kiss was slow and languid, his tongue dancing and caressing mine. When he broke away, my lips tingled.

"I bet we can make her come right here in this booth," Luke taunted. "Would you like to come, Katrina?"

Would I? Um. Yes, please!

Should I, though?

Glancing around nervously at the bar, I was unable to answer.

"She's shy," Caius spoke in my place. He removed the finger circling my clit, only to have it venture lower. The fat digit pushed inside easily, and his thumb resumed the little circles.

I braced both my hands on the table, trying in vain to act normally. These men drove me wild, my libido newly awakened in their presence. I stopped focusing on anyone else in the bar but them.

Luke kissed his way up my neck. My skin pebbled at the warm caresses. He nibbled on my ear, and I could feel it all the way to my core, heightening Caius's ministrations. "Make her come," he directed Caius. "Then we take her to my place, where we can worship her properly."

Redoubling his efforts, Caius added a second finger into the mix. I had to bite down on my lip to stifle a moan. I was close. It hadn't taken much at all, considering I went from barely liking or enjoying sex to actively anticipating having a three-way. What was a little heavy petting in public? I clawed at the table as my climax hit. Closing my eyes when the pleasure got too intense.

"Damn," Caius swore. "That was sexy as fuck."

"Mmm," Luke agreed. "Let's take our girl to bed. I think she deserves another reward for being so perfect."

"Would you like that, pretty girl?" Caius asked softly, his tone holding more than one meaning.

I'd wanted them both since the moment I first met them. Did it mean I was ready to enter into a full-time relationship with two men? Maybe not. I was still married, was a mother, and had an entire bag of issues to work out.

"Don't overthink it." Luke gazed at me with adoration. "Remember, all we expect is a chance. A chance to prove this life can work out for you. Let us worship you tonight. You're the center of our universe. Let us show you what that would feel like."

"That doesn't sound too terrible," I joked.

Having to subtly adjust himself when he stood, Luke winked down at me. "I'll take care of the tab. Finish your drink. I'm looking forward to showing you my home."

Immediate thoughts of ropes and a sex dungeon entered my mind. I gulped down my beverage in one swallow. *Yup. I'm doing this.*

Chapter Thirty-Two
Caius

We drove to Luke's apartment after having texted Kyle to make sure he was okay watching the boys overnight. My place was a total dump, so I had no objections about the locale. In fact, I was still in disbelief this was actually happening. If Luke hadn't flooded the bond with acceptance and confidence, I'd probably be second-guessing being here. Truthfully, Kate was better off without me, but I'd work to make sure she never thought it. If Luke was willing, knowing all about my past, to consider this relationship, then I would be nothing but grateful. Even if he was one bossy motherfucker, as long as it stayed mainly in the bedroom, I was in.

It got awkward fast when we reached the apartment. I pulled up my car when they were getting out of Luke's. Kate was acting skittish, scanning the street like she was afraid of getting mugged. Was she having second thoughts? Was she freaked about a relationship with two men? From what I learned, Aaron was the only person she had ever been with before Luke. A surge of jealousy batted at me, knowing he'd been with her first. I couldn't help the greasy thought. Luke raised an eyebrow at me feeling what I put out. I eradicated the emotion on the spot. I didn't want the anger I felt over Kate's husband to confuse Luke. I wasn't angry at him. He was a man of his word. We were here to make this right between all of us.

Luke's place was clean, almost bordering on military tidy. He lived the life of a Spartan man in more ways than one. The one-bathroom studio loft was all wood, metal, and glass. Having inherited money from his family, Luke only worked at the garage because he wanted to. He could actually afford a place much nicer than Miles could ever hope for. Instead, he spent his money on tracking the Order and security for our pack, and lived in a tiny yet well-kept apartment.

A pale gray L-shaped sofa was the centerpiece of the room. Dropping his keys on the kitchen counter, Luke strode to the couch and had a seat. Kate and I stood aimlessly by the door. From the way her attention darted all around, I'd guess she'd never been here.

"Your place is nice," she quavered. "Very modern."

Luke reclined back on the couch, both elbows resting high and legs spread open. Like a king on his throne, he was the only confident one in the room. "Take off your boots, baby."

Kate swallowed and twisted her fingers together before bending down and zipping off her knee-high boots. She stepped out of them and left them by the door. She made a move toward Luke, but he halted her with a raised hand.

"And the thong."

Her eyes went as round as saucers. "My panties?"

Luke nodded. "Take them off."

I sucked in a breath as she reached under her dress and shimmied a lacy black thong down her thighs. Holding them in her hand, she looked around.

"Give them to Caius," he ordered. "And come and sit on my lap."

A rosy blush spread across her cheeks. Without making eye contact with me, she thrust her soaked panties in my direction. Wordlessly, I accepted them. Timidly, she made her way over to Luke and stood directly in front of him. Leaning forward, he ran his hands on her now bare calves, pulling the tight sweater dress up past her knees, past her thighs, until the perfect globes of her ass were on display. Well, they had my full attention now. Adjusting myself with the hand clenching her thong, I rested against the kitchen counter to watch the show.

Luke quickly spun Kate around and yanked her onto his lap. Perched demurely, legs pressed together and hands clasped in front, she tried to protect her modesty.

"Tsk, tsk, tsk," Luke admonished. "We can't have that now."

His hands slid forward, grabbing her knees and yanking her legs open, her pretty pink pussy on perfect display for me. Throwing each of her legs over his own, he stretched her open an indecent amount. Kate didn't complain. She was panting with excitement. Eager. Luke ran his nails up her thighs, the scratch forcing Kate to arch her back in response.

"Do you need more of an invitation, brother?" Luke was watching me, a knowing smile tugging at his lips.

Still, I hesitated. Clearly, she was comfortable with Luke. Was I going to be a third wheel? Will she accept me as she had him? If we did this thing, the mate bond would snap into place for me. There was no going back. Mate bonds were for life.

Reaching back, Luke tossed a pillow on the floor in front of Kate. "Don't want to bruise your delicate knees." He chuckled at my confusion. "Come and worship our girl. You revved her engine earlier, but she wants more. She's a needy one."

I hungrily consumed the sight of her dripping core. Moisture glistened on her silky folds. Part of me wanted to tell Luke off for being bossy ... but the man had some truly inspired ideas. Eating up the floor in three large strides, I happily kneeled. Hell, I'd probably be happy to grovel if it meant she would consider being mine.

My hands traveled a similar path to Lukes. Scaling up from her calves directly to her center, I lovingly pet her bare mound. "Does Luke speak the truth, pretty girl? Do you want more?"

Her thighs were shaking, either from the strain of how widespread Luke was keeping her or excitement, I didn't know. Her pupils were blown out like she was lust drunk. She angled forward, reaching for me, until I stopped her with my hand around her throat. "Use your words."

The heavy rise and fall of her chest was my only response for a few seconds until she blurted out. "I want more. Please."

It was the please that got me rock hard instantly. "You never have to beg."

"Speak for yourself," Luke huffed. "I'm rather fond of her begging."

After rolling my eyes at the sick fucker, I resumed my soft caresses. Kate was straining to get closer, clearly not appreciating how gentle my touch was. Maintaining eye contact, I started kissing up one thigh, skipping where she was eager for me, and kissing down the other thigh. Her groan of disappointment had me smiling against her skin. She jolted when I gave her clit a little pinch and tried to close her legs. "Make sure she keeps them open."

"That's the plan." Luke chuckled darkly.

No more teasing. I went in for the kill. I thrust my tongue deep inside her opening before making my way up to her little bud. Kate writhed and squeaked adorably as I licked and sucked.

"Hands up," Luke ordered her as he pulled off the rest of her dress. Throwing it on the ground beside me, he flicked off her bra next, leaving her completely naked while we were both still fully clothed.

Kate was oblivious. She shut her eyes and lived fully in the moment. Gorgeous. Luke played with her perky breasts, twisting her nipples. Her heavy moans made my balls draw up tight. I quickly discovered what ministrations Kate liked most when her hand landed on my shaved head and her hips jerked wildly in my face. I added two fingers to the mix. Her tight channel greedily tried to suck me in. She came in glorious abandon, desperately grinding against me. A loud moan and my name spilled from her lips.

Rather pleased with myself, I sat back on my heels, watching her recover. Two orgasms, and the night was still young. Blinking her eyes to clear the post-climax fog, Kate pouted adorably. "Why am I the only one naked?"

Luke and I shared a private stare before we both burst out laughing. He kissed her softly on the temple. "You are simply too perfect."

Kate stretched, pushing out those perky tits and shifting that tight behind over Luke's groin. Oh, yeah. Our girl was a praise junky.

"Go give Caius a kiss and say thank you." Domineering Luke was back. I refrained from another eye roll. The man made some good calls. No need to interfere with his artistry of manipulation.

Kate slithered down from his lap. Ever the good omega, she didn't balk at a single one of his commands. She crawled to me, her eyes more on the bulge in my pants than on my face. "You are so fucking sexy." I sucked on my bottom lip, still tasting her nectar. My hand fisted in her hair as I pulled her head back. Swiping my tongue up her neck before finding her mouth. She opened without any hesitation, sucking on my tongue and making those cute moans.

Luke stood and unbuckled his belt. Popping the buttons on his fly while watching us make out. Shoving his jeans and underwear off in one go, he sat back down, working on his shirt. I pulled away from Kate's mouth, asking him silently what he planned for next. He was fisting his cock, seemingly content to watch us. Kate glanced over her shoulder at him with a wicked twinkle.

"Now what?" she asked cheekily.

He shook his head, smiling. "Now? It looks like we need to find a use for that mouth of yours."

She turned around fully, crawling back over to him, her peach ass on display for me. "And what would be the best purpose for it?" Her question was filled with hidden laughter.

"No one likes a tease." He leaned forward and nipped at her lip, pulling away and stretching it out with him. Then he softened the bite by running his tongue over it. "Suck me while you take Caius's cock. Think you can handle it?"

I made no move to get undressed while she assessed me. "Maybe?" There was a playfulness to her voice but also hesitation. "Is he bigger than you?"

I howled at the question. Luke's lips pinched together. "It isn't something I've ever compared," he stated dryly.

I called bullshit. We're shifters. Comfortable in our nudity, but nude often enough that you notice things. Admittedly Luke had nothing to be ashamed of in the dick department, but I was slightly bigger. I could feel the grin stretching across my face. "Would you like if we did a side-by-side comparison?" I teased our flustered mate.

"Fuck off and get naked," Luke groused.

"When you ask so sweetly." I batted my lashes.

Our banter dissipated Kate's nerves. "Can I see it?"

"See." I gestured. "That's how it's done? Can't say no to you, sweet girl." Without further ado, I pulled down the zipper on my overalls and stepped out of them. My T-shirt came next before I discarded my boxers. I thought I was hard before, but with Kate still on her knees before me, my erection grew painfully larger. Beads of pre-cum were weeping from my swollen crown. "Think you can take it?" I winked.

A sparkle fluttered through her eyes. "I'd sure like to try," she squeaked, causing both Luke and I to chuckle again. Her exuberance was fucking adorable.

"Come back over here, Katrina." Luke had a thing for using her full name. The way Kate perked up and arched her back when he said it showed she liked it.

Her lips surrounded Luke, and she was choking him down without being asked. He threw his head back against the couch and crunched his eyes tight as if in pain. Imagining only heaven would exist inside her mouth, I knew he was being well taken care of. I was more acutely interested in the body part she was wiggling at me.

Returning back to my knees, the front of my thighs grazed the silky skin of her bottom. My thumb dipped in and rubbed her puckered hole. A muffled exclamation from Kate had me reassuring her. "Don't worry. We'll save it for another time."

Kate was about to pull off of Luke's dick and speak, but he trapped her. "Both of you need to focus and get to work."

"Damn. Sir, yes, Sir." I saluted him before lining up at Kate's entrance. She pushed back in invitation. Dipping in and out of her entrance in shallow movements until she was ready to take me, both of my hands splayed on the globes of her ass. When I felt less resistance, I surged forward, causing her to suck Luke even further. Expletives and praise left him as he threw his head back again.

She was a tiny thing but managed to take me to the hilt. Her warm, wet core was gripping me tightly. I wouldn't last very long. At least not this first time. The mate bond hummed, twining around the three of us. Luke's eyes snapped open, staring directly at me. We vowed silently then. As we shared our mate between us, the bond unfurled and started to form around us, Luke and I understood. She would not feel this like we could. We needed to make sure to do everything to keep her happy, to keep her with us. Because after experiencing this ultimate bliss, the world would be a dull place without her heat.

Watching her swallow down Luke, I plowed into her. "Touch yourself. Rub that greedy little bud and come for us again."

Eager to please, her hand went right to work. As she rubbed in tight circles, her walls fluttered until she was screaming her pleasure on Luke's cock. The vibration must have put him over the edge. He grunted while shooting his load down her throat. I quickened the pace, not wanting to be left behind. Her pussy was still fluttering with sweet aftershocks when I spilled inside her.

The three of us, spent, breathing as one. This was home.

Chapter Thirty-Three
Kate

Between Mary acting as spy and Aaron's general lack of caring about his family, I managed to avoid seeing him for three weeks. Each time I went home I filled my car to the brim with mainly things for the boys. Having their toys, favorite blankets, and clothes made them feel more settled. My Christmas sales were through the roof this year, and I'd need to find time to head back home for a full clear-out of anything left there for my business. Akela's deal with the travel agency was working out well, but I was finding I needed even more storage than the spare room could offer me. The client gifts I'd made them had drawn new customers to my site. Potential big customers! I could see a possible avenue to some financial independence if I could land a hotel contract or country club chain.

Personally ... I was so freaking happy. I'd never known this kind of happiness before. It wasn't perfect with Caius and Luke. We were still working things out, but those men were good to me. The kind of good that makes a woman reassess every self-doubt. God, they made me feel cherished, protected, desired, and I was soaking it up like a sponge. Will and Tommy were blossoming as well. It had been a drought of male attention at home. Here, they were drowning in it. The pack loved the boys.

They helped put up a Christmas tree and surrounded it with presents. Will's eyes were as round as saucers as he pretended not to shake and peak at the gifts. It was Christmas Eve, and we were all heading to Austin's for the celebration. Christmas day would just be Luke, Caius and me with the boys. A day of gift opening, junk food eating, and movie watching sounded perfect. There was no need to fret about Aaron being upset. He had a deer hunting trip planned every year before the season came to an end. I usually spent Christmas at my mother's house.

The only fly in my ointment: the next full moon was coming the day after Christmas. There had been no more news on the Order. Austin's pack was going to stay inside the lab. Agreeing to cage their wolves for safety's sake. Raff's pack had a plan to camp miles away from home for the change. Miles had yet to discover any evidence their cabin had been located and the pact felt confident it was still a secure location.

I needed to decide to either drive to my mom's house or take the pack up on their offer and head to the cabin and watch them change. They assured me I'd be safe. Their wolves would not harm me. Physically, I believed. It was my mental status I was unsure about. Was I ready to enter their world so completely and eventually call it my world?

"There you are." Luke nuzzled me as his arms circled around my waist from behind. "I moved the car seats to my SUV. We can all drive together."

My car was too small to fit three adults and two car seats. My heart warmed seeing Luke make accommodations for Caius. They still bickered like boys over things, but transitioning to having two men in my life was fairly smooth. This bond they shared kept their heads on straight. Both had good enough poker faces to fool me, but sensing each other's emotions made it hard for them to fool each other.

"I need to pull the cornbread stuffing out of the oven, and I'm all set. Did you leave a space in the trunk for it?"

He nipped my shoulder blade, causing me to

shriek. "Yee of little faith! I didn't forget. You mentioned it twice."

To be heard. To be seen. It was a heady mixture. "Thank you." I blew him a kiss while heading to the kitchen.

It was a much different experience pulling up to Austin and Valentina's house from a month ago. I'd been lonely and desperate to find a connection, and now my cup was filled to overflowing. My guys handled the boys while I brought in my dish. My sister had arrived before me. After setting down my stuff, I went in for a hug.

"Mom make it here yet?" I whispered in her ear.

"Raff and I have a bet going if she shows her face at all." Chloe pulled out her phone looking at the time and checking for any text messages.

"What side are you on?"

She pursed her lips. "I said she would come. I think she misses this place. But Raff could also be right. Her guilt over dad's death could keep her away permanently."

"Do you think people will be cruel to her?" I fretted. My mother may have made some bad decisions, but she wasn't a bad person. Drama over the holiday was the last thing I wanted.

"They'll be on their best behavior." Chloe rubbed my back, reassuring me. "Valentina and I set some ground rules on topics to avoid."

"Auntie!" Will shouted as he barreled over to Chloe and hugged her legs.

Grabbing him and swinging around in a circle, my sister made him giggle-scream. "Hey there, squirt. You excited about Santa coming?"

"You think he can find me?" my son asked, a note of worry in his tone that pulled on my heartstrings.

Chloe settled him back on his feet and ruffled his

hair. "Oh, he most assuredly knows where you are sleeping."

"I believe it's *when* you are sleeping." I giggled. "The way you say it sounds creepy."

"But I want him to know, Mommy." Will looked up at me.

"He'll find us. Don't you worry." I peppered kisses all over his face while he protested and tried to wipe them away. He ran from me, squealing, and hid behind one of Caius's massive legs.

"Don't let her get me!" he pleaded.

"I got ya, little man. I'll even do one better. I'll take the kisses instead of you." Caius leaned his cheek out in my direction while wiggling his brows.

I swatted playfully at his massive chest. "You have to earn them."

A fire blazed behind his eyes. "Oh, I plan on devoting my life to just that."

I knew the words were corny, but dang, they worked! My smile was electric as I promised him without words that he would be getting plenty of kisses later. Chloe watched the interaction with keen interest. While she hadn't been able to visit with the security threat in her territory, we'd been talking almost daily. It was wonderful having my sister back in my life, even though she cautioned I was moving too fast. Caius scooped up Will and carried him to the den, where Luke was setting up toys to keep the boys occupied.

"You look happy," Chloe spoke gently. "Radiant."

My smile faltered. "I keep feeling this is only temporary. No one deserves to be this happy. I'm waiting for the other shoe to drop, mainly Aaron finding a way to make me miserable again."

"Hey." She held on to both my shoulders. "The

only power he has over you is the power you give him. It will work out."

I was prevented from responding by the arrival of Miles and Akela carrying way too many things. Both Cloe and I intercepted them to help bring food into the kitchen. Marta, Akela's mom, was helping organize the massive three-pack potluck and pointed out where we should set everything down.

"How are we going to eat all this?" Valentina cried over the mountain of dishes.

Kyle, who must have come with Akela, rounded the corner with another armload. He appeared flustered as we all shrieked at seeing even more food. "What?"

"It's the potluck to end all potlucks," Akela explained while helping him set down his burdens.

"All right." Valentina clapped her hands. "No men in the kitchen today. Boys, we have deep-fried turkeys and smoked briskets to tend to outside. So get." Most of the men hightailed it out on the alpha's orders, except Miles. He kissed Akela slowly, despite her mom standing right there, whispered something naughty enough to have her blushing, and then left. Valentina popped a bottle of champagne and started filling up flutes. Sliding over glasses to Akela and Chloe first. "A toast to our new alpha females as they head their packs into the new year."

Accepting a glass, I held it before me, wondering what Chloe's reaction would be. Both she and Akela clinked their glasses together in silly exaggeration before facing Valentina.

"To pack bonds," the older alpha female cheered.

"To pack bonds," everyone repeated. The words felt odd leaving my mouth. What the hell did I know about it?

Before the first sip could be finished, Valentina

steered the group to a topic she was eager to discuss. "You know, my dear." She smiled warmly at my sister. "A New Year's Eve wedding would be beautiful."

I could hear my sister counting backward from ten. "You mean next week?"

Eagerly, Valentina leaned forward on the counter. "It wouldn't be much trouble at all. I know you're not looking for a big wedding."

"Oh, I don't know." My sister played it a bit ditzy. "I always dreamed of a spring wedding. Better flowers."

Some of the eagerness dimmed from Valentina's eyes, but not all. "I can make spring happen, too. I just had some fun New Year's Eve ideas. Fireworks and such. But spring is pretty." She tapped at her flute with a long nail, a lopsided grin on her face. "But I'm glad you at least picked a date."

Chloe's mouth dropped open in shock. "I did not ..."

"I'd like a New Year's Eve wedding," Akela blurted out, interrupting Chloe.

Both Marta and Valentina did a double take. "What?"

Akela shrugged. "If you're being serious about it not being a problem to pull off a wedding in a week. Especially since we have the change coming."

Valentina simply looked stunned. Marta stared at her daughter misty-eyed. "Do you mean it, honey?"

"I was fighting the fact he was my mate since I was fifteen." The statement drew a frown. "There's no need for me to waste any more of our time. My pack having a mate ceremony here would mean a great deal to them. They've felt like outcasts and misfits too long."

The exuberance Valentina wore thinking about her son's wedding was replaced with thoughtful consideration as she regarded her niece. "Are you sure he'd want that?"

Shooting off a text, Akela pocketed her phone. "Only one way to find out."

We all continued to sip on champagne. Chatter turned toward the meal and any dishes needing reheating before Miles strode in.

He leaned cockily against the table, snagged a biscuit, and brought it to his mouth before he spoke. "You called for me?"

"I'd like to marry you. Next week. Here," Akela rushed out the choppy proposal.

The biscuit slipped from his fingers and bounced on the table. "You want to marry me?"

"Why not?" She giggled devilishly. "Unless you're having cold feet?"

"You're hilarious," he deadpanned.

"And you." She wrapped her arms around his waist and gazed up at him. "Are a wonderful man, and I want the whole world to know."

He searched her face as if wondering if this was a joke or a ploy. "A mate ceremony?" he asked again.

"A wedding on New Year's Eve. What better way to start our new beginning with a fresh new year? So?" Her puppy dog pleading eyes were set to maximum force.

A beaming smile lit up Miles's face brighter than the north star. "A wedding on the new year. Sounds nice." Awe filled his tone.

"It does, doesn't it?" Akela shared a secret glance before turning to Valentina and her mom. "What do you say, Aunt V?"

Marta's hands were covering her mouth as tears spilled freely down her cheeks. I was a bit misty-eyed, too. Valentina was more reserved, but obviously affected by the love she could see they shared. "My amazing niece, you deserve a wonderful day too. I'd love to plan this with you if you'll have it here."

"Thank you." Akela placed a hand over her heart. "It would mean a lot to me. To not only profess my commitment to this man but to have my pack accepted by you all."

"Of course!" Valentina hugged her niece and then Miles. Marta, Chloe, and I also jumped in on the hugs and congratulations.

"And then," mischief blanketed Valentina's tone. "Chloe truly will pick a date for hers, too, after seeing how beautiful your day will be.

Chloe groaned and chuckled. "The woman doesn't have an off button," she griped. "She never stops."

****

The mood for the rest of the evening was festive. Chloe won the bet and my mother arrived. Her visit was far less awkward than anticipated. She announced she would be parting ways with her current husband. Considering he lasted almost nine months, I'd say they had a good stretch. Valentina was happy to have her old friend back. The two of them were as thick as thieves, gossiping and catching up on life The alpha easily persuaded my mother to her side on the wedding campaign. My poor sister. Yet, if anyone could handle the manipulation, it was Chloe. She wouldn't bend unless she wanted to. Unlike me, she was not easily controlled by other people's desires.

I'd anticipated some hard-to-have conversations with my mother on my own marital demise or the fact I was openly dating two men. She took it more in stride than Chloe had. I suppose being raised as a Wa'ya, my mom hadn't found any of it unusual. She even went so far as to suggest I take the serum, causing the only violent reaction of the night. Chloe snapped at her and shut her down hard. My technique was always softer.

"I understand it was a dream of yours to feel fully part of the pack, but I have a lot to consider. There are hunters, the boys are human, not to mention I'm still married. I'm going to take things slow. I rushed into a bad marriage with Aaron. I need to make sure I'm making clear-headed decisions."

"Yeah." My sister slung her arm over my shoulder. "What she said."

Mom held up her hands in surrender. "I only want my girls to be happy." She plastered on a watery smile. "Lord knows I made some life-altering bad decisions."

Chloe's expression softened as she hugged my mom. "Would it cheer you up helping me plan a mate ceremony?"

Mom pulled back to search her face. "You mean it?"

Chloe glanced over to where Raff was sitting with his brother Rollin, both chuckling and shoving each other playfully over some joke. A goofy, love-struck grin morphed the scowl from her face. "He's the one, all right. But don't tell him." She confided in us. "He owes me a boatload of groveling still."

My mother and I winked conspiratorially. "Deal."

Chapter Thirty-Four
Kate

Christmas morning could only be described as the most magical I'd ever experienced. Nothing could compare with the bleary-eyed splendor of watching your children's excitement for the day. The holiday had always been nice at my mom's, but with Luke and Caius, I realized how much the boys and I were missing out. Having a partner to share in the joy with was amazing, having two, paradise. Caius was as giddy as the boys when they opened up new toys, never once complaining about the difficult assembly directions or building each new thing before the last had even been played with.

Luke kept me caffeinated and lavished me in more gifts than I felt deserving of. They were all thoughtful, too. Not your run-of-the-mill girl gifts, but things he understood I needed by observing me. Horrified when I broke down sobbing after opening up a pretty new schedule planner, he held me in his arms. "I'll return it," he spoke gruffly into my hair.

"I love it," I sniffled.

"Why are you crying then?" Using his thumb, he dried the tears on each cheek.

"You see me."

Understanding dawned on his features. "You're my mate. It's hard to see anything else when you're in the room."

My hand settled over his heart. "I wish I could feel what you do without taking such a scary risk."

"There's no rush." He kissed the tip of my nose. "Even if you are never ready, that's okay too. What we have is enough."

"It's more than I deserve," Caius called from the

floor, listening to our conversation. "We're both just grateful for you." He put down the directions he was prepping next and moved to sit on the other side of me on the couch. "But don't let your sister talk you out of considering the serum entirely. Luke and I have no doubt you are our fated mate. It would work."

"But do I want it to? I'm not sure about this turning into a wolf and losing my sense of self every month." My brows bunched as I looked at my children.

"I'm glad you agreed to come to the cabin, though." Luke played with my hair as he spoke. Twirling the long black strands through his pale fingers. "I think seeing us change, seeing us as a pack, will help you understand more about us."

"And you think it's safe to bring the boys? I shouldn't leave them at my mom's? She never offers, but for this, I know she would say yes." I nervously chewed on a fingernail.

"I promise they'll be fine," Luke answered. "Kyle has the place all stocked for you. He baby-proofed every outlet and bottom cabinet. We can bring some of their new toys to play with. It's going to be quiet out there but beautiful."

"Load up your Kindle," Caius suggested. "Keep yourself occupied at night ... at least until we can." He wiggled his brows, causing me to snort.

I covered my face in embarrassment, but Luke pried them away. "No hiding, pretty girl. Everything you do is freakin' adorable."

"Yeah, right." I rolled my eyes prompting a punishment of side poke tickles that had me jumping off the couch.

"Who's hungry?" I asked while wiping the tears from my eyes. Both my men smoldered at the question. I almost jumped right back to the sofa to sit between them.

"I'm hungry, Mommy." The high-pitched voice of my toddler doused any romantic ideas from my brain.

"All right then. Breakfast coming right up." I headed to the kitchen with a little more hip wiggle in my step than usual. Gotta leave them wanting more and all that.

****

Even though it was Christmas, Luke and Caius offered to work a few hours in the shop, finishing up two cars. Since we would be leaving tomorrow for the cabin no work could be done for four days. They needed to sort it all out before we left and have the cars ready for pick up in the morning.

I packed up for our little getaway, gave the boys baths, read bedtime stories, and finally got them tucked away for the night. Taking the baby monitor with me, I tiptoed downstairs to see if they guys needed anything.

Seemingly unbothered by the cold, Luke was working in only a thin white tank top and jeans, his Norse markings an inky black contrast over his arms. Caius lay on his back, half his body covered by the car he was under. I loved how his thighs were thick, straining against the seams of his coverall bottoms.

"Just checking on you," I called. "Wanted to make sure you didn't need anything."

Caius rolled out from under the car, giving me an exaggerated leer. "I can think of something I need pretty bad. What do you say, Luke?"

Luke was chomping on some gum and rubbing his knuckles under his chin. "It will be awful crowded in that small cabin. This might be our best opportunity to make our girl moan as loud as she can."

"I was thinking you might need a cup of coffee or a snack." I played at being demure, but my heart rate was thumping, and I did like being loud.

"Pass on the coffee." Caius prowled over to me, tucked two fingers into the waistband of my jeans, and pulled me forward till I bumped into his chest. "Yes, please, on the snack."

"You, sir, have a one-track mind." A peal of laughter slipped past my lips.

"Hmmm, call me sir again." He snapped his jaw at me in a mocking bite.

"Case in point." I tried to shove him playfully away, but the man was built from rocks.

He leaned down and captured my lips in a soft kiss. Lifting my arms to circle around his neck, I went up on tippy toe to deepen the kiss. Luke watched us with a lazy smile. "Me thinks the lady doth protest too much," he quoted.

"Agreed. Let's get to the loud moaning portion of the holiday festivities." Caius grabbed me and hoisted me over his shoulder.

"Oh my god," I squeaked as my flailing legs did little to persuade him to put me down.

Walking over to an empty hydraulic lift, Caius pressed the button for it to rise to his chest level. Swinging me around as I screeched, he sat me on the ledge. My feet dangled high off the ground. I wasn't dressed for seduction, wearing a long flowing cotton dress and fuzzy slippers. Caius gazed at me like I was on display in sexy lingerie. "I think we need to start a no panty policy whenever dresses are worn."

"Motion seconded." Luke finished washing his hands and joined us. "Take 'em off, baby."

The shop was closed, but I still looked out of the darkened windows. Worrying my bottom lip with my teeth, I hesitated.

"Katrina!" Luke's forceful tone had me sitting upright. "Panties. Off. Now."

It wasn't the easiest request while I dangled in the air, but I liked how my brain shut out all the worries in my desire to comply. I wondered briefly if this was some insight into my inner omega, the men alluded to. "Help?" A slight pout formed while I tried to figure out how to get the garment off.

Skimming his hands under my dress and up my thighs, Caius came to my rescue. "Lay back on your elbows and lift your cute little ass for me."

Teamwork makes the dream work after all. Caius divested me of my undergarments quickly, throwing my panties over his shoulder. They flew through the air and landed on the hood of the car he'd been working on. "I'll need those back later."

"Debatable." He shrugged before hoisting my dress up and diving his head inside. I giggled at his antics under my dress until his hot mouth latched on to me, and his tongue trailed around my folds. My thighs tightened involuntarily around his head while I threw back my head and released a moan.

"Such a good girl," Luke crooned, stepping behind me. "Already offering up those sounds I love to hear." He fingered my hair till he was cupping my head, his chin brushing against my nose. He delivered a punishing upside-down kiss, sucking hard on my tongue as I whined into his mouth.

While Caius lapped with little abandon, Luke pushed his hands under the top of my bra and tweaked my nipples hard. I cried needily as a bolt of lightning sailed from my abused nipples and traveled to my clit. Caius threw my legs over his shoulder as he penetrated me with his tongue, driving in as deeply as he could.

"You gonna come for us, baby? Shout, and I'll flip you over and fuck you deep, just how you like it." Luke's dirty words were almost enough to put me over the edge. Caius moved directly over my clit and sucked almost to the point of pain, but it worked. I tumbled into a climax, wiggling away when the orgasm became too intense.

The lift was digging into my elbows and lower ass, but the pain was muted as endorphins flooded my system. Distantly, I heard Luke command Caius to "Flip her." The world spun around, and I was on my belly. Luke was now behind me, and Caius in front. Caius's lips were turned up in an amused smirk at my befuddled expression. He settled his hand across my jaw while he plundered my mouth in a possessive kiss. As I was catching my breath, the hydraulic lowered till my toes were touching the ground and I could almost balance on them.

"Stop there," Luke instructed. "Perfect height." A playful slap had me glancing behind. His clothes were still on, but his jeans were opened and pushed down. He was stroking himself and licking his lips as he viewed me. "Looks like Caius got you all messy." He slapped my exposed entrance again. I yelped while blushing furiously at the wet noise. His fingers delved inside me and then rubbed the wetness all over my swollen clit. "Exactly right," he growled.

With all my attention focused on what Luke planned to do with me, I was startled to notice Caius was now fully naked. His massive, glorious body was on full display, made even more erotic by the strange setting of the garage. "Will you open up for me, baby?" He asked while his monstrous cock brushed my cheek. It seems I was at the perfect height for him as well.

I nuzzled, kissed, and gave little licks but did not open. "It's gonna be like that now, eh?" He chuckled darkly. "Luke, our girl thinks she's a tease."

Luke, who had been about to thrust inside me,

halted. "Oh? You done for the night, Katrina?"

I shook my head, making sure my mouth brushed over Caius's dick with each move. He hissed at the contact, making me inordinately pleased with my performance. Luke withdrew fully, reached under me, and pinched my swollen bud. Hard. I lurched forward, mouth open, about to protest, when Caius used the action to press his way in. Mirth sparkled in his eyes when I glared up at him.

"Were you about to say something, baby? I might have missed it." Thrusting even farther till I almost gagged, he continued to gloat over his victory. Lightly, I grazed my teeth over him. He stilled his movements, and we engaged in a staring contest. I could take that smug look off his face rather quickly. His eyes widened a fraction, almost sensing my thoughts. Instead, I giggled, the vibrations in my throat causing him to close his eyes and fist my hair. I wiggled my butt, telling Luke he better get started and then began sucking in earnest. "Fuck," Caius sighed out as he struggled to find his rhythm.

Never one to disappoint, Luke entered me in one deep thrust, pushing Caius even further into the back of my throat. Effortlessly, my guys found their rhythm. Sensations engulfed me. The light scratch of Caius's nails on my scalp. Luke's long fingers squeezing my ass. The salty taste of precum mixed with my saliva. The wonderfully sensitive spot deep inside me Luke managed to find with every plunge. The sense of time being replaced with pure sensation, until the moment of climax.

Caius went off first. He slipped from my lips, and his legs gave way, the organism taking him forcibly. Luke's hand left my ass and traveled to the back of my neck, pushing me further down while he increased his pace. My toes lifted from the ground, and my body rocked forward with each movement. This new angle, though? My clit ground against the cold metal edge of the lift. It only took a few thrusts before my vision sparkled with twinkling white lights, and I shouted, unable to keep the emotion contained inside me. My walls clamped down hard, bringing Luke over the edge with me. He slumped, his head resting in the center of my back. Still pulsing inside me, his hand clasped firmly on my neck, he didn't move until his breathing slowed.

Managing to find his underwear and coveralls, Caius finished dressing. "You're crushing her, man," he griped.

Luke released me and pulled back. "You okay, baby?"

"More than okay." I beamed. "But I would like to get off this thing. It's digging into my ribs."

"Shit," Caius cursed as he pushed the button, bringing me back to the ground. He didn't let me stand, though. Instead, he scooped me up bridal style.

"I'm capable of walking."

"You sure about that? Your legs are shaking."

I shrugged. He might have a point.

"Besides, I want to give you a bath. No sexier way than to end the night watching my blissed-out girl covered in bubbles." Cuddling me closer, her rubbed his nose over the top of mine.

"By all means." I laid my head on his chest, brandishing my arm toward the door. "I won't stop you."

Chapter Thirty-Five
Luke

As we drove to our cabin for the change, I couldn't stop looking at Kate in the rearview mirror. She insisted on taking the back seat so she could feed the baby in the car. I'd much rather have her up front with me than Caius, but I saw the logic in her choice. It was a whirlwind trying to get out the door. We'd all overslept after another marathon session post-bath. Multitasking was needed to get up to our place in time and not instantly abandon Kate in the middle of the forest before our wolves emerged.

As calm as I appeared to be, I freaked out inside. My promise to Kate that she would be safe was weighing on me. We'd done everything we could to ensure the pack wasn't being actively hunted, but the Order was crafty. The idea of leaving Kate alone with the boys in the cabin wasn't fully settling right in my stomach, but neither was the idea of having her stay behind. There was a live wire thrashing around, making me jumpy. When Kate cursed from the back seat, I immediately slammed on the brakes.

"Shit!" she exclaimed, frantically searching around in her bag and the floor. "I think I left my cell phone charging in the kitchen." We were well over an hour away from the apartment. No time to turn around.

"You'll have plenty of cell phone options to choose from," Caius soothed her. "It's not like any of us will be using ours over the next three days. I'll give you my password, and we can make sure you have all the contacts you need."

"But I need to manage my online store." Her voice still held a note of panic.

"Did you forget your laptop too?" Caius asked.

She relaxed back in her seat, blowing out a breath. "Right. Laptop. I have it packed." She scrubbed at her face and giggled. "Guess I'm nervous. My head's not on right today."

Pulling back onto the road, we made eye contact with each other in the mirror. "Everything will be fine. I've set up a crazy stupid number of recording devices. There will be lots of provisions. The living room had been baby-proofed."

"It will be like a mini vacation." She parroted the next line I'd been about to say. I guess I'd been a bit repetitive.

I wanted to call her a smart ass, but Will was likely to repeat any bad word I accidentally uttered. "Exactly."

"Do you think Chloe will be safe?" A slight tremor spoke of her fear.

"They plan to do an eight-mile hike today and set out camp. Should be far enough from where we spotted the hunter." It wasn't ideal, but the plan was sound.

"I still don't understand why they just couldn't come here as well." She looked outside the window, craning her neck, as we left the paved roads for dirt.

"Ha," Caius barked. "Miles and Raff barely get along in human form. They'd flat out kill each other as wolves."

"Two alpha males is one too many," I answered. "Our animal side is territorial. They would fight for dominance. It wouldn't be safe for either pack."

Shivering, she zipped up her jacket. A light dusting of snow was on the ground. I wasn't looking forward to waking up naked, lying in it. No matter what the rest of the pack thought about me being impervious to the cold, having your junk covered in snow was never fun.

"Mommy! Snow!" Will shouted, delighted. "Can we make a snowman?"

"Oh, there isn't enough for that, honey. Maybe a snowball or two if it doesn't melt today." She blew on her hands to warm them, and I adjusted the heat in the back.

The omega in her never complained. "Tell me when you're cold, baby," I admonished lightly.

Caius looked back at her with a frown. "Iceman here was made for freezing temperatures. You need my hoody?" He was already taking it off before she was able to respond. We were both locked in her orbit.

"I can feel the heat now. Keep your clothes on." Her peal of laughter had us both grinning.

My packmate and I looked at each other with the same thought. Wouldn't be enough time to get naked again in the fun way before the clothes had to come off for our wilder side. A few times as a kid, I refused to take off my underwear outside in the cold. Miraculously, once, it had stayed somewhat on me, but it was beyond disgusting when I returned to my human body. I made sure to not have my wolf suffer the humiliation of a three-day-long cloth diaper again.

We were the last car to pull up to the cabin. Kyle and Xan had driven up after Christmas Eve dinner to get everything ready. Miles and Akela were still unpacking their car, so they couldn't have beat us here by too much.

"You made it." Akela waved at the boys in the back seat making goofy faces at them.

I stretched as soon as I left the car. Popping my spine before opening the back door for Kate to climb out. Will tumbled out of the passenger side and promptly started making those snowballs.

"Too slushy," he pouted, displaying his hands with the watery mush.

Akela took a knee in front of him. "No worries, little dude. This is the old melty stuff. It's supposed to snow again tonight. In the morning, you will have the perfect snow."

Giddy at the idea, Will spun around in circles. Or maybe he was just thrilled to be out of his car seat. Man, he was adorable. Kate held Tommy in her arms. He was nothing but snuggly, eyes drooping as nap time approached. I had a flash then of Kate, belly rounded with child. I wondered if she would want any more? If she would want them with us? After my family was slaughtered, I'd never once thought about being a father. Now? The idea warmed me up on the inside like a shot of whiskey.

"It's freezing," Kate chattered. "Will, let's get inside. You don't have a jacket on."

"I'll take him back out to play for a bit," I offered. "After we get you settled."

"But not for too long," she pleaded. "I want to spend time with you before ... " Her voice trailed away. I knew she was scared about tonight. No matter how many times I assured her, the fear was there.

Running a comforting hand down her spine and settling at the small of her back, I escorted her in, hopeful this wasn't just a visit but her entry into a new life.

Chapter Thirty-Six
Kate

The remainder of the day passed without anything remarkable happening. It felt like a cabin retreat crammed together with friends. As the sky got darker, I noticed small changes. They talked less. Everyone kept freezing in their actions and staring out the windows, mesmerized before shaking off the effect and carrying on. The guys would trail Miles around from room to room as if he were about to perform some miracle. It was odd, and I was the only one to notice the irregularities in behavior.

"You okay?" I asked Caius after a rather long bout of him staring off into space.

His forehead scrunched at my question. "Sure? Why you asking? I should be more worried about how you're feeling."

"Well." I shrugged. "Ya'll are acting out of it."

"Ah." It dawned on him then. "Our wolves are close. We feel them entering our minds bit by bit until they take over. It's the same when we transition back. They don't leave right away. Remnants stay with us the day we return. It's like a waking dream sometimes. Growing up with it, I don't even notice anymore when it's happening."

Swallowing loudly, I grabbed at his hand. "I'm a little scared. You're certain your wolves won't attack me if I'm outside?"

"There are shiftless females with the packs all the time. The wolves will recognize you as one of us, even in human form. Luke and I will still know you're our mate. Be prepared for a belly rub request," he chuckled.

My eyes grew wide. "Seriously?"

"We could get in a little practice now if you like?" He pulled up his shirt and stretched, showing off the cut lines over his abdomen. I couldn't resist going in for the kill. My fingers poked and fluttered over his stomach. Caius jumped a foot away. Served him right. A ticklish man should never tease!

"Our wolves may approach you, but they will be gentle." Luke joined us in the room. "I've spoken to other mated couples about it. It's why I know you'll be safe."

"But not the boys," I clarified. Having no intention of them joining me tonight, my statement was more about the future. Keeping this from them when they were small would be easy but much harder when older.

Luke nodded. "Best to keep them away for now. We can always use a more controlled environment if you wish to try another time."

"Let's just get through tonight," I sighed out the words.

As it was the end of December, the days were short, and the nights were long. The moon would be out before the boys usually went to bed, but I rushed through the nighttime routine in order to be able to go and see the pack transformation. There was still a small part of me that needed to see it to truly embrace it.

I hustled outside when finished. The pack, unable to wait for me, had already undressed and gone out. It was hard not to blush at all the nudity. They were standing about a hundred yards from the cabin, staring at the sky. An eerie quiet settled over the forest. I could no longer hear the crickets chirping or the leaves rustling. Something was coming, and the night was holding her breath.

As if pulled by an invisible string, both Luke and Caius turned in unison to me. It wasn't affectionate or comforting like I'd come to expect. It also wasn't vacant. It was an acknowledgment of my presence. A sense of acceptance settled over me, allowing me to ignore my first feelings of intruding. Our eyes met, my heart beating wildly. Boom. Boom. Boom. The organ was as loud as a drum to my ears. Everything else was silence.

The moon reached its zenith, the silver light refracting through the clouds. A flash, like a camera, blinded me, and complete whiteness blanketed my vision. Blinking until I could see again, I rubbed my face. Wolves yipped. The humans gone, except Kyle. He stood shivering in his nudity, the wolves circling him in what I could only describe as playful. They were massive, bigger than any dog I'd encountered. The most massive nudged at Kyle's legs, pushing him toward me.

Kyle chuckled at the wolf. "I'm as surprised as you are, alpha." He turned and started walking toward me, but before he reached me, two wolves sprang past him, a shaggy gray wolf with a partially chewed-up tail and a pure white wolf I'd only ever seen in documentaries on Alaska. I fell to my knees, no fear at all in my body. I may not sense the mate bond, but I knew who these wolves were to me. Caius reached me first, running his huge tongue across my entire face. Luke nipped his hind, causing Caius to yelp and sidestep away. Luke then proceeded to headbutt my hand until I buried my fingers in his coarse hair and scratched behind his ears. His tongue rolled out to flop to the side of his jaw in a wolfy smile.

"Not too different as wolves, huh?" Kyle was standing before me.

Yanking my coat off, I tossed it to him while averting my eyes. I might be getting comfortable with being in a relationship with two men, but I wasn't ready to live the nudist lifestyle.

Chuckling, Kyle covered up his junk for me. "Sorry. As shifters, we get used to it."

"Why are you still this?" I gestured to his body with my hand.

"Akela and Miles see you as pack." He spoke as if that was an explanation.

"I'm flattered and all, but I still don't get it."

The mountain of a wolf sat on its haunches and howled. All the playful yipping stopped. Caius and Luke left me to return to the alpha. Miles then darted full speed toward the lake, and the pack followed.

"We're both omegas," he continued the conversation.

"Still not getting it."

Kyle started heading back to the cabin. "There are young here to protect. That is the job of Omegas. I didn't shift since the boys are here."

"But my kids are human. They're not Wa'ya."

"Are they any less your family since they were adopted and not from you genetically?" he probed.

"No, of course not." I couldn't imagine being capable of loving anyone more.

"It's the same with us. Packs form not because of biological similarities. We are an entire pack made up of strays. When we sense young in our territory, under our protection, omegas don't shift."

"Do you mind? Not being with them?' I looked back but could no longer see where the wolves had traveled to.

He touched his chest. "I'm still connected to them where it counts." A huge grin split his face. "I'm going to love being all warm and cozy when they wake up in these frigid temperatures. This could be a fun change of pace. I expected it would happen soon with a new alpha pair in the pack. Children are always sure to follow. This is just giving me a head start. And." He had a sparkle in his eye when he spoke. "I'll have you to do it with. Thank God! As far as Omegas go, I'm a bit of a lost cause. I've never been around children until yours. Us Omegas are as rare as alphas. Once Akela completes nursing, she will shift, and then it would have been just me. I thought I'd be doing this all alone."

"So, even if I take the drugs, I won't change?"

He cocked his head to the side. "You'll change. You just won't shift unless there are no little ones present. Our animal side senses when those weaker than us need protection. Omegas are submissive to alphas by nature, but we're fierce in protecting the weakest members of our packs."

"How would I know it even worked then?" I mused.

"Oh, you'd feel it. The bonds are like a warm hug that never leaves you. It gives you insight on what you need and alerts others of your needs. There's no human experience to compare it to. But if you dropped off your kids at your mom's and came here without them, we would both probably shift then."

Would I even want that? Could I get this amazing pack bonds experience, and stay with this pack caring for kids and never worried about the alien nature of shifting into something else? Would that make me want to try more?

We made it back inside. I was grateful Xan had gotten the fire started earlier. It was blazing, chasing away the cold an older, draftier cabin was prone to have. "I'm grateful for your company. I was nervous about being here completely on my own with the boys. It's pretty far away from anyone else," I admitted.

"As the sole member of the pack that lives here full time, I understand. I like the quiet, but no one else spends more than a week here without needing to be back in civilization."

"Oh, I didn't mean to insult your home." Feeling awful, I covered my mouth with my hand.

He gently pulled my hand down. "I wasn't insulted. How about a cup of hot chocolate." He grinned like a little boy on Christmas. "Didn't get to have any earlier and was thinking about it just before the change. Wishing I had, that is. And now! Here I am. Hot cocoa not three days away but three minutes."

"I'm relieved you're taking this well. We should talk about the next full moon and what you want. I could stay with my mom if you're missing out. You also don't have to feel obligated to do things with me over the next three days. I don't want to be in your way," I nervously rambled.

"Kate." He threw his arm over my shoulder to reassure me. "Relax. I'm thrilled. This is part of being an omega. When you embrace being a Wa'ya, you embrace the natural flow of things. I'm here. Therefore I am meant to be here. Done."

"That simple?" I still fretted.

"Yes," he answered easily.

"Either way, I'll need to think about what to do with the boys for all of this. Will is clever and curious. They are small enough now that none of this will register with them. But what about when he's older? Do I tell them? Can I?"

Kyle squirmed, unsure how to answer. "You'll need to ask Miles. I think if it was just you and the kids, it wouldn't be an issue to have them know. Raise them with the knowledge, have them live the lifestyle with the packs. But if your kids attend school or see your husband, they might let it slip. Being young, they would not understand the implications of unveiling us to humans. It would be too great a risk."

I didn't like thinking their life would be filled with lies. Keeping such a huge secret from my own children bothered me. Kyle was right, though. Until I knew what kind of relationship they would have with my husband, it was safest they remained unaware. I could only imagine how quickly I would lose custody if they told their father Mom was a shifter. Not because he would believe them but because he would assume I'd gone crazy.

Chapter Thirty-Seven
Luke

We woke in increments. Senses modified from primal to high reasoning. The comfortable feeling of a pack huddle in a snowy landscape changed to the reality of Caius's head buried in my underarm and my chin resting on Xan's bare ass. Gotta love pack life. We truly had no boundaries. My first thought was gratitude we were not completely buried in snow followed quickly by a sense of wrongness.

Clutching his chest, Miles was the first to jerk upright. I scrubbed my eyes, gauging our surroundings. "Where's Kyle?" I asked, alarm settling into my tone. The pack bonds were distraught. We all cast a hectic search for the omega.

Xan's usually calm demeanor slipped as he cursed repeatedly. "Fuck, fuck, fuck! Do you think hunters have him?" The bond was freaking us out. We knew he wasn't dead, but something was very wrong.

"Wait," Akela called. "I remember seeing Kate, and ... " She trailed off as she tried to pull back the fog from the change. "Kyle stayed human. He didn't change with us."

Miles breathed out. "Yes. I have the same memory. I was thinking Kate and the boys should have more protection. They are pack."

The gratitude I felt at my alpha's words was short-lived. "Then Kyle is with her." A boulder settled in my stomach. "And the bonds are saying something isn't right."

"Xan," Miles barked out, and Xan took off. He was our best tracker and could decipher our location quickest. He was also responsible for planting supplies and clothes for possible change spots. I hated waiting while he ran out, but running off after him wouldn't help matters.

"She's going to be fine," Caius spoke with more confidence than the bond suggested he felt. "We just found her. We won't lose her now."

An agonizing amount of time elapsed before Xan returned with a hiker's backpack and duffle bag slung over his shoulders. He was wearing a beat-up navy hoody, gray sweats, and canvas slip-ons. Not ideal for hikes, but we had to pack what we could in a few different places. "We're farther than normal. The snow must have pushed us away from our usual spots. I'm lucky I even stashed anything here."

"How far?" Mile's tone was grim.

"At least five miles." Xan's grimaced.

We were all thinking the same thoughts. Kyle was alive but distraught. Something must have happened to Kate. I was the first to unzip the duffle, grabbing out anything I would fit into, Caius only a heartbeat behind me. Usually, the first thing after a shift all we could think about was food and getting clean. I felt no hunger. The state of my body had no bearing on my urgency. Making sure Kate was well was the only thing my brain could focus on. Miles had to force me to eat a protein bar and chug a bottle of water. I resented the time spent in the act, unable to stop glaring at him while I chewed and swallowed.

"We are depleted and need fuel for the journey back. You won't be doing anyone favors if you collapse on the way." His admonishment was slight, his reasoning sound, but I still felt like a horse chomping at the bit needing to run.

The snow was deeper than expected, making our trek even more slow going. None of us were dressed for such an extreme hike in these conditions. The canvas shoes quickly became soaked. Blisters formed as my feet were rubbed raw. The only benefit of the cold was after a mile, I could barely feel them. I gritted my teeth and kept pace. At this rate, it would take us almost two hours before we reached the cabin. Every minute was agony.

Miles flooded the bond with assurance and comfort in the hopes that Kyle would calm down. It worked for a while, then crushing despair would flare up. It was hard to breathe when it hit. It felt too close to grief. A promise of a painful death. Were the hunters at the cabin waiting for them to return? Did they have our omegas?

While Miles blazed the trail, stomping down the snow and finding us the safest routes to cross, I prayed to every deity known to man that Kate and the boys were okay. Guilt sat like a leaden weight on my shoulders. I'd been the one to assure her she would be safe. What if, yet again, the Order had managed to take away everything dear to me? I'm not sure life would be worth continuing. If my girl was harmed, I would spend every penny I had tracking down the Order's headquarters and go in guns blazing. The only good ending would be taking as many of those fuckers with me.

Over an hour in, our mad dash back, Xan tripped and rolled his ankle. He could put weight on it, but he was limping. "Go without me." He waved us on.

As much as I didn't like the idea of leaving him alone, I could only think about Kate. Gut clenching, I stared at Miles while he was clearly processing his options. I might have to go against my alpha if he decides we should stay together.

"Get to the omegas," Akela ordered. "I'll stay with Xan and help him back." To prove her point she hefted her shoulder under Xan, bracing him so they were able to continue. The woman was badass.

"Babe, you sure?" Miles was already looking ahead to the path.

"Time could be of the essence. Xan and I will manage just fine," she assured us.

Miles administered a fast, hard kiss on her lips. "You know I love you, woman?"

A lopsided smile dangled from her lips. "What's not to love?"

About another twenty minutes in, we could see smoke billowing from the chimney in the distance. We started moving double time then. Sweat poured off me from the exertion. My breathing was as labored as a kid with an asthma attack, but we pressed on. Till the most glorious site in the word was before me.

Kate left the cabin and was all out sprinting towards us. She reached Caius and me at the same time and threw her arms around us. "Oh, thank God! You're alive! Kyle told me you would be, but I was worried. He was worried too when it was taking you so long to get back."

Kyle ran out of the cabin as well and skidded to a stop. "Where's Akela and Xan?"

"Xan twisted his ankle. They're coming." Miles appeared mystified at the clearly two healthy and unharmed omegas. "What the hell, Kyle? We thought something happened to you. Your end of the bond was like a knife to the chest."

Visibly, Kyle paled before he scrunched his eyes, bracing. "Raff's pack was attacked by the Order. They must have been tracking them in some way. Miles ... I ... " he trailed off, seemingly at a loss.

Kate wiped at her tear-stained cheeks. "There was a fight early this morning. Chloe, Lowe, and Tate were all shot." She sobbed, unable to speak for a moment.

"Tate is the worst off." Her face scrunch as if she was debating whether to continue. "They don't think he'll make it."

Miles dropped like a stone to his knees, disbelief blanketing his features. "Where are they?"

"Chloe and Lowe just got out of surgery. They're in the ICU, stable right now. Tate had to go under again. They're having difficulty stopping the bleeding. He was the only one with multiple gunshots." Kyle placed his hand on our alpha's shoulder.

I squeezed Kate to my chest. Her little hiccups and sniffles tore at my heart. "And the others? What of the hunters?"

"Raff said they must have showed up before the dawn. The hunters attacked, and his wolf defended them, but he transformed back in the middle of the fight. He managed to wrestle a gun away from one of hunter, and the others fled, but not without causing as much damage as they could." Kate sunk her head back on my shoulder. "Poor Chloe. This was her worst fear come true."

"Where did they take my brother?" Miles was shaking.

"Raff is at the hospital with them now. He has his cell phone on, waiting to speak with you," Kyle spoke gently.

Caius helped our alpha up, and we made our way into the cabin. Snatching his phone off the counter, Miles waited with a gritted jaw while it rang. "Hey." A muffled voice on the other end was all I could hear. "Your mate will be okay? Good. Your omega?" I watched Miles absently nod. "What hospital are you at?" He motioned for a pen. Kyle ran and grabbed him one so Miles could jot down the info. "What about the others?" A much longer discussion was being had on the other side, answering. My hands clenched into fists at my side.

"And you'll call me when you have news?" The first note of distress entered my alpha's voice. He'd been strictly business till then. "I'll call Rollin. We can be over there in a few hours. Talk soon."

Miles hung up, needing a moment before he could address us. "They airlifted the injured to a military base hospital. Austin has contacts in the government that work with him. They're still trying to save Tate."

"What can we do?" Caius asked.

"Rollin and Weylin stayed behind. They're hunting the Order," Miles began.

"I'm in," I interrupted. "I've been hunting them the longest. They need my help. None of us are safe until we route them out."

Kate clutched me, shaking her head. "Luke, you could get killed." Her fingers were like talons gripping into my shirt. Tremors racked through her body.

I lightly kissed her brow. "I know that better than most, baby."

Miles cleared his throat. I could feel him wrestling with grief and anger through the bond. He pushed it down deep so it would not affect us. "They could use our help. Austin's government contacts are assisting with protection and medical, but they won't go after the Order. Austin's pack is valuable to them. He offers research. The rest of us are on their own. The official statement was they aren't convinced it was anything but poachers or simple hunters," Miles grunted his derision. "We can't get access to the base. I won't be able to see Tate." He ground his teeth while sucking in a lungful of air to calm down. "But you're right, Luke. Our pack has more experience with these bastards, especially you and Xan. We need to finish this before any more of our kind get hurt."

As if summoning them Akela and Xan entered

the cabin. Xan must have made the ankle worse by pushing it, their pace wasn't too far off of ours. "Is everyone okay?" Akela asked.

Miles pulled her in for a hug. "We're okay here, babe, but Raff's pack was attacked. Chloe and Lowe are recovering from gunshot wounds. Tate's not doing too well."

Akela grew up with Tate as her foster brother. They were even closer than Miles was to his biological brother. She took the news hard. Tears fell freely as her hand covered her mouth to stop any sobs. Miles pressed her tighter to his chest. "I need you to head to your Uncle's place and stay there," he spoke into her hair. "Austin has protection set up for any that go there. Take Kate and the boys."

As she pulled away, Akela searched his face. "Where will you be?"

"The rest of us are meeting up with Rollin and Weylin. We're going to hunt the hunters."

Chapter Thirty-Eight
Kate

Miles had everyone dressed and out the door in under an hour. There wasn't even time to protest as Luke and Caius packed the boys into Akela's car and escorted me to the passenger side. I didn't want to leave Luke and Caius, and I was terrified this might be the last time I saw them. Chloe was still in the ICU recovering from surgery. There was no way to speak with her. No one seemed to want to talk about this vigilante plan in motion. I couldn't understand the amount of risk involved in going after the Order. From what I gathered, they were well-funded, well-armed, and difficult to find.

"How long will you be away?" I grasped Luke's jacket in my hands, refusing to sit in the car.

"Depends on if the trail is cold or leads to a dead end," Luke answered calmly.

"You don't have to do this," I whined. My stomach felt like acid. "What if more of you get hurt. Is it worth it?"

He mulishly puckered his lips. "We do have to. They won't stop unless we stop them. You haven't seen how they decimate packs. We could easily be next."

Akela left the cabin with a bag slung over her shoulder. She marched straight to the car and put it in the trunk. Miles stood at the cabin door, arms folded over his chest, looking resolute. There were no sweet words of goodbye to his mate. From the stubborn set of her jawline, Akela apparently had issues with being sent away, too. I thought I heard fighting earlier behind closed doors. "Let's go." She sighed at me before staring at my guys. "You watch out for each other. Call us with any news immediately. Xan, that ankles not in great shape.

Stay off it."

"Yes, alpha," they replied in unison.

Tears pooled in my eyes while Luke and then Caius kissed me goodbye. I was outvoted. This train was on the tracks, and I couldn't derail it. My boys, sensing the tension, whimpered and fussed in the back seat. I needed to put on my big girl panties and comfort them, even though deep down, all I wanted to do was sob as we pulled away.

The drive was relatively quiet, Akela and I living out worst-case scenarios in our heads. Will was engrossed in his iPad, and Tommy finally fell asleep. "I need to stop at the apartment. I left my phone there and need to call my mom and let her know about Chloe. Tommy also has a bad diaper rash, and I think there's more of his medicated cream in my other diaper bag. Poor guy is pretty miserable."

"No problem." Akela changed lanes to head in the direction of the garage.

When she finally pulled up, both Will and Tommy were still passed out. "I'll just run in and grab it. Unless you need to use the restroom?" I asked.

"I'll wait with the kids," she offered.

"Thanks." I ran up the stairs and spotted my phone. Powering it on I had a few texts from my mom and my neighbor Mary, none from Aaron. He should be getting back from his trip with his buddies either today or tomorrow. I wasn't sure how to deal with him during this crisis, but I needed to come up with a solution soon. He thinks I've been at my mother's this whole time, and I know he expects me to return home eventually.

I ransacked the place, searching for the cream for Tommy, with a sinking feeling. It was in my extra diaper bag, but that bag wasn't there. It was still at my house. I grabbed a few things, locked up, and walked back to the car. The boys were still passed out.

I tapped on the driver's window, signaling she should roll it down. "Hey, I need to head to my place. I know it's out of the way, but if you take the boys, I can drive my car there, grab what I need for the baby, and be about an hour behind you. It might be best if I have my car, either way. Do you mind if the boys stay with you a bit longer? I'll be much quicker without them."

"I don't mind keeping the boys with me. Your husband going to give you shit?"

"He shouldn't be back from his annual trip quite yet. I think I can get in and out. It's the fastest way to get the stuff Tommy needs. The pharmacy doesn't always have it in stock and the medicated one clears it up in a day." I played with the keys in my hand feeling guilty about adding to her pile on top of all the stress.

Akela settled her hand over mine. "Truly, Kate. I don't mind. Having them with me will be a good distraction."

"Thank you."

She shook her head while she smiled. "There's no need. We're pack. I'll see you at Austin's place. My folk's house is a few down on the street. We might stay there tonight."

"Okay, see you soon."

I texted Mary before getting in my car. It was weird not being able to confide in my good friend, but she needed to stay removed from this new world I found myself in. I kept it simple, hoping she had a good holiday with the family and asking if Aaron was home. There was no response. I knew Mary had family over from out of town and might not see my message. I couldn't wait for an answer, though.

In and out. That was the plan.

"Kate?" I heard my husband shout my name

when he opened the door.

Fuck a duck! I was only in the house for five minutes. What lousy timing. A nice note saying I needed more time before we talked would have been supremely preferable to the conversation I'm sure we were going to have. "Hey!" I shouted. "I'm in the nursery."

Aaron appeared rumpled and a bit worse for wear. He leaned on the doorframe, watching me pack up stuff for the baby. "Where are the kids?" His voice was softer, less aggravated than usual. He peered down the corridor.

I couldn't tell him the truth. He seemed docile right now. I wanted to keep him this way. "They're at my mother's. I ran out of diaper cream and needed to pack up a few things."

Resting more fully on the door frame, he sighed heavily. "It's been a month. I thought you'd be home by now. Instead, you're packing even more stuff up." The usual rage was absent from his tone. "I think it's time we truly talked. Come down to the kitchen? I'll make us tea."

It was weird seeing nice Aaron make a return. Not since our newlywed year had the man made me anything. "Are you okay? You look a little bruised?"

A sheepish chuckle proceeded a wince. "Got home early from my trip and decided to work on the house. I was cleaning out some clogged rain gutters and fell from the ladder. In fact, I just returned from the ER." He pointed to a bandage peeking under his cuff I'd missed earlier. "Had to get some stitches."

"Oh, Aaron, I'm sorry. Do you need pain meds? Can I get you something?" Guilt settled over me. I'd expected him to make it easy on me. Continue to be a jerk about everything, and I'd happily tell him it's over. Instead, he was injured and calmly asking to speak with me.

"I'm good. Don't worry about it." He signaled behind him with his head. "I'll get the kettle on. Why don't you finish up and come downstairs?"

"All right," I agreed quietly. Appearing dejected and exhausted, he walked away. My stomach clenched at the conversation about to go down, but it was past time I ended it. I had a new family waiting for me.

As quickly as I could, I grabbed what I needed for Tommy. I should get this over with. The packs were in crisis mode with the hunters. Maybe there was some small way I could be of help. It hadn't occurred to me about playing it safe and staying away from them. It wasn't even a consideration, not only because of my sister or Luke and Caius but because they all welcomed me like no one ever had. I didn't need to act perfect with them, and it was wonderful allowing myself to be myself. The danger the Order represented was chilling but worth the risk of having a full life. This last month proved there were things in life I was willing to fight for.

Carrying my bag to the door, I took a steadying breath before entering the kitchen. Aaron was reclined on a chair, tilted back on just two legs. He sat up straight when I entered the room. Offering a tentative smile, he pushed the mug of tea across the table to where I usually sat.

"Thank you," I offered a timid smile in return. The tea was bitter, overbrewed due to my packing time. Cringing at my first sip, I added more sugar rather than complaining.

"I tried calling you when I fell," he started talking as he watched me drink. "I was hoping you could drive me to the hospital, but it went straight to voicemail."

"Oh," I exclaimed. "Sorry about that." I fished it out of my back pocket. "I left it at a friend's house and picked it up on my way here. It was completely dead." I hadn't noticed a miss call from Aaron.

"That explains it, then." He cleared his throat. "I thought maybe you were blocking my calls."

"I wouldn't." Taking a last gulp of my tea, I set it aside and placed my hand over his on top of the table. "We should be able to have a better relationship than that. The boys deserve parents who communicate."

His focused on our hands, then shifted to my cell. "Would you text your mom? Tell her we have stuff to work out. I don't want you to leave tonight."

I shifted uncomfortably in my seat. Maybe Caius would understand, but Luke would freak out if I stayed the night to patch up my relationship. Even if it would only be for the kids to not see us fighting during our separation. I told Akela I would be only an hour or so behind her. I couldn't thrust caring for my boys on her like that. "I can shoot her a text later if necessary. She isn't expecting me back soon."

"And that is where you've been? With your mom?" His eyes narrowed slightly. "Or with this friend you left your phone with?"

Unease flittered up my spine. Mean Aaron was peeking through. "I don't want to make this into a fight."

He held up his hands in surrender. "Who said anything about a fight? I'm just wondering where my family has been the last month. You've evaded telling me." He stood before I could respond and walked to the counter. Grabbing a letter sized manilla envelope, he returned and set it on the center of the table but made no move to open it.

Could it be divorce papers? My lips felt numb as I tried to address the elephant in the room. "What's in the envelope?"

With an upturn of his mouth and a cold glimmer

in his eyes, he tore open the envelope and pulled out photo paper. At least, I assumed it was photos as he flipped the pages and made appreciative sounds. The images were faced away from me.

Loudly sucking on his teeth, he leered. "I gotta say. Maybe we could have had more fun over the last few years. You were such a rag doll, boring in the sack. It was an effort to get it up. I truly didn't know you had any kinky in you." The pictures spilled from his hands and landed on the table. My vision swam as image after image of me in the garage with both Luke and Caius slid across the table.

"Where did you get these," I stammered. My skin was flushed. Sweat was beading on my forehead, and I was beginning to feel faint.

"If only I'd known you had such a freak flag! You were such a cold, dead thing beneath me. Holding out on me, eh?" a dark chuckle accompanied his words.

"What is this?" Confused and hurt, I licked nervously at my lips, still tasting the bitter brew he made.

"Well, this ... " He picked up a photo and held it in front of me. "Is called being spit roasted. I guess you don't have to know what it's called to do it, though, huh?"

I attempted to swat the picture from his hands but missed, much to his delighted cackle. "You had me followed? Spied on?" My words were as jumbled as my emotions.

"Followed? No." He tapped on my cell phone. "You kindly shared your locations with me."

"What the fuck is this? Blackmail of some kind? What do you want?"

"From you?" He stabbed at an image. "I want this fucker's name and location."

It was difficult to focus. My mind was racing.

Aaron was pointing to a picture of Luke. "What does it matter? I don't need to get a lecture from you after all the years of you cheating on me. Obviously, this marriage is over." I tried to stand but instead slid to the floor. My limbs were no longer working properly as the room spun. *Shit! He put something in the tea.*

"Oh." He smiled wickedly while towering above me. "Thank fuck! It is finally over."

The earth turned on its axis, and reality warped sideways. One second, I was flailing on my butt, and the next, I was face down on the kitchen tile. Promptly after, I lost consciousness.

****

Waking wasn't instant. Whatever drug Aaron put in the tea wasn't strong enough to knock me out entirely, but enough to prevent me from speaking or using any of my extremities. My eyes briefly opened as he dragged me down the cellar stairs. Being much smaller than him, he could have lifted me. It was pure cruelty as he pulled me down by my armpits, my hips banging with each step.

Managing to drag my eyelids open again, I watched passively as Aaron tossed me onto a metal folding chair and tightened my wrist behind my back with a zip tie cord. A pair of handcuffs circled around my ankles till the skin pinched enough for me to feel it in my drug-induced stupor. Satisfied with his efforts, he walked up the stairs before I drifted again.

****

Our unfinished basement was cold most of the year. As it was the end of December, it was freezing. Shivers wracked my frame forcing me to alertness. A needle-like pain was piercing my skull, no doubt thanks to the side effects of whatever crap was in the tea. I had to blink several times before I was able to see clearly.

Perhaps it would have been better if I hadn't. Aaron stood before me with a large bucket, gauging my reaction. I was dripping wet. The full-body shivering made sense now. I guess he was impatient. He'd doused me in cold water to get me up.

"Oh good, you're awake," his tone all dry humor as if this was the funniest of jokes.

"What's going on?" I freaked out seeing the set up in the basement. He'd been busy while I was out. There was a small dog sized cage in the corner and what looked like a wolf inside. It was snarling as Aaron stood in close proximity to it. Rolls of plastic covered the floor under me. A saw table rested near me with an open toolbox sitting on top. I may not have been a *Law and Order* fan, but this looked like a room for murder. I started hyperventilating as I struggled against my bindings.

I stared at my husband, realizing I knew nothing about him. Only a stranger stood before me. Dressed in what looked like a hazmat suit, gloves, and rubber boots, he had his hair tucked under a tight cap.

"I don't understand. You've been cheating on me for years," I sobbed. "Why do you even care I'm with someone else? This is insane! Let's just get a divorce. I won't ask for anything from you."

"How can you be this clueless? You think I give a crap about who you're fucking? This"—he gestured around the room—"is because of *what* you are."

I stilled. "What're you talking about?"

"I know you are a monster, Kate. Correction, I know you're a broken monster. After I get the information we need from you, I'll let my little friend here out of his cage to finish the job. Your warm blood will be awfully tempting since I've been starving him. Then dump you in the woods your kind loves so much, and voila, I am finally done with this sham of a marriage I was forced into."

The full horror of my situation was slowly poking through my foggy brain. "What do you mean?" I stammered. "Are you a hunter?"

"The Order serves mankind. We are not just hunters but defenders of humanity. Eradicating freaks has been our great purpose. Men are hunters by nature, and your kind has made the most interesting prey. Wa'ya packs are crafty though, hard to find. Austin's pack has been known to us for years, but since he works for the government," his lips pulled into a tight sneer. "Getting close to him had been difficult. Your mother was on our radar, too. I'll admit when I first volunteered to attempt to infiltrate, I thought I was getting the slutty older sister, but the general thought you would be the easier conquest."

"You married me to find other Wa'ya? I didn't even know I was one!"

Aaron flipped around a folding chair and sat across from me. "That was a bit of a letdown for sure. At first, we assumed I needed your trust for you to let me in on the family secret. When it was obvious you were clueless, the Order wondered if you were human, but the bloodwork we did on you confirmed what you truly are."

"When did you take my blood?" How could I have been married to this man all these years? He was clearly unhinged. *What a complete fool I've been.*

"The fertility doctors I took you to." He made quotation marks for fertility. "They told the Order all we needed to know about what you are." He sneered, disgusted at the idea.

"Why stay married to me all these years? Why adopt children?" A ragged sob tore from my throat, thinking about my boys.

"I was the sacrificial lamb per se in the great experiment. After you were unable to provide the introduction we had hoped for to other packs, the Order wanted to see if eventually you could provide an in. Most of us just want your kind dead. Interacting with you is the least desirable thing. But after we wiped out a few packs. It became harder to find you little freaks. You make such a good sport. Shame to have future generations unable to share the rite of passage of the first hunt." He looked away wistfully as if killing was a fond memory. "So, I was told to stick it out, just in case you were ever contacted by them."

"Boy how I'd wish they assigned me your sister for that task. She's a walking wet dream. But I was assigned mousy little Kate. You were younger, more eager to please, more malleable. Sadly, for me, frigid. I got boring real fast, though. Thank fuck your kind and mine can't breed. There was talk about seeing if it was possible. I never fully agreed with the idea but followed the orders given to me. I thought they would let me get rid of you years ago, but no." He glared at me as if I should feel bad since he wasn't allowed to murder me sooner.

"They were convinced you could still be a pathway to finding more packs one day. Unprotected packs. Then your mother finally told you what you were, and you went straight to Austins. Finally, we had an exact location. We knew Austin's research was government-funded. We just didn't know they cared enough to protect him from us. We took our shot at his pack last month. What a waste of a hunt that was. We were excited when we spotted wolves, hoping they were freaks. But sadly, all we got were dead wolves and this one here in the cage. So, we waited to see if you could bring us some outlier baby packs. Ripe for the picking."

"I'm glad I didn't tell you shit then," I spat, disgusted more at myself for ever thinking I loved this man.

"You didn't need to, idiot. You took your phone with you and let me find your sister and her pack. I'd hoped you would send me to your lover's pack, but you left your phone behind. I thought you were on to me."

"I'm the reason you attacked Chloe's pack?" My gut clenched, thinking it was my fault if Tate died. *They'd been safe until I showed up at her door.*

He cackled and rolled up the cuff of his shirt to show me his stitches. "Your bitch of a sister actually bit me. I wish I'd put a bullet in her brain, but her mate shoved her out of the way."

My blood went cold. All Aaron's hunting trips took on a new disgusting meaning. He might even have been responsible for the killing of Luke's entire pack. His excuse for cleaning the gutters had sounded hollow earlier, but I didn't question it. My husband had come close enough to kill my sister, and it was all my fault. How could he be this callous about the life we shared together?

"I've been your wife for almost six years. We have a family." My stomach revolted. I thought I might vomit.

He shrugged. "I agreed to adopting kids because at least they'd be human. Made sure we only adopted boys. That way I could bring them in the Order. When they're older and hear about how you were brutally murdered by those freaks, they'll be dedicated to the cause. Sons I can be proud of. Not monster freaks with no right to be alive. This hungry wolf here will provide all the evidence their little brains will need. If they falter in their dedication, I can whip out the photos of your mangled body to incentivize them."

I shook my head in denial. Images of my sweet boys becoming warped and twisted like Aaron flashing before me. "Never," I hissed over his cruel laughter. "Why not kill me now, then? Why tell me all of this?"

The hatred in his eyes seared me. "To prolong your suffering, of course. I had to put on an act for six long damn years. I wouldn't want your final moments on this earth to think anything we shared was real. I want you to experience misery. It's the least you could do for me."

"You're bat shit crazy," I shouted. "I was a good wife to you. I put up with your cruelty, your cheating." A sob tore through me. "I don't deserve this from you."

"The only thing your kind deserves is a bullet through the brain on the full moon. We usually only kill you in animal form. Makes the sport much better. But you're not only a freak but a reject, too. This shape will have to be how you leave this world."

I struggled as he approached. With my hands bound to the chair, I had little chance of breaking free. The idea of my boys growing up with my killer, being turned into a man like him because of a misplaced vengeance for their mother, had rage coursing through my body. I may not have a link to my animal side, but at that moment, I could feel my wolf restless inside me, wanting the taste of blood.

"I haven't fed him in two days," He kicked the cage, and the wolf snapped, jaws dripping drool. "I imagine if I slice you up just a little, he won't be able to resist taking a bite or two. Kind of poetic if you think about it. Bleeding out is a slow way to die. Payment owed for the last six years of my life being forced to live with a freak." His hatred was a living thing, suffocating any air between us. I panted, looking between him and the wild animal in the cage.

Instead of reaching for an implement of torture among his tools, he lifted up a photo of Luke. "Who's this pale asshole?"

"Why should I tell you anything? Your mind seems set on killing me." This man had taken much from me. My confidence. My self-esteem. Soon, my life. I wouldn't leave this world giving him anything else. I was scared shitless, but I was resolute.

"He's a murderer. He's killed true humans." Shoving the picture under my nose, he yanked my head back by the hair.

Scalp stinging, my eyes watered unable to see the image of my lover, my mate. "Turnabout is fair play, then. His was an act of self-defense and preservation. You're the murderer."

"It's only murder if it's human," he scoffed, releasing my hair. Lovingly, his fingers trailed over the tools near me. My stomach clenched at the sight of hammers, saws, and blades.

"How do you think to get away with this?" The pleading tone spilled from my lips. "I have friends and family. They will come looking."

"Oh, I'm counting on it. To snuff out this fucker would be a huge feather in the Order's cap. This torture is all on you. If you'd taken your phone with you, we'd have all we needed. Since I know now it was an accident, then this asshat still has no clue who I am." He shook his head in disbelief. "If you remain unwilling to give me their location, then your dead body in Chloe's pack territory will send a clear message to the monsters."

"You're fucking sick. You're the monster." My chest was heaving as I tried to calm my breathing. I didn't want my death to give Aaron any leverage. I most certainly didn't want to leave my children without a mother and an insane man as their only parent.

The doorbell chimed upstairs. Instantly, my thoughts went to Mary. Maybe if I screamed, someone would hear me. "Hel ... " Aaron stuck a dirty rag in my mouth until I gagged.

"Hold that thought." Holding up a finger, the jerk had the gall to wink at me before heading upstairs.

The oil-stained rag was causing me to cough. Hot bile filled my mouth, not improving the horrific taste. Using my tongue, I pushed out the rag bit by bit until I was finally able to dislodge it. Sucking in a clean lungful of air, I spat before managing a solid scream. "Help!"

The cellar door opened, and heavy boots descended to join me in the dimly lit room. My heart pulsed an uneven rhythm when I noticed it wasn't my husband but his boss from work. "Oh, thank God! Mr. Anderson, please untie me! Aaron has gone crazy," I sobbed in relief.

"Quiet, animal!" he shouted. A quick backhand to my face had me seeing stars. Blood poured from my cracked lip, body drooping as I realized this man was another enemy. Of course, my entire life with Aaron was a lie. His job, also being a farse, shouldn't have surprised me.

The wolf growled and pawed at the cage in Mr. Anderson's presence. Poor thing seemed to dislike him even more than my husband. Speaking of the devil, Aaron descended downstairs with my cell in his hand. "Where the hell are my kids, Kate? They aren't at your mother's."

"You don't have any children." Leveling him with a glare, I prayed Akela had taken them to her parent's place as planned. Aaron would think to search the garage.

"Those are human children, animal." Mr. Anderson loomed over me. "They should be with their own kind."

Half delirious, I convulsed. "I guess this explains why I thought you never liked me."

"What information have you gotten out of her?" The older man addressed my husband.

"I was just getting started." Aaron was repulsively delighted at the prospect. He reached for an extendable blade and pliers. "She's not used to pain. I say we can start small, the fingernails."

Before asking a question, Aaron strode behind me and twisted my arm at an irregular angle. I groaned at the sensation of my shoulder, feeling like it was going to pop out of place, but it was nothing to the agony of him taring my thumbnail right off. I'm not tough. I cried out instantly. "Please stop!"

He moved onto my index finger, slicing with the blade first in order to give the pliers leverage. Unable to see and only able to feel what was coming, I still squeezed my eyes closed in wait. The second nail gave. It hurt even worse than the first one.

"Where's your lover boy?" Aaron whispered in my ear.

Choking sobs were the only sounds I could manage. Drool left my mouth in long strings as I cried.

"Where are the children?" Mr. Anderson barked. When I didn't respond, he delivered a solid punch to my jaw, his ring splitting open my lip even further. Blood gushed.

The older man stared meaningfully at Aaron behind me. "We need to keep her alive till they're found. Missing wife found dead, we can cover up. The children out of our control will raise suspicions with police and media."

"There's plenty we can do to her. She'll cave," Aaron stated. A third nail was forcibly removed, this time my ring finger. I thrashed in my chair as he went for a fourth. I could hear the popping noise before I registered my shoulder went out of joint. A tidal wave of pain followed. Screaming till I was hoarse, I swayed in the chair on the verge of passing out again. Black spots danced before me.

"Boys need their father," my husband tsked at me. "This is only going to get worse for you."

The sound of crashing glass saved me from answering. Aaron and his boss both bolted up the stairs. I pushed against the restraints until the chair toppled over. Without anything to brace me, my head cracked against the floor, making my vision swim. In a daze I heard shouting but couldn't distinguish any words. My heart stopped at the booming sound of gunfire. The wolf growled menacingly from the cage I'd fallen beside. Sucking in panic breaths, I strained to pull my ankles away from the bars in case the animal could reach me.

More gunshots. I scream-cried with my face pressed against the plastic-covered cement floor. Images of Luke and Caius being gunned down by my insane husband on repeat in my mind. Were their dead bodies even now lying on my living room floor? My heart beat wildly, adrenaline pumping, electrifying me to move, but the cuffs and zip ties kept me immobile.

"Kate!" A muffled shout.

"Baby, where are you?" Closer now.

"Basement," I tried to yell through my tears, relieved to hear their voices.

The creak of the door was followed by violent cursing. I couldn't see from my angle who was descending in a run. "Oh, baby. Shit! Are you alright?" Caius gently righted my chair.

Unable to form a single word, all I could do was whimper. Caius was alive. I wanted to hurtle questions at him. What about Luke? What happened upstairs? But I was still in shock.

"There's blood," Caius spoke to another barreling down the stairs.

"Those fuckers." Luke hands clenched into tight fists. "I killed them too quickly."

I sobbed even louder, seeing my other mate. They were both alive.

"Only our girl matters now," Caius snapped at him. "Find something to cut the zip ties. We need the keys for these cuffs on her ankles unless there's a bolt cutter down here."

Luke approached, and gently stroked my cheek with his thumb, settling me enough to stop the ugly cries. "We're here, my love. You're safe. Hold tight, and we'll get you out." Turning to Caius, he spoke again. "I'll go search them for the keys."

"They're dead?" The words rattled out.

"Yeah, baby," Caius answered gently. "He'll never hurt you again."

Caius searched the toolbox while Luke ran back up the stairs. The poor abused wolf snapped at the bars, causing the both of us to jump. Glowering over his shoulder, Caius shook his head. "Why in the hell is there a wolf here? Did he think it was one of us? Full moon is over."

"No," I licked my dry, blood-crusted lips. "He wanted it to maul me so he could tell my boys I was killed by Wa'ya when they grew up. Oh god." The cursed tears flowed again. "How could I've been blinded to what he was all these years?"

"Hey, hey," Caius soothed. He selected a blade and sawed at the ties. "None of this. And I repeat. None of this is your fault."

He freed my undamaged hand first before turning

to the one where my nails were removed. "Jesus," he cursed. Moving slowly so as not to touch my open wounds, he removed the tie from my other wrist.

Both arms free, I stumbled forward. He caught me, but I screamed in his embrace, my shoulder dangled uselessly out of joint.

"I'm sorry!" he exclaimed. What did I do?"

"My shoulder. It popped out."

"Oh babe, we gotta wait to set it back in place. It's gonna hurt like hell to move, but we got to get out of here." Caius grimaced.

"What about the wolf? I don't want to abandon the poor thing down here." The creature appeared as pitiful and beaten as I was.

"This place will be swarming with cops soon. Someone will see to it." Caius placated me.

Burying my face in the crook of his neck, I felt his pulse jumping. A sign he was alive. We were all alive. "Thank you for coming for me."

He pulled away, his beautiful face pinched. "I wish we realized he had you sooner. It's killing me. We didn't keep you safe."

I offered a watery smile. My lip was swollen where Aaron's boss hit me. Caius's mood darkened the more he observed my battered body. "I'll be okay. Nothing is permanent."

"Found them." Luke returned with the keys in hand. He trailed his gaze over me and the setup of the room, paling even more than his usual light complexion. "Sick fucks," he ground out before tossing the keys to Caius to uncuff me.

I tried to stand but my legs were Jello. Caius scooped me up and held me nestled against his broad chest. My bad shoulder facing away. "I got ya, baby girl."

"My boys?" I asked worried knowing Aaron might have someone trying to find them.

"Safe at Austin's compound. Once we get you patched up, we will take you to them."

"You might want to look away," Luke spoke gruffly when he opened the basement door.

I didn't heed his warning. A Jackson Pollock installation of blood splatter decorated the walls. The sightless eyes of my dead husband greeted me before Caius tucked my head back against his chest. "What's the plan?" he asked Luke.

"Drive her car. There's no time for cleanup today. I'm surprised the cops aren't here yet, considering the gunshots. This one is going to get ugly. Her blood's downstairs. There's no way to hide this. We'll need Austin to come through on his government connections." Luke kissed the top of my head. "I'll be right behind you, then you're not leaving my arms till my heart can settle back into my body."

Caius gingerly placed me in the passenger seat and buckled me in, mindful of my shoulder. It was still hard not to moan at every small movement. He ran to the other side while I heard sirens blaring in the distance. "Don't drive out too fast!" Luke warned. "They might pull you over. Stay calm."

Caius audibly swallowed before starting my car. My neighbor Mary ran out the front door when she spotted me. I rolled down the window and shouted as we drove past her. "I promise I'll call you. Don't say you saw us, please!"

She covered a hand over her mouth in shock at my blood-splattered appearance but managed to nod. I hoped the promise would hold once she was told there were dead bodies in my house. I'm not sure any friendship is strong enough to lie to the cops over a murder wrap. I didn't want the guys to go to jail because they saved me from my own stupidity. "Will Austin be able to help us? Maybe we should stay and talk with the police ourselves? It was self-defense."

"This will be way too hard to explain without going to jail. Cops don't know about our kind, baby," Caius spoke softly. "We need Austin's contacts on this one. He has government agents assigned to his work. They can offer us some immunity while an investigation takes place. Otherwise, a black man and a foreigner just killed two upstanding white citizens in the South. Trust me. We can't stay here."

Sighing, I reclined my seat back and tried to slow my erratic heartbeat. Caius stayed away from the main roads, taking every side street to evade the sirens we heard approaching. Luke had driven in the other direction. I fretted over whether he'd be safe, only breathing again fully when we reached the highway and I spotted his car a few yards ahead. Eventually, the adrenaline faded. As the miles rolled by, my body succumbed to exhaustion.

Chapter Thirty-Nine
Kate

I spent a night in a hospital bed in Austin's lab before I was able to see my kids. It was another week before I could see my sister and Lowe. They'd been placed in an inaccessible government hospital. Tate was still there. He was in a coma.

Needless to say, the New Year's Eve wedding of Miles and Akela didn't happen. The men from all three packs spent the majority of their time hunting the Order, desperate for a break in their location before the next full moon. Luke and Caius were at the center of things, but they made sure one of them was always with me and the boys. I could have protested the coddling, but I needed it. I was an antsy mess when left alone. My body was healing from the torture, but my mind was still on red alert.

With three packs all crammed in on Austin's compound and no good news on Tate, tensions were high. The packs were working well together, but tempers would flare up over small things. Snide comments about the lack of coffee in the pot or a battle over the setting of the furnace stat were simply inevitable when people were forced to share space. Mile's pack, being relatively new friends with Austin's, kept us all feeling like we were walking on eggshells.

I had to close down my storefront. There was no way to manage it. We were staying low and letting Austin's connections handle everything that happened at my house. Agents questioned me while I was in the hospital, as well as Luke and Caius. Miraculously, even though we fled the scene, the self-defense plea kept my guys from prison.

Like a complete coward, I hadn't told Will his father was dead. He never asked about him. Tommy was too little to understand. I wondered if Will, after a year or two, would even remember Aaron. Could it be that easy? We just never mention him again and move on with our lives? I felt a twinge at the idea, remembering my mother had just stopped talking about my father to me.

"Hello, Katrina?" Luke sauntered into the bedroom. I was sitting cross-legged on the bed, checking a few things on the laptop. His use of my proper name always caused the butterflies to stir in my belly.

"Putting the website on a semi-permanent close," I sighed as I shut the laptop.

Luke was wearing low-cut jeans, no shirt, while carrying Tommy wearing only a diaper in his arms. Might be the mom in me, but there was nothing hotter. While I appreciated the view, when I left them, they were both clothed.

"What happened?"

"This little monkey." Luke tickled Tommy till he squealed. "Decided he was not fond of the split pea soup Kyle made. He doused us both pretty good with it."

I covered my mouth to hide my smile. "Sorry. Want me to grab you a new shirt?"

Luke nodded before tossing Tommy up and catching him. "And something for the split pea-asourus here."

"Dada!" Tommy chirped before burying his face against Luke's chest and blowing a wet razzberry.

We both froze and stared at each other. I sighed when Luke's usually somber face lit up. "Is that okay?" I whispered.

"Babe." He shook his head in wonder. "It's better than okay." Luke's adoring gaze at Tommy played havoc with my hormones. "I get to tell Caius I got a Dada first!"

"Luke." I tried for stern, but couldn't hide the giggle. I reached over to grab a shirt from the dresser, but held it in my hand rather than pass it to him. "Not sure you need a shirt. You look pretty hot."

Tommy gurgled up at Luke, patting his chubby fist over the wet mark he'd made on Luke's chest with his razzberry. "Dada!" he yelled again.

Much to Luke's delight, Caius walked into the room at the exact moment. "No fair! Did he call you dada?"

"Yup," Luke gloated while drawing out the single word and popping the p.

"Little dude!" Caius patted his hand over his heart. "I thought we had a special bond?"

Tommy pointed at Caius and giggled. "Dada." My beautiful lover lit up like a firework at the proclamation.

"That's right, little dude. We'll share the title." He turned and winked at me. "We are very good at sharing."

"But I was first," Luke mumbled playfully.

Caius frowned and shot him a glare before turning puppy dog eyes at me. "He gets all the firsts," he playfully whined.

"I don't know what you want me to do about it," I giggled.

Caius rubbed at his chin and pondered. "I think I need to have a first of something to even it out."

"Will is a bit older. It might be a while before he comes around," I replied with a worried frown.

Caius searched around to check if the little man was around, then used his hands for "earmuffs" over Tommy. "I was thinking more along the lines of anal." His pearly white grin split his face in two.

My eyes flew wide open. "Oh my god, you did not just say that!"

"Ah, let him have it, Katrina. He'll work his way up to it." Luke wiggled his eyebrows. "I bet you'll like it."

I rested my hands on my hips. "What, no competition for it?"

Luke shook his head slowly, a devilish glint in his eyes. "Nope, I think I will rather enjoy watching you take him."

"Ugh," Caius groaned. "Does this mean you'll get all bedroom bossy?"

I clamped my legs together tightly at the erotic image. I loved it when Luke was bossy. Guess it was the omega in me.

Luke landed a playful punch on Caius's shoulder. "Don't pretend you don't enjoy it." Luke handed the baby to Caius and pulled me close, yanking the shirt from my loose grip. Before putting it on, he leaned in and whispered loud enough for Caius to hear. "But the first time you take us both together, that little hole is mine."

The idea both frightened and excited me. These men remade me. They knew my body better than I ever did. I'd gone my entire life unaware there could be such pleasure. While I stared open-mouthed and in a trance-like state, a shout came from the living room.

Hurriedly, Luke threw on his shirt, Caius handed the baby to me, and we were all running to the living room. We were staying with Akela's family. Her mother and father were on the couch, holding each other and sobbing. Akela was listening to the phone pressed tightly to her ear as Miles stood beside her, hands balled into fists.

"Thank you, Doctor," Akela quavered. "I appreciate the call." She hung up. "Tate woke up. He's confused and lost some memory apparently, but the doctor thinks it's a temporary effect of the coma."

"Can we see him?" Miles asked.

She shook her head. "Not yet, but he can have one visitor at a time in a couple of days."

Our big, strong alpha collapsed on the couch. "I thought fate couldn't be so cruel to give me my brother back only to take him away again."

Akela rubbed her mate's shoulder. Tears spilled freely down her face. "It will be a long recovery," she warned. "We'll need to be patient."

"Oh, I'm a patient man," he replied meaningfully, glancing at Akela, who had kept him at arm's length most of their lives, not accepting him as her mate.

She leaned over and kissed the top of his head. "Yes, Yes. No one knows that more than me, my love."

"What happens to injured Wa'ya when it is time for the shift?" I asked.

"We shift," Luke answered plainly. "We have to be careful with the injured, though. Often, we cage them before the shift and keep them someplace safe. Otherwise, they may not be with us when it's time to shift back."

"And how will anyone be safe this next shift?" I was out of my mind with fear, thinking I would watch them change, not knowing if they would be hunted down.

Miles scowled, clearly unhappy with the reminder of the Order. "If we cannot ensure our pack lands are safe, we will all need to be caged for the next shift. The omegas and the shiftless will need to watch over their packs. But it is only a measure I will take if absolutely necessary."

The idea of them tucked away and kept secure had me feeling a sense of relief, but I could tell none of them liked the idea at all. Their animal side wanted freedom, not imprisonment. "It would be a relief knowing you were protected rather than out in the wild where anything could happen to you," I confessed to the group.

"People die in car accidents every day, yet we don't freak out when we watch someone get in a car." Miles squeezed my shoulder. "Life in a cage isn't a life."

"I might have a plan for the Order, Alpha." Luke looked somber, his eyes swimming with guilt as he glanced at me. "I got some news today, too. My contacts might finally have tracked down their main area of operation. Mr. Anderson was the general they all spoke about. His eldest son looks to be the next in charge. I had him followed this morning."

"What are we waiting for then?" Miles practically growled.

Luke's mouth set in a grim line. "They have more firepower than I had ever guessed. We will need backup and lots of it. Like all the packs. Including your parent's."

Miles crossed his arms over his barrel chest, looking pensive. He gnawed at his bottom lip while I held my breath. I didn't like the sound of any of this, even one little bit. I knew why Luke had held back this information. It would mean both he and Caius would need to leave me behind and put themselves at risk. It would break me to lose them.

"I understand." Miles sighed. "I'll let Austin and Raff know. We have to call in the alphas. It's time we declared war."

To be continued...

BONUS EPILOGUE

Kate
Four Years Later

Five days ago, I took the serum. Many more Wa'ya females had successful transformations with no negative side effects. I held out as long as I did for my boys. I needed to be sure it was absolutely safe. As much as I loved life with my guys, I wanted to experience the sense of pack they spoke about. While we suffered losses and experienced great hardships, we also learned a lot in the last three years. Not only was the serum safer now, but we have the ability to protect our pack lands. I hadn't gotten pregnant like many expected. Akela and Chloe have lapped me on the children front. Akela had three, and Chloe was newly pregnant with her third. The serum will make me extra fertile. Not only would I feel a sense of pack, but maybe, if lucky, I could have another son or daughter.

How we took the serum had also evolved. The initial injection was done under sedation. The first five hours of the transformation stage were the hardest, and therefore, we slept through it. Once I woke up, I felt achy, like after a fever. I was weak and lightheaded for about a day before feeling entirely myself again. Feeling myself, though, was the problem. I worried if it worked at all.

Three days ago, we headed up to the cabins, and the pack shifted. Being an omega with tons of children around, I did not. All females, while pregnant or nursing, never shifted. Only the omegas stayed human till there were no longer any children around to care for. Akela, still nursing her youngest son, hadn't shifted this full moon either. She was currently sitting on my couch, attempting to keep me calm. The pack should be changing back to human this morning. My stomach clenched with unease at not feeling any bonds.

"It won't happen till the pack returns, and we're all together again," she reiterated for the tenth time, trying to pound the truth into my brain, but I was still a wreck.

"I know," I replied while chewing on my fingernail and staring fixedly out the front window.

Our pack had grown considerably, and we no longer all fit in the main cabin. Luke, Caius and I were the first to move out and build a small two-bedroom next door. It wasn't our main home, yet the nine hundred square feet felt like a cozy getaway every month.

It was a warm summer morning, and my boys were outside playing with Akela's three-year-old twin daughters. Kyle, our other omega, was outside watching and trying to get them all to play the same game. They were kicking a ball around. Some with intentions, like my oldest Will, others as a distraction, mainly the twins. Obliviously happy giggles spontaneously erupted, causing my frown to shift slightly and my lips to turn upward.

While my boys, being human, would never experience a shift, it was still to be seen if Akela's twins would shift naturally at age five or have to wait till they were adults and find their fated mates.

"Would you be distressed or relieved if the girls don't shift?" I asked timidly, not having broached the subject before. The girls were still two years away from shifting age, but that still felt crazy young to go off into the wild.

"As long as they both have the same experience, I'll be content. If one shifts and the other does not," Akela cringed. "It would make things difficult between them. They're so incredibly close. I wouldn't want anything to change for them."

"It doesn't make you nervous thinking about them like little pups out in the wilderness?" I continued to question, wondering how I would feel in the situation.

In typical Wa'ya fashion, Akela accepted the natural order. "Their wolves will look fully grown. We believe it's why it takes them five years for the shift to happen. Removing any weaknesses, like small pup bodies or pregnant females, from shifts."

"Then you might stay human when it's time for the girls to shift if you get pregnant again?" The idea of staying back and watching my kids shift sounded terrifying.

Akela nodded, nonplused. "Miles, as alpha male, will take good care of them. My mother watched me shift, as well as Aunt Valentina for almost all her boys. The bonds are a comfort when it happens. I will feel my girls in here if they shift." She patted her hand over her heart. "Nothing would make me happier to be connected to them on that level. Honestly, the energy spent worrying about it simply isn't worth it. Whatever happens, happens." She shrugged.

I couldn't contain the eye roll. "I can't help but feel that remark was directed at me? After waiting over four years to take the serum since I was worried about doing it, I hardly think I will stop worrying about every potential outcome now."

"The omega in you." She stood and started burping the baby. "The omega is a protector of the young, a job requiring fast thinking and planning." Akela suddenly performed a megawatt movie star smile and angled her head at me. "And how are you feeling now, Kate?"

"Daddy!" A shrill, happy cry could be heard through the closed windows as the twins spotted Miles.

A tsunami of emotions washed over me. I sank to the couch, my legs no longer able to support me. Excitement, joy, nervous anticipation, and a more delicate emotion of growing arousal all bombarded me.

Akela huffed before she chuckled. "Your mates are eager to see you." She took in a calming breath, and all the emotions melted back till only excitement remained.

Wide eyed, I blinked at her. "What did you do?"

"Alpha males control the pack when we are beasts. Alpha females control the pack bounds when we are people. The pack can push out emotions to others and sense those around them, but if the flood of feelings is too intense, I can tapper it, or if the emotions are too abrasive, I can negate them. Alpha females also tie off the bonds to mated couples or, in your case, throupple. It allows you all to have a stronger connection the rest of us do not have to feel." Akelas' eyes sparkled with mischief. "I keep the main pack bond open for communal emotions. Gotta keep it PG for the kiddos, ya know. But ... I sense your thread to the pack now and can tie it off to your mates. Are you ready for it?"

I wanted to run outside and jump in their arms. The bond filled me with nervous excitement. I hadn't realized how isolating my previous existence had been. The bond was like an endorphin high. "I think I kept us all waiting long enough. I'm ready."

Akela closed her eyes to focus once again. I'm glad I remained seated. When she was done, the floodgates reopened. I could still sense the entire pack like a delicate silken spider web, but the threads pulling me to my mates were solid chain links anchoring our souls together. Luke and Caius were excited to see me, worried for me, hungry, but mainly needy. Lust jolted through me, and I had to stifle a moan. I shot off the couch and wrapped my hand around the front doorknob before I was even aware I'd moved.

"Go on," Akela urged, a knowing smile tugging at her lips. "They're waiting."

I flung open the door and saw our pack members returning. Miles had been the first to reach the cabin. He had both the girls danglingly in utter delight from his tree trunk arms. Tommy and Will had used the situation to take back the ball for a mock game of soccer. My eyes found Caius's warm, smiling ones before sailing to greet Luke's intense gaze. Both men had the ability to soak my panties with a look before but with the bond in play? An embarrassing amount of heat and wetness assailed me.

"Oh boy," I muttered weakly.

Akela grinned. "I'll have Kyle take the kids to the main cabin for cartoons and pancakes. That should buy you some time." She winked.

I was too desperately horny to even be embarrassed. "Sounds good to me!" I ran straight to my guys, eager to be held and kissed. Luke caught me around the waist and twirled me around.

"My beautiful Katrina. I can finally feel you inside me." The look of wonder and joy on his face was amplified by the reaction in the bond.

Caius stepped up and sandwiched me between them. He placed a kiss on the back of my neck. "Did I hear our gloriously devious alpha correctly? They are taking the kids this morning?"

"Yup!" I spoke with cheeky delight.

"Then we're wasting daylight." Luke threw me over his shoulder and jogged back to our cabin door.

I was out of breath with laughter by the time he set me back on my feet. Caius made quick work of divesting my clothes before we even made it to our bedroom. No complaints from me. I wanted to feel them inside me in every way possible. "Want you both," I panted.

Their eyes sparkled at my demand. I usually had to work up to taking them at the same time. Caius used to tease me it was special occasion sex when we did it. I couldn't think of a more special occasion than finally feeling on a deep cellular level I was a part of the pack, but most importantly these men were my fated mates. I needed them as much as oxygen.

"I'll get the lube." Luke winked before heading to the bathroom.

"I'll get us started," Caius shouted at his retreating figure. In record time, he got naked and laid out on our big king-sized bed, goofily making mock snow angels while I finished undressing. His cock was beautifully erect, jutting up past his navel. When he noticed me staring, he began to rub it up and down. "You gonna get over here and climb on? Or is this a more a liking to watch moment."

"I'm coming." I giggled as I crawled over to him.

"Not yet, baby, But I promise it will be soon." He closed his full lips over mine, licking his way in, slowly circling my tongue.

I grabbed his dick, delighted to hear him groan in response. Eager to have him fill me, I rubbed his fat head over my slit until I was dripping for him. Too big to ever plunge in one thrust, I worked my way down him until he was fully sheathed. My eyes closed in the sheer bliss of being connected. Of feeling full, just not as full as I would be after Luke joined us. The bond thrummed a happy vibration in my chest. I could feel Caius's overwhelming love for me. The well was endless. I moved up and down in a trance-like state, feeling him in my body and surrounding my soul.

So distracted by the experience, I hadn't noticed Luke enter the room until lube slid down my crack. He pushed his thick fingers into my tight, puckered ring. My eyes flew open at the sensation. Double penetration sex was always intense. I needed to be in the right headspace for it.

Caius searched my face for clues, slowing down his thrust till he barely moved while Luke lined up behind me. Luke leaned over my back, peppering hot kisses on my neck and working his way up to my ear lobe. He nipped me. "You're going to take me now, Katrina."

I shivered as his warm breath skated over my flesh. "I'm ready," I replied breathily while he removed his finger from me and positioned the head of his cock at my opening. My legs quivered in anticipation, waiting for him. Luke gently stroked my back, calming me, before adding more lube over himself. I barely noticed the cold liquid. My core was on fire for my guys.

Spreading my cheeks further apart, Luke pushed through the ring of muscle. I tensed up at the overwhelming fullness. Caius stilled entirely while Luke worked his way in. A warm, wet mouth suckled one nipple while a devious hand twisted the other.

"Relax, baby," Luke grunted behind me. "Let me in."

I let go of the muscles I hadn't realized I was clenching. Luke slid further inside. I could feel them both inside me, rubbing against each other, with only a thin membrane separating us all. Caius threw back his head and resumed thrusting. It always started as a push-or-pull game. One sliding out while the other slid in. I remained on all fours, doing little more than riding the wave of ecstasy their movements generated.

Caius shoved his hands between us, pinching my slippery clit and making me see stars. My orgasm hit almost painfully, and I clenched hard as the little shocks rode through me. Both the guys groaned loudly at that. Without needing to speak, they both picked up the pace, plunging in and out of me in unison. Boneless, my body surged forward with every thrust, Luke's firm grip on my hips the only thing keeping me from falling on my face. My inner thighs burned with the stretch of being astride Caius's larger frame. I welcomed the pain. It kept me present. It kept me from floating away.

"You're going to come again for us, Katrina. We need to feel you grip us like that again." Luke's stern tone made me want to obey. My body was his to command.

The tingling in my spine alerted me a strong climax was coming. My men kept up the pace, pounding the sensitive spots in me over and over until I complied with Luke's wishes. This orgasm was a slow build to an intense crescendo. I cried out my pleasure while I convulsed. A string of expletives left Caius's mouth, followed by his hot semen spilling inside me.

"Such a good girl," Luke crooned as my eyes glazed over. He always managed to be the last to come. Such a control freak, but I loved it.

As Caius and I both whimpered at the oversensitivity of his continued movements. He shushed us. "You can take it."

I could feel Caius trying to pull out, but if I could endure, he could, too. I clenched down even tighter to keep him in, but it also had the added benefit of pulling Luke over the edge. His grip tightened on my hips with his final deep thrust. Chuckling darkly, he slapped my ass. "Naughty girl."

"Hmmm," I hummed happily, collapsing on Caius's chest. He embraced me and kissed the top of my head, mumbling nonsense endearments into my hair. Luke leaned over pressing his lips to mine, a rare smile lighting up his serious face.

I didn't think I'd ever been more content in my entire life. My children were growing up surrounded by love, I was closer to my sister and mother than I ever was before, and I felt adored and cared for. No matter where we were, if I was with my guys, I was home.

The End

MARIA MERCURIO

EVERNIGHT PUBLISHING ®

www.evernightpublishing.com